love's Secret torment

STACY L. DARNELL

Cover Design: Robin Harper, Wicked by Design
Editor: Nancy S. Thompson
Cover Photographer: Mandy Hollis, MHPhotography
Interior Designer: Integrity Formatting

Dedication

To my husband and son,

Mike and Austin Darnell

*for the endless hours I've had
my laptop with me wherever I go.*

*Your support, encouragement and
belief in my dream has meant the world to me.*

CHAPTER 1

How It All Began

Sam

It was the summer before my junior year of high school, five years since the worst day of my life, the day my cousin died, taking another life with her. My family had experienced a great deal of sadness and heartache in those five years, not to mention guilt and that everlasting question—what if?

But as awful as that day was, as painful as the knowledge that Jolie's decision to drink then drive had not only robbed our family of a loved one, but another's as well, if it weren't for that worst day, I never would have experienced the best day of my life.

Since her death, members of my family have volunteered to help raise funds for drunk driving awareness. I'd always wanted to help, too.

One afternoon while walking our chocolate lab, Gage, I saw a flyer on a telephone pole advertising a charity event for the cause. I snapped a picture of it with my cell phone. Later that night, I called the number listed and signed up to help. I wanted make a difference.

Making jewelry was one of my passions. Susan, the foundation president, said they were having an auction and needed items to bid on. I was so excited, I signed up right away.

As I organized my supplies scattered in piles on the table, the wind blew across the park, knocking down my sign. Thankfully, it wasn't my charms. I bent down to pick up the sign when I saw a flash of light in my peripheral vision.

I looked up and saw it was sunlight reflecting off the leg of a chair being carried by a hot guy. My heart stopped for a second. He stood with his back toward me, picking up stacked chairs. The way his muscles moved under his skin was so sexy, I caught myself holding my breath as I stared.

It was a hot, sunny day. He wasn't wearing a shirt, and as the sweat dripped down his back, I could see he had a strong muscular body. His fine ass was attached to sexy, long legs. When he turned around, my eyes focused on his toned abs, my skin tingled, and I completely lost track of what I was doing.

As my attention traveled up his body to his face, I immediately recognized him from school.

Alec Morris.

He was in my junior class. My friend Heather, and I always lusted over Alec, but I was shy, and neither of us ever had the nerve to talk to him. There was always something about him that just wasn't approachable.

The three of us had gym together last year, but other than that, we'd never had any classes together. And let me tell you, that class was *definitely* my favorite of the day. It fast became my favorite class of the year. Maybe of all time.

As I struggled to tear my gaze from him, I finished my jewelry pieces. But I couldn't keep from peeking up at him. I felt like such a creeper. His messy hair and crystal blue eyes made my cheeks feel hot, and I dropped my pliers when I noticed him walking in my direction.

"Hi. Samone Lang, right?"

I blinked several times, not quite believing he was standing only a few feet away, shirtless, sweaty, and talking to me. Swallowing hard, I attempted to speak, but apparently, the English language had become a distant memory. Thank God my instincts kicked in and I nodded.

"I'm Alec, Alec Morris. We had gym together last year."

He stared at me like I was his favorite dessert, his gaze roaming from my lips to my eyes. It made me squirm in my chair. I'd never experienced someone looking at me the way he did.

"You can call me Sam. All of my friends do."

"Well, I really like your name. It's pretty. Unique. So . . . if it's okay with you, I'd like to call you Samone," he said as he put his foot up on the bench, wiping his forehead with a wet towel.

"Umm yeah." I nodded. "That would be kind of cool actually."

I smiled up at him. I prayed that the sesame seeds from the bagel I'd eaten earlier weren't stuck in my teeth. That would be my luck.

He seemed nervous, fidgety as he looked away. He acted as if he wanted to say something more. I was relieved when his amazing lips formed a beautiful smile.

"You know what they say—you only live once—and . . . well, I've kind of wanted to talk to you for a long time. So maybe we could have lunch together when we wrap up here? I'd love to know why you're volunteering, and I know a great café. We could take my truck." He winked.

I knew I was in for it. He was so much nicer than I had imagined. I just couldn't match up this Alec with the aloof, standoffish version from school. He was always getting into trouble during class for not paying attention. But he had the right answers when the gym teacher asked him questions, usually about whatever game rules we were just given. It made me wonder if he was purposely acting guarded from the world in general. Heather would never believe he came over and talked to me, let alone asked me out.

"That sounds great. I should be finished here soon." My grin was permanently plastered to my face.

"Really?"

He looked surprised . . . as if I might have actually said no.

"Awesome, okay. I just have a couple more tables to move

for Susan, and then I'll be ready. Why don't we meet over by the gazebo? My truck is parked there. It's the old, green one. I'm going to rinse off in the showers by the pool and change into some clean clothes, but I shouldn't be long."

My mind was stuck on the visual of him rinsing off in the showers when he pulled me from my thoughts.

"Samone?"

"Oh, sorry. That sounds good. Umm, no worries if it takes a bit. I can just catch up on my reading."

He cocked an eyebrow and looked around. "Reading?"

"Kindle app. Three hundred books in one small package."

He laughed lightly and nodded. "All right then. I'll be just a few more minutes."

I gawked at his sexy, tanned back as he walked away. Hurrying, I packed up my beads. I'd never been so excited to abandon my hobby. But I couldn't wait to finish so I could get to the gazebo and meet Alec.

Walking to the gazebo, I could see him pacing. He was on his phone and didn't look happy. I wondered what or who could've changed his mood so dramatically in just ten minutes. He shoved his phone in the front pocket of his jeans, roughed his hands through his hair, and moved the nearest table into position.

I walked over and sat on one of the benches. When I pulled my phone out to check for messages, the lock screen showed three texts. My best friends, Alison and Tamron, were demanding to know what time I'd be done and my sister, Tricia, wanted to make sure I'd be around when she came home from college the following weekend.

I sent a brief text to Tricia confirming I would be and we needed to fit a pedicure in while she was in town. Then I sent Alison and Tamron a group text saying I didn't know what time I'd be done. I had a lunch date, and even though I was ditching them for a hot guy, under no circumstance should they see the new Robert Downey Jr. movie without me.

I wasn't surprised when the rapid-fire text messages started coming in. It was their typical twenty questions. I loved those girls, I really did, but I swear, sometimes it felt like there was a big age difference between us when, in reality, they were only a year older. I decided to appease their curiosity, knowing they would be digging out the yearbooks to look him up.

Me: His name is Alec Morris.

T: He hasn't been approved.

Me: Seriously Tamron? Alison, is she for real?

A: He's not on the list, Sam.

Me: Are you kidding me right now? There's a list?

T: Yes, there's a list. He's not on it. Tell him you forgot you already had lunch plans with your besties.

A: Chicks before dicks, Sam.

Me: OMG. Sorry girls, but I'm going.

A: Wait Sam, you can't.

Me: Meet at my house. Maybe I'll stop drooling by then. Preview . . . sexy, tanned, muscular back. YW.

T: Ah—hell.

A: Go. Have lunch. Just lunch.

Me: Ha ha, I should've started off with that. Love you both.

When I looked up, I noticed Alec leaning against the gazebo, watching me with a smirk on his face. It was an improvement over the scowl he wore when he was on his cell earlier.

"So the book you're reading, is it funny?"

My face must have been red. I felt the heat in my cheeks.

"Oh . . . no, it's actually a romance." I smiled. "I was just laughing at my best friends. They wanted to know when I was going to be done here because we're supposed to meet for a movie. They kind of freaked when I told them I had a lunch date . . . uh . . . I mean . . . plans . . . and didn't know what time I'd be done. They're kind of a force of nature."

I didn't miss the triumphant smile and light in his eyes when I'd slipped and said date.

"Date huh?" He grinned.

My God, it was the most adorable expression ever, whether at my expense or not, I couldn't deny it was sexy. I fumbled over my feet, getting up as he came over and offered me his hand. When we touched, tingles spread over my entire body. We walked to his truck. He even opened the door for me. He was such a gentleman.

Mesmerized, I watched him saunter around to the driver's side, and I almost had to pinch myself to prove I wasn't dreaming. He slid his long legs into the seat and started the truck. The powerful muscles in his arms rippled as he shifted it into gear. He was absolutely mouthwatering.

Turning on the radio, Billy Joel's "Uptown Girl" started playing through the speakers. He looked at me and winked. I didn't realize it then, but that moment was the beginning of something amazing.

CHAPTER 2

Captivating Brown Eyes

Alec

My hands began to sweat as we pulled into the parking lot for Reveille Coffeehouse and Café. I glanced at the beautiful girl sitting in the passenger seat of my truck.

Yup . . . she's really there. Holy shit.

Her hands were in her lap, and she was fidgeting with her bracelet. She was nervous. Well, that made two of us. I had no idea what the hell I was doing. There was no room in my life for a girl. I was damned, and the people I loved tended to suffer for it.

Her sweet voice pulled me from my thoughts.

"So, have you eaten here before?"

I pulled into a spot and shifted my truck into park. Leaning my head back against the headrest, I closed my eyes. Her soft hand slipped into mine and she exhaled a shaky breath.

"If . . . if you don't want to go in, it's okay. I can get a ride back to the park to get my car."

"No, Samone. I'm sorry. It's not that. I want to be here with you. It's just—complicated."

"Oh. Okay."

"And I would never make you get a ride anywhere. I'm not

an asshole."

"No, I didn't mean that, I'm sorry Alec."

"It's okay. I know you didn't mean it, but wanted to make sure we were clear. You don't ever have to worry when you're with me."

Her shoulders relaxed and she smiled.

"To answer your question, yes, I've eaten here before. It's really good. Let's go in, okay?" I said as I lightly squeezed her hand.

Her beautiful brown eyes captivated me as she sat in the booth across from me.

"So . . . what's good here?" she asked with a quiet voice.

"Everything I've tried is great, but my favorite is the ham and cheese omelet."

"Oh good. Thanks." She nodded.

After the waitress took our order, I looked up at Sam, her brown gaze staring at me. She startled when she realized I caught her and looked everywhere except at me.

"Will you look at me?"

She blushed a crimson red but focused those beautiful eyes on me. "Why are you staring at me?"

"I don't know," I said in raw honesty.

"Oh."

"You're the most beautiful girl I've ever seen." I smiled as I watched her cheeks turn several shades of pink. The way her smile lit up her face was enough to make a sad man happy on his worst day.

"Thank you. You're pretty handsome yourself," she said with a coy smile.

Her eyes lit with curiosity. "So why were you volunteering?"

"It was just something I needed to do, that's all," I muttered.

Damn it, I clenched my fists. I wished I hadn't told her I wanted to know why she was volunteering. That was a quid-pro-quo type of question, and I wasn't about to open that can of worms. But I was grasping at straws when I asked her out

8

and had a case of verbal diarrhea.

"Let's not talk about that right now. Tell me about you. What movie are you ditching your friends for me for?"

Her lopsided grin was perfect. "Robert Downey Jr.'s new movie. But they're waiting to see it with me. He's one of my favorite actors. I kind of fan-girl over him."

I cocked an eyebrow at her as an embarrassed look spread across her face.

"Oh my God. I didn't just say that." She covered her face with her hands. "Forget you heard it, please."

"It's okay, Samone. I like to know my competition ahead of time," I teased.

CHAPTER 3

Hello My Name Is

Sam

One day, a couple months into our junior year, while we were waiting for a movie to start at the theater, Alec leaned over and put his arm around me. "Samone, I'd like to meet your parents."

"Oh. Umm, okay," I replied. "They asked to meet you, too, but I haven't found the right time."

"That's okay. I've been meaning to ask for a couple weeks now," he said. "I just want to officially introduce myself before we get much further into our relationship."

"Relationship, huh?" I teased.

"Yes, relationship. We've been dating a few months now. You. Are. Mine," he said as he looked directly in my eyes.

"Yes . . . I am," I replied with a smile. I hesitated because he was always so closed off about his own family. "Alec, can I meet your parents, too?"

The set of his shoulders stiffened, and he let go of my hand, leaving a sense of cold behind.

"No. That's not possible," he snapped.

I couldn't understand his reaction. But I let the subject drop. I rubbed my hands together, wishing I could take the question back.

"You know, I want you to meet Alison and Tamron, too. They're driving me nuts about meeting you."

I saw him relax into his seat and breathed a sigh of relief. I didn't want to upset him.

"Cool. Maybe I could come in and meet your parents when I take you home later. And I'd love to meet your friends."

"Yeah well, meeting my parents will be easy as pie. It's the girls you have to worry about," I teased.

"Nah, they'll be fine. The way you talk about them, I am sure they've already stalked me around town to make sure I'm not a serial killer or something." He laughed in a fake nervous way.

I smacked him on the shoulder. "They're not that bad. Just . . . okay, well maybe borderline." I giggled.

The movie started, and I leaned over and rested my head on his shoulder as we watched. He held my hand in his and gently rubbed his thumb over mine. I relished in the feel of his touch.

When the movie was over, we passed a Starbucks on the way back to my house. Alec took the drive-thru and ordered us lattes before continuing on to my house.

Mom and Dad were sitting out on the front porch when we pulled into the driveway. Alec parked and dashed around to my door, helping me out of his truck. As we walked up the front porch steps, I saw my parents watching me with expectant eyes. I guess this meeting was going to happen whether we'd planned it or not.

"Hey, Mom, Dad."

"Hey there, Princess," Dad said.

As I leaned into Alec's side, he gave my hand a light, reassuring squeeze. I felt relieved when I looked up at his soft smile, and turned back toward my parents.

"This is Alec Morris. I've been meaning to introduce you for a while. Just . . . you know me. I keep getting distracted."

Mom and Dad smiled as I laughed nervously.

"He said he wanted to meet y'all tonight, so we came back early."

"Yes, we've been wanting to meet him, too." Dad looked at Alec and raised his hand. "Alec, it's nice to finally meet you. This is Sam's mom, Maggie, and I'm Vance."

"Hello, Mr. and Mrs. Lang. It's a pleasure," he said, shaking my dad's hand and kissing the top of my mom's.

"Maggie and Vance is fine. There's no need for formalities here," Dad said.

"Okay, sir," Alec said with a nervous smile. "I mean . . . Vance."

We sat and talked with my parents as we sipped sweet tea and snacked on some Mom's famous ginger snaps.

Gage came out and met Alec. He kept trying to sit in our laps while we sat on the porch swing. But it wasn't working since he was eighty pounds of crazy puppy. He finally settled on lying at our feet.

"Well, Mr. and Mrs. Lang—Sorry . . . I mean, Maggie and Vance." He smiled. "It's been nice meeting you both."

"For us, too Alec," Dad said.

"Yes, come see us again sometime," Mom added.

"Yes, ma'am." Alec smiled.

My parents went inside the house. I walked Alec down to his truck wrapped my arms around him. "Thank you for a wonderful evening."

"You're welcome, Samone," he said as he pulled me into his arms. His lips gently pressed against mine. His fingers wound through my hair. My mouth opened to his, the kiss was warm and caused shivers to run down my spine.

"I had fun, and your parents are really nice. I'm helping my Aunt with a few repairs around the house tomorrow, but I'll see you at school on Monday."

"Okay. Drive safe going home." I lightly squeezed his hand.

"Will do," he said then climbed into his truck and drove away.

The following Saturday, we made plans to meet up with Alison and Tamron for lunch at Reveille Café. I was excited for

Alec to meet the girls. I loved him and hoped they would, too. He was that guy, the one you can't help but like. He was sexy, funny, caring, and always made sure I was happy.

We got there early and had the hostess seat us at a booth. I slid in on one side and Alec scooted in beside me. He put his arm around me and kissed the top of my head.

"Relax, Samone. There's no need to be so nervous."

"Easy for you to say," I murmured.

The waitress came and took our drink order while we waited for the girls to join us. I smiled nervously when they walked around the corner toward our booth.

"Hey, girls!" I called.

"Hi Sam, Alec," Alison said, looking from me to Alec and back.

"Hey there," Tamron replied as they slipped into the booth and got settled. The waitress returned with our drinks and a couple extra ice waters for the girls.

"Would you like anything else to drink?" she asked them.

"Yeah, I'll have a Coke," Tamron said.

"Do you have Diet Pepsi?" Alison asked with hopeful eyes.

"I'm sorry, just Coke, miss," the waitress said.

"Just Coke products? What kind of a country are we living in when one of its citizens can't exercise their freedom of choice in their local eating establishment? How dare you discriminate against my beverage of preference? I know we're in Atlanta, the epicenter for Coke. But the last time I checked, Atlanta was still a part of America."

"Relax Alison," Tamron urged. "It's not the waitress's fault. Geez."

"Right. Sorry. I'll have a lemonade," Alison deadpanned.

The waitress walked away and the girls looked across the table at us and smiled.

I cleared my throat. "Girls, this is Alec. Alec, this is Tamron and Alison," I said, motioning to them in turn.

"It's nice to meet you both."

"Thanks, Alec. It's nice to *finally* meet you, too," Tamron retorted.

The table jolted as Alison kicked her under it.

Alison smiled. "It's nice to meet you, Alec."

"I know, girls. I'm sorry. Things just kept coming up. He just met my parents last week."

"Well Sam, you can't fall off the face of the earth just because you met a hot guy," Tamron scolded.

I looked at Alec and could have sworn he was blushing. I smiled to myself. "I know. We've just been doing so much on the weekends."

"It's okay, Sam," Alison said. "We're meeting him now."

After the waitress came and took our orders, the girls swung their heads in unison to look directly at Alec.

"Okay, Alec, we need to have a talk," Tamron began.

I inwardly groaned as I twisted at the cloth napkin on my lap.

"Okay," he said.

"If you hurt her. At all. Ever. You will regret it," Alison said.

"I won't hurt her. There's no need to worry. In fact, I'm finding myself falling madly in love with her," he replied, looking at me with a smile.

Heat flooded my cheeks as my head snapped up to his then slowly turned and stared doe-eyed at the girls. They looked back with approving amusement.

"Well then. That's settled. Let's catch up," Tamron said matter-of-factly.

CHAPTER 4

Those We've Lost

Sam

J unior year was one of the happiest years of my life. Alec was always sweet and made me laugh. We spent hours talking and it seemed like we learned something new about each other every day.

We dressed up as Jack Skellington and Sally from the movie *A Nightmare Before Christmas* for Heather's Halloween party.

When Thanksgiving came, we each had dinner with our own families, and the next day, Alec took me Black Friday shopping for one of those digital photo frames for my parents for Christmas, earning him "The Most Patient Guy Ever" award.

We were talking one afternoon during one of our park dates under the shade of our tree. The sun was peeking through the clouds as I lay on the blanket with my head in his lap. He played with my hair, one of my favorite things. I loved the feel of it as his fingers twirled around the long strands.

I enjoyed going to the park with Alec. I brought a small, insulated basket with bottled water, pastrami sandwiches, and fresh fruit I bought from Mrs. Barrett at the street market that morning. Every free day we had was spent at the park. We never went to his house.

I'd heard that he lived with his aunt. I wanted to ask about his parents, but I always felt his profound sadness on the rare occasion when he mentioned them, which was always followed by a quick subject change.

"I love nature and being outside. It's my favorite place to be. What about you?" he asked as he lifted my hand to his mouth and kissed each finger, making me feel lightheaded.

"Oh, you know, I love nature, too. Breathing in the fresh air and seeing the birds fly and listening to their songs. Lying under the stars and dreaming. My favorite part of the day though, is walking Gage around the neighborhood or taking him to the dog park."

"What's your favorite subject in school so far this year? Mine is definitely English."

"Hmm, how about any class with you?" I giggled. "So I guess that means English and Algebra are tied since we have them together. You know, I could see you as an English teacher someday."

When he didn't respond, I looked up at him. He was staring straight ahead like he hadn't heard me.

"Alec? Did you hear what I said?"

He finally looked down at me and smiled, but it didn't look like his normal smile. "Yeah, sorry. I guess I was . . . lost in thought."

"It's okay, I, umm, need to head back home to study for a science exam I have this week," I murmured.

"Okay."

We packed everything up and headed back to my house.

Sometimes I wasn't sure what to make of him. He liked to have fun and was the most carefree person I knew. But other times, he seemed guarded. Like there was a piece of him he wasn't willing or ready to share. It showed at school in the way he acted when teachers thought he wasn't paying attention. I knew full well he was, but he was also somewhere else in his mind or heart, somewhere he kept closed off from me. I hoped that he would trust me enough to let me in someday.

During one of our afternoon park dates, we had eaten lunch, and were lying under our tree. Alec finally asked me the question he'd evaded answering during our first date at the café so long ago.

"Why did you decide to make and donate your jewelry to the charity auction?"

I curled into his arms as we lay there. Birds were chirping in the trees as I gathered my thoughts.

"A few years ago, my cousin, Jolie, was driving home from a party drunk. She blew through a stoplight and hit a car head-on. The accident was indescribable. I still don't know how they were able to separate the cars. The couple in the car she hit had been celebrating their first wedding anniversary. The husband lived, but his wife died instantly. Unlike in most drunk driving accidents, so did Jolie. I miss her terribly."

Alec handed me a napkin from the basket and I wiped at the tears as I cried.

"We'd always been close, more like friends than cousins. She never made me feel like a little girl the way everyone else did. Anytime we had the chance, we'd watched movies together, or she'd style my hair and do my make-up. My mom and Aunt Olivia, Jolie's mom, always laughed at the mischief we got into.

Aunt Olivia tours the country, speaking at high schools. She talks about the consequences of drinking and driving. About Jolie, and the couple she hit. How it changed the husband's life and affected the families of all those left behind. I lowered my eyes so he couldn't see the hurt and inhaled deeply. "I miss her so much. I wish she never got into that car. There's never an actual 'okay enough to drive,' ya know. I mean, if someone's been drinking then they just shouldn't drive. Period."

Alec was so sweet, he hugged me close. "I'm so sorry for your loss, Samone."

But when I asked him the same question, his answer stole the breath from my lungs. "So why were you helping set up that day at the charity?"

His eyes lost some of their light, and his mood turned somber. It was so slight, I would've missed it if I hadn't been staring at his handsome face. He reached down and caressed my face with one hand, while the fingers of his other played in my hair. It felt like he was seeking comfort or strength. I think he needed both.

"Samone, do you remember when our sophomore year started, and I wasn't there at the beginning?"

"Yes, you came after Labor Day, I think. I remember Heather talking about 'the smoking-hot, new guy' in her English Lit class." I giggled. "Hadn't you just moved here?"

"Yeah . . . but it wasn't a good move. Believe me, I'm happy we did move here, specifically because of you. But my older brother, Emjay and I moved up here from Southwest Florida. Just before my sixteenth birthday, my mom and dad were . . ."

He paused and looked down at me, caressing my face. His brow scrunched together and his chin began to quiver. I knew this wasn't going to be good, and I didn't want to cause him pain.

"Hey, it's okay. You don't have to tell me if it's going to upset you."

"No, Samone, I want to tell you. I want you to know all about me, because I want to know all about you, too. I don't want us to have any secrets."

He pulled my hand up and pressed his lips to the top of it, weaving his fingers through mine as he continued his story.

"My parents were on their way home from the airport. My dad had gone to pick up my mom. She'd been visiting her sister, my Aunt Robin, here in Atlanta. She had a late flight. They were at a stoplight when a drunk driver going eighty-five miles an hour hit their car."

I couldn't believe my ears. It felt like a bag of rocks had settled in my stomach. I lay there frozen in his arms as he went on.

"The coroner said that Dad died instantly. But Mom didn't. When the ambulance got there, she was alert and begging my dad not to leave her and their boys." He leaned his head back and pinched the bridge of his nose. "They had to use the jaws-of-life to get to her, and by the time they did, she was gone, too. My best friend's dad was one of the EMTs on the scene, and he told my brother and me later that she died holding Dad's hand." His breath caught. "And her last words were 'Tell my boys I love them.'" He squeezed my hand and looked up to the sky. "The drunk driver lived and is now serving a sentence at a state prison in Florida."

I couldn't breathe, and my chest hurt as I watched the tears flow freely down Alec's face. As my own tears fell, he held my hand tighter.

"Since Emjay was eighteen, I was able to stay with him. Mom and Dad both had hefty life insurance policies. Our inheritance was enough to get us moved up here with Aunt Robin. We still each have money for college with savings left over."

He gazed down at me as I gently rubbed my thumb over his fingers.

"But we both had to get the hell out of that town. Everyone was nice and helpful, but everywhere we looked, we saw pity in people's eyes. Just when we'd have a day we were able to get through without falling completely apart, all it took was those sorrowful looks from neighbors or the postman. It would bring it all crashing back. It made the pain of losing Mom and Dad even worse."

Alec startled me when he jumped up and leaned against the tree.

"I've never been able to talk about this with anyone before."

"I'm so sorry, Alec. You must think I am such a baby for being so sad and missing Jolie like I do since *she was* the drunk driver in her accident." I choked on a sob.

"No, no . . . definitely not," he said as he sat back down and held me close, kissing the top of my head.

"In life, no matter the cause or who's at fault, all deaths leave wounded hearts and broken loved ones behind. People make mistakes; it's part of living, Samone. But it doesn't mean that we shouldn't mourn them when they're gone."

His words choked me up. They reached into my soul and made me feel whole and hollow all at the same time. It was like he spoke out of one of his old English poetry books. But I knew the words came from his soul directly to touch and heal mine.

"I love you, Alec," I whispered.

He smiled down at me. "Love you always."

How he could have experienced the devastating loss of his parents and still hold compassion in his heart amazed me and left me in awe of him. I realized then that this incredibly sexy, sweet guy was also a beautiful old soul, and I was so grateful that he was mine.

CHAPTER 5

The Sky, Balloons And Other Things

Sam

Our love continued to grow with each day. As the summer before our senior year came to an end, Alec surprised me with something I'd always dreamed of. The sound of tapping woke me up. I cracked my eyes open, waiting for everything to come into focus. The sun peeked through my bedroom curtains. It was such a beautiful morning. Shaking my head with a wry smirk, I crawled off the bed, knowing only one person would be plinking pebbles at my window.

I shuffled to my window and spread the curtains wide. Smiling up at me was my Alec. I didn't know how it was possible and had never experienced anything like it in my life, but damn, I loved him.

He waved me down, and I noticed he had a Starbucks cup in his hand. He knew me too well. I was a coffee and hot tea junkie and thanked God every single day that we had a Starbucks within five miles from anywhere in town. I threw my bathrobe on over my sleep shorts and tank top and ran downstairs to see what my sweet guy was up to.

"Hi baby," I said as I wrapped my arms around him and my body molded into his.

"Good morning Samone," he said back as he smiled. "I have a surprise for you," he chuckled, knowing how I loved surprises, especially from him.

"Tell me please, please, please. Alec, don't make me wonder this time. I'm dying to know."

He handed me my crème brûlée latte, bringing a smile of appreciation to my face.

"How about I just give you a hint?" He smiled down at me and squeezed me tight.

"Oh, okay" I drew out the last word before I took a drink.

"It's such a nice day, and the sky is so clear, I thought looking at the mountains would be amazing from a higher vantage point."

"Hmm, cryptic much?" I pouted.

"Why don't you go inside, grab a shower, and get dressed, maybe a light sweater would be a good idea, too."

A light sweater? Was he crazy? It was in the high seventies outside, not hot, but certainly not cold enough for a sweater. In fact, it was my favorite time of year. It was absolutely beautiful outside.

I ran inside and showered. I dressed in my favorite jeans and his worn Falcons t-shirt. It was so comfortable, and I was going to keep it as long as possible. My sweater caught my eye as I walked out of my closet. I shook my head and grabbed it before leaving my room.

When I walked downstairs, Alec was having a cup of coffee with my mom and dad. They were outside, my parents at the porch table and Alec sitting on our swing, all of them laughing. He patted the seat beside him, and I walked over and sat down. When he handed me my latte, I smiled knowing he'd heated it in the microwave for it to still be nice and hot.

"Well we better get going, Samone. Mr. and Mrs. Lang, always a pleasure." He kissed the top of my mom's hand and shook my dad's.

Mom laughed. "Alec, you're such a charmer."

"You kids have a great time today," my dad replied as he slipped a folded paper into Alec's fist when they shook hands goodbye.

I looked at Alec, curious what that was all about.

We drove for about forty-five minutes. I watched out the windows, looking for some clue to where we were going. Finally, we came to a field with a lone warehouse and something I couldn't quite make out in the distance. The sign, however, answered my ever-growing curiosity, and I squealed with glee.

"We're going on a hot air balloon ride!"

He chuckled as he pulled his truck up into the parking area.

We went inside, and he signed us in as Alec Morris and Samone Lang. I smiled as my mind flashed to the inside tab of my school folder where I had doodled Mrs. Samone Morris about a thousand times.

We took a seat in the waiting area. Alec rested his hand on my thigh as I flipped through an issue of Travel and Leisure they had in a magazine rack. The man behind the counter called our names, and we walked up and had to show our ID's. It was then Alec pulled out the folded piece of paper my dad had handed him. It was a parental consent form since I was still seventeen. I looked up at him and he winked. Smartass always thought of everything.

The man led us outside behind the warehouse, and we rode in a little golf cart out to the large object I couldn't quite make out earlier. It was a hot air balloon. They were just now lighting the fire in the basket to begin filling the balloon with air while it laid on its side on the ground. As another man walked over, I smiled up at Alec and squeezed his hand. He kissed the top of my head.

"I love you," he whispered in my hair.

"I love you right back."

The new man was introduced to us as our pilot. We listened to the safety rules, and when he finished, I looked over and saw that the balloon was fully upright. Holy hell . . . it was gigantic. My heart started hammering with anticipation, and I could hardly wait to get in the basket and start our ride.

He squeezed my hand in his. "Are you excited?"

"Yes, I can't wait! Oh Alec, this is the best! Thank you so much for this amazing surprise!"

We followed the pilot in, and as the balloon rose, the earth grew smaller. When I shivered in the cool air, Alec helped me into my sweater. Wow, he really did think of everything. He rubbed my arms, and hugged me close as we looked out over Georgia. The landscape was beautiful. There were green trees everywhere. We sailed over Red Top Mountain and Allatoona Lake. I'd never realized it before, but it wasn't shaped like a typical lake. It was a big body of water, but it weaved through the land like a finger tracing a squiggly line. As we drifted toward Fort Mountain, there were ponds and smaller lakes scattered about the land. We saw baseball, soccer, and football fields. The cars and trucks seemed so small from the balloon. It truly felt like we were floating on a cloud, and the sky was clear and beautiful.

We were in visual range and saw Fort Mountain. It was even more breathtaking from that vantage point. He pointed out a lake we'd camped near once. Alec held my hand in his and we talked of our plans for after graduation and watched the birds flying below us. He pointed to different landmarks and noted where we were gliding above.

"I have an idea. What if, after we graduate, instead of staying on campus at Kennesaw State, we got an apartment together? My inheritance is enough that it would cover the cost of a simple apartment. We wouldn't need anything fancy." Alec said.

"Oh, yes!" I squealed.

"Do you think your parents will be okay with us living together?"

"Well I'll be eighteen then, and they've always encouraged me to follow my heart. Plus, it helps that they adore you."

I was so excited I couldn't wait to start looking at ads in the newspaper. I just hoped Mom and Dad would go for it. Alec was serious about school, so I knew it wouldn't get in the way of my studies.

I hoped we'd get accepted at Kennesaw State.

"Have you chosen a major yet?" I asked him.

"Yeah, English, I think. I'm sure you're not surprised." He laughed. "I've always wanted to be a teacher, and you know English is my favorite subject, so it just makes sense. I'll do something that encompasses the things I like best. My dad always said if you love your job, that's more than half the battle of life since you spend so much time of your day doing it. What about you?"

"I think I'm going to study psychology. I've always wanted to help people, and there are so many psychological illnesses. It's misunderstood, and a lot of people need help with it. I'd like to help them have and live happier everyday lives and feel better."

He smiled at me with that grin of his. "Samone, you'll make the best psychologist ever, I can't imagine anyone with a bigger or more caring heart."

When the ride ended, it felt too soon, and I didn't want the trip to be over. We thanked the pilot for an amazing excursion, and Alec drove us to our park.

With the excitement of my surprise, I hadn't noticed the cooler in the back of his truck. As he grabbed it, I picked up the blanket and small basket sitting beside it.

We walked over to our oak tree, which was thankfully clear of people. Spreading the blanket on the ground, I opened the basket as Alec pulled bottles of water out of the cooler, an apple, pastrami sandwiches, and a small baggie of cheddar cheese cubes. We sat and ate our lunch together under our tree. After we finished, Alec leaned back against the tree and I lay down with my head in his lap. He combed his fingers through my hair with the most delicate touch. Between the balloon ride and our lunch under the tree, it was the most beautiful day ever . . . one I would never forget.

The next morning, Tricia came into town for Jolie's memorial dinner, and I couldn't wait to spend some quality time with my sister.

"Hey, Tricia!" I called as I came downstairs to see her at the table having coffee with Mom and Dad. She got up and gave me a hug.

"How's my little sis? Looking adorable as usual, I see. Are you ready for our spa day?"

"I'm great, thanks, but what about you? Did you have a good drive down? When did you get here?" I replied as I stretched my arms up above my head.

"Yeah, it was good, and virtually no traffic, so I got here early and had a cup of coffee with Mom and Dad while waiting for your sleepy head to wake up," she said, making us all laugh.

"We should get going soon, or we'll be dealing with the Atlanta traffic."

"Yeah, just give me a minute. I'll be right back."

I ran upstairs and grabbed my sandals then met Tricia outside. She owned the cutest car, a red Nissan Juke. I hadn't seen it before; she bought it after her last visit home. Mom and Dad were outside checking it out.

"Wow! Your new car is amazing! I love it."

She smiled. "Thanks, Sam. Now let's get in and go so we aren't late."

Traffic was light. I told her about the hot air balloon ride Alec had taken me on.

"Damn, he sounds like a keeper."

"I know. I'm in love with him. He asked me to get an apartment with him while we go to KSU. Hopefully, we'll both get accepted. If Mom and Dad are okay with it, he wants to start looking right after graduation so we're ready and moved in before classes start in the fall."

"Wow. So you really think Mom and Dad will be cool with that?"

"Yes, I do. Tricia, they love Alec. He's kind of an old soul, and I think they can relate to him. Plus, he's responsible about everything; I think they'll feel better knowing I'll be living with him rather than on my own."

"If you say so. Damn. That never would have flown with me. 'No, Tricia, this; no, Tricia, that.' It's true, you know, what they say . . . that the babies of the family are spoiled with the lax rules." Narrowing her eyes in my direction, she added, "You're lucky I love you so much."

As we picked out our nail polish, we giggled at some of the colors they had available. When they called us back to begin our pampering treatments, we looked at each other and sighed. Our facials were heavenly, the manicures, and pedicures were just what we needed to unwind.

After we finished, we grabbed a late lunch. Then spent the rest of the day walking around the mini-mall.

"Sam, check out that window display in Cindy's Boutique."

"Oh, wow! That's really cute."

She smiled. "Yeah, let's go see if they have our sizes."

We walked inside and went directly to the sales rack with the window display clothing.

"Awesome! Let's go try these on." I said.

We walked back and waved to Cindy. She was the sweetest lady and always had the latest, trendy clothes to choose from. As I slipped my dress on, I imagined how Alec's face would look when he saw me in it, I suddenly felt flushed and excited.

"Tricia, I want to see your dress, so come out when you've got it on," I whispered.

"Okay."

I was standing at the tri-mirror, looking at the front, back, and sides of the dress. I loved it. Tricia came out of her changing stall, looking like a runway model. She was beautiful.

"Wow, you look great!"

"Thanks. I really like it," she said, blushing.

She looked me up and down with a sly smile. "Yours looks fantastic, I bet that boyfriend of yours will love it!" She wiggled her eyebrows.

"Oh God, Tricia, stop. You're embarrassing me."

"I'm just saying how I see it. Besides, he's a guy. Of course he's going to love the way it hugs your curves."

"Now you're just making it worse," I deadpanned.

"Okay, okay." She raised her hands in surrender. "Geez."

We changed back into our clothes and walked to the

counter to make our purchases.

Putting our bags in the back of her car, she held her hand against her chest in mock disdain, "Good Lord, now I'm gonna have to find a guy to take me somewhere to wear this dress, you know that, right, Sam?"

I blushed. She was perceptive as always.

"Yes, yes, I know, you already have Alec," she teased.

My phone beeped with a text message. I looked at the lock screen and saw it was from Alec.

> **A:** Sorry I took so long to reply. I can come to dinner.
>
> **Me:** Great! I'll see you tomorrow.
>
> **A:** Ok.

I shook my head. Usually he ended our texts with *Love you always*.

> **Me:** I love you.
>
> **A:** You, too.

"Huh," I muttered to myself.

"What's that?" Tricia asked.

"Oh, nothing. Umm, Alec is coming to dinner tomorrow though."

"Sweet." She drew out the word.

"God, Tricia, please don't embarrass me."

"Stop, you know I won't," she admonished, "Let's call Mom on the way home, and see if she needs anything from the store for tomorrow's dinner. Aunt Olivia should be arriving soon," she said.

"Okay, sounds good."

CHAPTER 6

Strange

Sam

Senior year was flying by. I was on my way to my car after lunch to get a bracelet I'd made Heather for her birthday when I saw Alec getting out of his truck. He'd been acting strange for a couple weeks.

"Hey, baby," I called as I ran up to him.

"Huh? Oh. Hi Samone," he murmured.

I paused and stepped back, looking up at the guy I loved. "Alec, why are you just getting to school? It's lunchtime. Is everything all right? You've been acting weird lately."

"Everything's fine. I've just—been busy. Not a big deal." He roughed his hands through his hair. "Look, I'm running late as it is. I'll catch up with you later."

He brushed past me, heading toward the school office. I leaned back against his truck and wondered what the hell that was all about. I had to find out what was going on, whether he wanted to tell me or not. This evasive crap had to stop.

I met up with Heather in my last class of the day and gave her the bracelet I'd made.

"It's beautiful, Sam! Thank you." She covered her mouth, looking around, "Phew, I thought for sure Mr. Meade heard me."

"You're welcome. I'm glad you like it," I said as I put my head down on my desk with a thunk.

"Hey, what's wrong?"

"I don't know. It's Alec. Something's not right, and I wish I knew what it was."

"Oh, he's just a guy. Who knows what causes their mano-pausal mood swings." She laughed.

Heather pulled a chuckle from me, too, half-hearted, but it was better than nothing.

"Sam, that guy is in love with you. Everyone knows it. We can all see it."

"Yeah, I guess you're right," I whispered.

The bell rang, so we made our way to our cars. As we walked by Alec's truck, we saw Peter standing at the front passenger side.

"Peter!" Heather called as she ran up and hugged him from behind.

He turned around and kissed her.

"What are you doing?" she asked.

"Just checking out Alec's truck. I was on my way to my car when I noticed it looked like he'd wrecked it." He looked up at me. "Oh . . . hey, Sam."

"Wrecked? What? Let me see," I shrieked.

"There." He pointed to the front bumper.

I gasped and my hand flew to my mouth as I saw the damage.

"Maybe that's why he was weird this morning," Heather said.

"No, well yeah . . . maybe, but he's been acting weird for a couple weeks." I groaned.

"Ah Sam, don't worry about it. He probably just slept like shit," Peter said as he took Heather's bag. "We gotta get going. See ya around."

"How can I not worry?" I murmured.

"It'll be okay. Remember . . . he loves you. I'll call ya later."

"Okay, bye guys." I waved.

I stood there, staring at the mangled metal. I decided to wait for Alec to come out. As the minutes passed, I was torn between being worried and angry. Finally, he walked out to his truck. The grim set of his mouth made me momentarily consider letting the issue go, but I had to make sure he was all right.

"Alec, are you okay? What happened to your truck?"

"I'm fine. I'll get it fixed. Don't worry about it."

My jaw hung open as I looked at him, not quite sure I knew who was talking to me anymore.

"Of course I'm gonna worry! You were late for school . . . again. Clearly, you were involved in a car accident. One minute you won't talk to me, and the next you're taking me on hot air balloon rides. Just tell me what's going on, please."

He ran his hands through his hair and sighed. "I'm sorry. Yes, I ran into a road barricade this morning. But I'm fine. It's just a little damage to my truck. That's why I was late." He pulled me to him and wrapped his arms around me. My shoulders relaxed as he leaned down and kissed me softly. "Love you always."

"I love you, too."

CHAPTER 7

Fresh Air
And Happiness

Alec

I'd never had a girlfriend longer than a few months, let alone over a year. It was nearing Christmas, and we were almost half through our senior year. Classes were good, especially the ones I had with Samone. School was easy for me. Sometimes it was too easy, and my mind would drift back to when I lived in Florida. It would always dwell on the worst day of my life.

At least in the classes we had together, she would pick up on my mood change and distract me from my own personal hell. The way her soft, rose-colored lips would turn up in a smile, and the look of love in her eyes affected me in those dark moments, was a miracle in and of itself.

I left to pick up Samone for a hike at Sweetwater Creek State Park. My truck ran a little rough, so I knew it was time for a tune-up. I didn't mind though. I loved working on my truck. It reminded me of when Dad taught Emjay and me about engines, and we started working on his Camaro together. That was a fun project with good memories, it meant the world to me, especially now. I made a mental note to take some time tomorrow morning and give it a good look over and an oil change.

Pulling into Samone's driveway, I saw her sitting on the front porch swing. The way her face lit up when she saw my truck made me smile. It made me feel like an asshole, too. She was right. Something was wrong. I just couldn't talk to her about it yet.

She was amazing and the most beautiful girl I'd ever seen. She had the kindest heart and was extremely smart. Her level of creativity was remarkable. I had no doubt she could sell the jewelry she'd made.

I was glad we'd run into each other at the charity event. I'm not sure why, but I had to talk to her that day. I had to know her. Now I did, and my feelings for her were unlike anything I'd ever felt before. I could see us together for a long time, maybe even forever if we were lucky. I knew a good thing when I saw it, and Samone Lang was definitely that.

"Hey, my uptown girl," I said as I got out of my truck.

"Hi yourself," she said, smiling up to me.

"Are you excited to go hiking? The weather is supposed to be perfect."

"Yeah, I packed us a little lunch for when we reach the old mill." She winked.

I walked over and pulled her into me. Wrapping my arms around her, I kissed her softly on the cheek. She looked up at me with wide eyes, her mouth splitting into a broad grin that showed me how excited she was to see me.

"Ready to go?"

"Yup, let me just grab our food."

I watched her run back up the steps to the porch swing. I couldn't stop myself from staring at her sexy, little ass.

She walked back down the steps, carrying two narrow CamelBak backpacks containing what I assumed were our lunches and water. I took them from her and set them in the back of my truck.

I opened the door, and she brushed against me. Her touch shot currents of heat across my body and felt electric to my soul. I felt connected to this girl. I didn't understand why, but it made me feel alive, and I loved it.

I ran around to the driver's side and hopped in, relishing in the way she watched me slide into the driver's seat and put my key into the ignition. She glanced up and saw me staring at her then blushed a crimson red.

I rested my hand on her knee as I backed out of her driveway, hoping it might relieve any anxiety. She squeezed my hand in reassurance as I drove off.

It was early in the day, and we made record time driving down toward Atlanta. Even on the weekends, the traffic was typically stop-and-go. I pulled into the park and left my truck in the lot near the office.

"Which trail do you want to take?" Samone asked.

I smiled. "I was thinking either the yellow or white. Sound good to you?"

"Yes, sounds good. We could do both if you want to."

"Yeah, let's do that," I said

I handed her the purple CamelBak, putting the black and red one on my back. We walked hand-in-hand toward the trailhead.

I smiled to myself as we went along the water's edge and stopped every so often for her to take pictures. Sweetwater Creek State Park was one of Samone's favorite places. I loved bringing her here. When we reached the mill, we stopped at the lookout for lunch. I was surprised when I saw her pull a mini thermos out of her pack.

"What's in there?" I asked

She blushed pink in her cheeks as she looked up at me with a small smile. "It's a . . . umm . . . a mocha latte."

I laughed before I could stop myself. "I'm sorry, but . . . isn't it a little hot outside for a latte?"

Her eyes narrowed, and I worried I'd offended her.

"It's an iced mocha latte, thank you very much. And it's small. I only brought it for the taste. I'm kind of addicted to them," she finished, casting her eyes down.

"Oh. Okay. Sorry. I was just surprised. Sometimes I forget

how much you love them. Most kids our age aren't into coffee drinks."

"It's okay. I know I'm not normal," she pouted.

I reached out and lifted her chin. Locking her gaze with mine, I leaned forward and gently kissed her soft lips. "No, you're not. You're unique, and that's even better. I don't want a cookie-cutter girlfriend."

Her eyes snapped to mine, and she smiled, biting her bottom lip. I couldn't stop watching her as we ate the rest of our lunch.

"That was really good. Thanks," I said.

"You're welcome. I figured we could stay a little longer than last time if we're not so hungry."

"Good idea. Let's get moving so we can finish both trails."

She stepped up on her tiptoes and gave me a quick kiss on the cheek then started skipping down the path. As I took off behind her, I couldn't remember a time I was so content in my life.

I wondered when the other shoe would drop and everything would be taken away. I was becoming too attached to her. I pushed back thoughts of slowing down. I wanted our relationship to grow and was determined not to let my idiocy get in the way. It was okay to let someone in. It was okay to let Samone in.

CHAPTER 8
Much Needed Family Time

Alec

I woke up early. I couldn't sleep. Emjay was coming home from college to see Aunt Robin and me. It had been months since he'd been home. I loved my brother. We'd always been very close, even closer after Mom and Dad died. For a while, we only had each other, until we moved up here to stay with Aunt Robin. She traveled a lot with her boyfriend, Kent, but knew I was responsible enough to stay out of trouble while she was gone.

I walked downstairs and smelled cinnamon rolls baking and coffee brewing. Clearly, Aunt Robin couldn't sleep either.

"Good morning Aunt Robin."

"Oh, good morning. Did you sleep well?"

"Yeah, it was good. Just woke up early. I guess I'm a little excited to see Emjay today," I answered.

"Me too, dear. Me too. We really need to go see him if it's going to be this long in between his visits home."

"That's a good idea." I smiled.

"Alec, hey!" Aunt Robin startled me.

"What?" I asked, surprised by her worried tone.

"Are you okay?"

"Yeah, I'm fine," I answered confused. "Umm, hey . . . do you need any help with the cinnamon rolls? I can put the icing on for you," I said, my mouth watering as she pulled them out of the oven.

"Yes." She looked at me skeptically, with her brow scrunched down. "Thanks, but that doesn't mean you get to eat one early. You can lick the icing spoon though," she smirked.

I laughed. "Okay."

I took the icing from her and set it in the microwave for ten seconds for easier drizzling. Aunt Robin set the table for when Emjay got there. She always liked to entertain when she was home. I wished that was more often than not.

I heard Emjay's car pull into the drive way and his door shut. Aunt Robin rushed to the front entry to greet him.

"Hey, Aunt Robin."

He sounded older than the last time we'd seen him.

"Hello, dear. We've missed you."

"Are those your homemade cinnamon rolls I smell?"

She laughed. "Yes, they are. See? You should come home more often."

They rounded the corner, and I looked up and saw my brother. I couldn't help the swell of pride that filled me. It had only been a few years since our parents died. For a while, I wondered if he would even go to college. He withdrew into himself. I know he thought the same of me, too. It was, and still is, hard to deal with the death of our parents. To see him coming home from college with a smile on his face gave me relief. I wondered if that happiness had anything to do with the overabundance of beautiful girls on campus.

He walked up and gave me a solid brotherly hug. "Missed ya, little bro."

"I missed you, too, man," I replied. "How long are you staying?"

"Just a couple days," he said. "Then I have to head back for my shifts at work."

"Cool. Well then, Aunt Robin can we eat? I've been smelling these since I woke up and I'm dying to have one," I said as I licked the icing spoon.

She laughed. "Okay, okay. You boys sit down. Let's eat."

"So, Alec has a steady girlfriend since last year, don't you dear," Aunt Robin blurted.

Emjay swung his head around and looked at me, his eyes wide with shock. "Wow, you never told me about her. Why's that?"

"They seem like they're pretty serious too, if you ask me," she said.

"Really, bro? A serious girlfriend . . . for that long? She must be something to break you out of your hermit shell," he teased. "Congrats, man."

"I can interact with the outside world," I deadpanned.

"She's adorable, too," Aunt Robin chimed in.

"Yeah, she's amazing. We met at a drunk driving charity event we were both volunteering at."

Emjay smiled, and I could tell he was happy for me, but he was definitely curious.

"I'd seen her in school before, but . . . well, you know . . . I'm not exactly a social person. Anyway, she's great. Just the thought of her makes me smile. I feel like a goober, but I don't care."

Emjay's eyebrows perked up. "Ha ha! Goober! Can I call you that now?"

"Not unless you wanna wake up to a wet bed from having your hand soaked in warm water."

"Okay. Damn. I was just kidding, ya brat."

"Anyway, her view of the world is innocent and pure. It's refreshing. She doesn't condemn people for the mistakes they've made. She has a pure and forgiving heart."

"Nice! It sounds like you are . . . in love," he said.

"Yeah, I definitely love her. She makes this whole, sometimes very ugly world, better."

"Well that's good. I'm happy for you."

"We all deserve some happiness," Aunt Robin said. "Kent and I are going on a trek across Europe this year, and I, for one, can't wait."

"That's great, Aunt Robin."

"That's awesome," Emjay added. "Take lots of pictures to show us when you get back."

We each ate our breakfast and caught up on each other's lives. When we were done, Emjay and I headed out back to look at my truck.

"It's been running hard on and off for a while. I've gone over it with a fine-toothed comb, but I'm just not sure what the problem is."

"Well it could be a bunch of things. I'll have a look. We can take my car to the auto parts store if there's anything we need."

I turned on the radio, and we both dove into auto repair mode.

CHAPTER 9

The Swimming Hole

Sam

I was sitting at the park having lunch with Heather when I got a text message from Alec.

A: Swimming hole at 4pm. I'll pick you up?

Me: Sounds great! I'll be ready. Love you.

A: Love you always.

I smiled and looked across the picnic table at Heather. "Hey, do you and Peter want to go to the swimming hole with me and Alec? Maybe Marchello and Emily can come, too."

"Oh, hell yeah! Let me text Peter and Emily. She and Marchello were going to walk the trails at Sweet Water. What time should we meet?"

"Alec said he would pick me up at four."

"Okay, count us in. I'm pretty sure Emily and Marchello will be there, too"

"All right, I'm going to head to the mall. I want to get a new bathing suit. I'll see you there." I stood up and gave her a hug.

"Laters."

When I got home, Dad was sitting on the porch talking to

Mr. McGraw from next door. I walked over and kissed Dad on the forehead and waved to Mr. McGraw before walking inside.

I headed upstairs and took a quick shower.

I washed my hair and shaved my legs while the conditioner worked its magic on my unruly hair. As I rinsed the suds off, I thought of Alec. I hoped he would like my new bathing suit. I had only ever worn a one-piece bathing suit around him, so I was a little nervous.

When I got out of the shower, Mom was walking into my bedroom. I showed her my new bikini.

"It's adorable, Sam."

I covered my face with my hands. "Thanks, Mom."

"Is something wrong?"

"Not really. I just haven't worn a two-piece around Alec before, and I guess I'm kind of nervous."

"Oh dear . . . well, you're as cute as a button, and that boy adores you, so I am sure it'll be fine."

"Yeah, I know. So you really like it?"

"Yes, the colors are great. Listen, I'm gonna go downstairs and get dinner going. Will you be back in time?"

"No, I don't think so. Alec isn't picking me up until four. So we'll probably just eat out tonight."

"Okay, have fun and be careful. Love you," she said as she walked out of my bedroom.

I decided to wear my new bathing suit under my clothes. When I put my shorts and shirt back on again, I stood and stared at myself in the mirror. It really was cute. I just hoped Alec would think so. If I was being honest with myself, I was just as excited for Alec to see me in it, as I was nervous.

Alec's horn honked, and I smiled. I looked at my watch and saw it was exactly four pm on the dot. Damn, he was good.

I walked downstairs as Dad was letting Alec in the front door. He stood in the foyer wearing board shorts and a white t-shirt. His tanned legs were mouthwatering, and I suddenly felt other things deep within me at the thought of Alec seeing me in my new bikini.

He looked up at me coming down the stairs in my shorts and thin white t-shirt, through which he could see my bathing suit. I noticed his expression change from happy to surprise, as his jaw went slack when he realized my suit was a bikini. His smile gave me the extra confidence I needed.

I felt goose bumps spread across my skin. He looked in my eyes, his brow slightly raised, his stare intent, and I gave him the "*not here in my parents' house*" look. Shaking my head, I took his hand as he pulled me down the last step and looked around to make sure we were alone. He pulled me into his arms and kissed the top of my forehead.

"You look beautiful," he said, smiling down at me.

"Thanks. You look kind of great yourself," I teased.

He cocked an eyebrow at me and smacked me on my ass, steering me toward the kitchen where my parents were talking.

"Mr. and Mrs. Lang, thanks for letting me take Samone out. I promise to have her home at a decent hour. I do have special plans for dinner, she doesn't know about yet. So it may be later than usual if that's all right."

My head had jerked up when he mentioned special dinner plans.

"Yes, that's fine, Alec," my dad said.

My mom gave me a wave and put a pan in the oven.

"You kids have fun and be careful," Dad said as we walked to the foyer.

"Thanks, Dad. We will. Love you guys,"

I followed Alec out as he held the screen door for me.

"Oh, Alec, wait. I need a change of clothes for dinner," I said as I stopped at the stairs. "What kind of outfit should I have?"

"Anything semi-casual is fine."

"Umm, okay. I'll be right back."

I could feel his eyes on me as I ran upstairs. I quickly grabbed the new dress I bought with Tricia. I threw in my make-up bag and hairbrush for good measure. Running downstairs, I saw him waiting for me. He smiled with that sexy smirk of his.

As we got to his truck, he leaned over and captured my mouth with his. Feeling his hands in my hair as he pulled me closer to him was exhilarating.

"Mmm, kissing me like that in my driveway where my dad can see could get you smack-full of buckshot, mister," I teased

"Ha! Never. Your parents adore me."

"Yeah, that's true, they do."

"So, to the swimming hole then dinner. Where did you say we were going again?"

"I didn't say, little miss sneaky. You'll find out when I'm damn good and ready to tell you."

"Fine. Don't tell me." I stuck out my lower lip in a pout I knew he couldn't resist.

"Okay, this time I'll tell you. I swear, Samone, you're spoiled rotten." He winked. "We're going to have dinner at The Sundial Restaurant in Atlanta."

"Holy crap! Seriously? I've always wanted to go there. I can't wait."

"Good, I'm happy you're happy."

We arrived at the swimming hole a few minutes later. Everyone else was already there. It was good to see our friends. I jumped out of the truck and waved to everyone while I stripped down to my bikini behind the truck door. That's when Alec walked around and saw me.

He stood there staring at me with his mouth hanging open. It made me feel empowered to insight such a reaction in him.

"Wow, you look—incredible," he breathed.

My cheeks felt hot. "Thanks. I . . . was hoping you'd like it. I just bought it this afternoon after your text."

"Well, you did great picking it out," he said as his eyes roamed all over my body.

I felt tingles and heat everywhere.

"As much as I want to just stand here and look at you, we should probably head over, before they start staring at us."

"Okay." I laughed nervously.

"Hey, everyone," I said as we walked over to them.

Alec sat down on a big tree stump and he pulled me onto his lap. His hand was running up and down my back, finally resting near my waist. His touch left a heated trail all along my skin.

"Who's in first?" Alec asked

"Always me!" Marchello yelled as he jumped on the rope swing and dropped into the water, leaving a big splash that soaked Emily and Heather.

We laughed as the girls shrieked from the cold water hitting them. We each took our turns swinging from the rope and dropping into the water, swimming and having fun. As it got later, Alec whistled for my attention. I swam over from the girls to meet him, and he wrapped me up in his arms.

"We should get going," he said between kisses, "if we're going to make our dinner reservation."

"Oh." I smiled. "Let's go."

We made our way to the bank where the others had gathered.

"Hey, we're gonna take off. I have dinner reservations and definitely don't want to get stuck in traffic," he said.

"Okay, we'll see you guys next time," Peter said, and the others waved.

Alec climbed up the bank and helped me out. He ran over to his truck and grabbed our towels, meeting me halfway back. I wrapped the towel around me and warmed up. Drying off, it occurred to me I had nowhere to change or deal with my wet hair.

"Alec, where am I going to change?"

"I thought we could drive a little down the road and you could change in the truck. I'll change outside behind the truck bed."

"Oh, okay. That'll work."

We drove down the road to an overgrown section of woods. He got out and grabbed a duffle bag out of the truck bed. I dried off the excess water and changed into my dress.

I couldn't stop myself from peeking in the side view mirror and gasped when I saw Alec pulling his pants up over his cute ass. He turned around and caught me looking, and I threw my hands up over my face. It was my own fault I peeked and he'd caught me looking.

He turned to me "I brought an extra towel for your hair. It's right here in my bag."

"Oh thanks. That'll help."

He always thought of everything.

"Thanks, Alec. It's been an awesome afternoon. I can't wait for dinner."

"You're welcome. I can't wait either."

I couldn't help but notice as his voice sounded nervous, and the way his thumb tapped the steering wheel as he drove.

CHAPTER 10

Firsts

Sam

We got to the restaurant and rode the elevator up to the top of the building. It was beautiful seeing the city lights through the walls of glass.

"Wow, it's so pretty here. Look at the view," I whispered.

He smiled at me. "I was hoping you'd like it."

"Have you been here before?" I asked. "I wonder what's good. I bet everything's delicious."

"No, I haven't eaten here before. But I'm glad my first time is with you." He smiled softly, taking my hand in his.

"Me, too. It's just so beautiful with the sunset. You couldn't have picked a better time to come."

My eyes locked back onto Alec. "This is so romantic. Thank you for such a fun day and amazing dinner."

"Anything for you, Samone."

My heart warmed, and I felt the smile spread across my face. The way he looked at me, his intense stare, made me feel complete.

"I love you."

"Love you always."

As we ate our meals, I kept peeking up to catch him

watching me. I felt like we were passing on to a new phase. I just wasn't sure what that phase was yet.

When we left, Alec took the highway home. He passed the exit for my house.

"Where are we going?"

"Well it's pretty early still, and . . . Aunt Robin is in Europe, so I thought we could hang out at my house for a few hours, maybe watch a movie before I take you home," he said in a shaky voice.

I wondered what could have affected his usual confident mood.

"Oh, okay. That sounds great."

We pulled up to his house. I'd only been there once before to meet his aunt. It was strange though. There weren't any family pictures on the walls. There was artwork, the walls weren't bare, but maybe they didn't want the constant reminder of the loss of Alec's parents. In my house, we had family pictures scattered all around.

Alec put his truck in park and things began to suddenly feel very real. With his Aunt out of town and his brother away at college, we'd be alone. In his house. Quite possibly . . . in his bedroom.

I felt flushed with anticipation that tonight could be the night we gave ourselves to each other. I loved him with every ounce of my being. If it felt right for him, too, and we both wanted to, I decided then and there that I would do it. I loved him. I wanted him. I wanted this next step in our relationship.

As he unlocked the front door, my nerves skyrocketed. He held my hand in his as we walked inside, smiling back at me, and I felt relieved.

That's how Alec was; he could wind me up and calm me down all at the same time. I followed him into the kitchen, the big empty house silent. He poured us both a glass of sweet tea.

"Would you like to watch a movie?"

"Sure. Whatever you want," I said as my hands started to fidget at my sides.

He got that sexy smirk back on his face. "Whatever? So—

anything I want, is that what you're saying?"

I felt my cheeks flush as I slowly nodded.

"All right then," he said as he tilted his head in thought, "Let's . . . watch a movie."

He led me to the couch in the living room. Sitting down I looked around and saw a chaise lounge near the fireplace. It's funny, the things you notice, and focus on when you're nervous.

It had gotten chilly outside, so he lit the fireplace. As the fire crackled, we sat on the couch.

"What sounds good?"

"I don't know. Anything really," I said

"Well, let's see what's on. Hmm . . . how about *The Notebook?* That's one of your favorites."

"Yes, I love that movie, Alec, but it's as chick flick, as chick flicks get. Not exactly one you would like. We can find something else."

"Nah, that's okay. We'll watch this. It doesn't really matter to me."

My stomach fluttered. I looked up into his eyes as he held my gaze.

"I just want to spend time with you, and hold you in my arms for a while, before I have to drive you home."

We settled in to watch the movie, but I couldn't get comfortable on the couch, so Alec moved us to the chaise lounge by the fireplace. I snuggled onto his lap, his long legs stretching out beneath me. While the movie played, his fingers weaved through my hair, and he occasionally kissed the top of my head.

I felt safe and loved in his arms. I leaned back against his chest, and he tipped my mouth up to his, kissing me softly.

"I love you Samone," he said as he stared into my eyes.

"I love you, too," I whispered.

He ran his hand up and down my back, into my hair, and settled on caressing my face. "I want to make love to you. I want us to be our firsts."

My breath caught in the back of my throat. "I . . . I want that, too Alec."

"Really?"

"Yes, but . . . I'm not on birth control." I said nervously as I twisted at my bracelet.

"It's okay. I have it covered."

He shifted me off his lap and stood up. I held my breath as he reached into his back pocket and pulled out a foil packet. His expression was one of nervousness mixed with love, and I felt my eyes open wide as I watched him place it on the side table.

"I . . . uh, bought them when I realized I wanted to share this part of me with you," he stammered.

My mind raced a million miles a minute. What if it wasn't good? What if *I* wasn't good? Was it going to hurt? I'd never done this before.

"Oh, stop, Sam." I muttered aloud.

"What's that?"

"Oh, umm, nothing. Just . . . talking to myself."

"Are you all right?"

"Yeah, I'm good."

He brushed his hand down the side of my face. "Let's go up to my bedroom," he whispered.

I looked around and shook my head.

"It's okay. We don't have to do this, if you're not ready."

"No, that's not what I was shaking my head about. I . . . I just don't really want to go up to your room right now. I mean, we have the entire house to ourselves, and this beautiful fire is right here. It's . . . pretty romantic, Alec."

"Oh. Good. You mean right here? On the chaise?" He looked surprised.

I felt my cheeks flush. "Yeah, I mean, if that's okay."

"Anything you want is good with me, Samone."

As I thought of what we were about to do my stomach fluttered.

He stepped back and grabbed the hem of his t-shirt, pulling it up and over his head, only breaking eye contact with me momentarily. I watched as the muscles in his abs and chest flexed with his movements. As he kicked each shoe off, my pulse began to speed up.

Okay, it's my turn. Just take my dress off . . . I can do this.

I looked up at him then, standing there, watching me. He gave me a small smile, and I felt his love, his complete adoration. I slipped my hand in his as he held it out to me, and I stood on shaky legs. He gently rubbed his thumb back and forth. His gaze never left mine as he reached down and freed the button of his jeans. When he began to lower his zipper, I found the courage I needed to slip my arms through the straps of my dress, letting it slide to the floor. I dropped my eyes while he looked at me standing there.

"Please don't look down, Samone."

I glanced up at him, as he stood there with his eyes roaming over my body.

"You're absolutely beautiful, and most importantly, the girl I love. I want this to be special between us. Always"

"Me, too."

He pulled me to him, wrapping me up in his arms, and kissed me. It was a kiss like nothing I'd ever felt before. We melded together, and he held me in a possessive embrace. He lowered me onto the chaise, kissing me tenderly. As he hovered over me, he looked into my eyes. My gaze held his as he gently laid kisses on my cheeks, the tip of my nose, and finally settling on my mouth.

"Love you always," he breathed.

"I love you, too," I whispered.

When our bodies met at first, I flinched.

He stopped instantly, as a look of terror spread across his face. "I'm so sorry. Are you all right? Is . . . this okay? Do you want me to stop?" he rambled.

"No, I'm good. It just hurt a little. But it's okay now." I kissed him as he looked down at me with wonder.

He took his time and made sure we both felt our love and

passion. I hugged him to me and kissed each corner of his mouth, running my hands down his strong arms, winding my fingers in his.

We moved together as one, cherishing each other and making love by the fire. Our bodies wrapped around each other in tangled limbs. I didn't think I could ever feel any closer to another human being than I did at that moment with Alec.

CHAPTER 11

Bliss

Sam

It had been four weeks since we'd discovered our passion. We were studying for our exams, cramming everything we could into our overworked brains. It was exciting being seniors in high school. The world was truly at our feet, as the old saying goes . . . we just had to choose our path.

With only half days remaining, Alec met me for lunch one day after class. As we left hand-in-hand, he led me around the side of the café in the alley.

"So, I was thinking . . . maybe we could hike Sweet Water Creek this weekend," he said.

"That sounds great."

"We could even bring Gage with us if you want."

"Oh, yeah, let's bring him!"

He stopped suddenly and pulled me into his arms, kissing me deeply. I was breathless, staring into his eyes as he stepped back.

"I just had to kiss you," he breathed onto my lips.

"Oh, Okay . . ."

It was all I could say before he leaned in and captured my mouth again. His hands ran up my back and into my hair as he held my head in place.

"I cherish you," he said between kisses. "You're my everything."

He dropped his hands from the back of my head and hugged me to his chest, and I melted into him, wrapping my arms around his waist.

"I love you Alec," I whispered.

"Love you always."

We resumed our hand-in-hand walk back out of the alley and into the parking lot, the sun shining down warm on us.

When we got back to Alec's truck, I watched as he got in. I always got lost in his fluid movements. I was utterly mesmerized by him.

"Where are we going next?"

"I thought we could go see that Robert Downey Jr. movie you've been talking about," he said.

I covered my face. "Oh my God, how did you know that?"

He laughed. "When I walked into the cafeteria, I overheard you talking to Heather about it."

I couldn't look at him. I was so embarrassed. He reached over and turned my chin toward him until I met his crystal blue eyes with mine.

"It's okay. I've known about your infatuation with him since our first date, remember?" he teased.

I smiled and rolled my eyes. "Why don't we just go watch that new action-thriller we both want to see? You did watch *The Notebook* with me a few weeks ago."

"Well Samone, there wasn't much movie watching going on that night," he said as he waggled his eyebrows at me.

My cheeks heated. "Yeah I know, but you intended to, so that counts just the same."

We drove over to the theater, bought our tickets to the movie, then bought a soda and popcorn. When we settled into our seats, he put his arm around me. I snuggled into him and smiled.

"I think we'll have to start catching the late matinee more often. We practically have the theater to ourselves," he whispered in my hair.

"I think so, too."

We watched the movie and shared popcorn. It was another awesome afternoon with Alec, and I was so happy to have him in my life.

I'd been checking the mail for weeks, waiting to see if I'd been accepted to Kennesaw State. The girls had begged me to apply to Auburn as well, so I could be with them. I gave in, as always with them and applied. My acceptance letter for Auburn came in the mail the week before. I didn't tell Alec about that. It's not as if I was actually planning to go there.

When the mail truck stopped in front of my house, I ran downstairs and out the front door to check. I flipped through the envelopes until I found it. My stomach did somersaults as I worried what the contents would say. I pulled my phone out and sent Alec a quick message.

Me: OMG, my KSU letter came!

A: Well, what's it say?

Me: I don't know. I haven't opened it.

A: What are you waiting for?

Me: I'm scared. What if it says I wasn't accepted?

A: I'm sure it won't. You're brilliant, and you have the GPA to prove it.

Me: I just can't open it.

A: Okay, I'll be over shortly.

Me: Thanks. I love you.

A: Love you always.

I sat on my front porch swing while I waited for him to arrive. Tracing my finger across my name and address on the front of the envelope, I prayed it was a yes. I was so lost in my mind, I didn't even know Alec had arrived until he stepped up onto my porch.

"Penny for your thoughts?"

I smiled. "I have about a million at the moment. Did you have one in particular you wanted?"

He laughed and walked over, sitting down on the swing beside me.

I handed him the envelope. "Will you please open it for me?"

He smiled reassuringly and he took it from me. I felt like I was going to throw up as he ran his finger along the top and ripped it open. My eyes were glued to the side of his face. I tried to gauge his reaction while he unfolded and read the letter. His demeanor was as expressionless as his voice was monotone while he read it aloud. Giving me no hint as to the contents until he spoke the words.

"Dear Samone,

Congratulations and welcome to The Owl Family! You have been accepted as a freshman to Kennesaw State University for the Fall Semester to the College of Humanities and Social Sciences."

My mouth hung open, and I watched as he re-folded the letter and slid it back into the envelope. He leaned forward and set it on the table near the swing. When he sat back, he pulled me into his side and held my hand in his.

"Wow. I really got in," I whispered. "Now we just have to wait for yours."

He stiffened slightly. "No, we don't. My acceptance letter came last week."

"What? Why didn't you tell me?" I playfully smacked his shoulder.

He chuckled. "Because I knew it would only make you worry more if you'd known. So I waited for yours to come."

"What . . . what if mine said I wasn't accepted?" I narrowed my eyes at him.

"Then I would have applied to Auburn and hoped I got accepted in time for the fall semester," he said with a lopsided grin.

"Auburn?" I squeaked.

He shook his head and laughed, "Yes, Auburn. You only left your acceptance letter laying open on your dresser. I saw it the last time I was over when we studied for that English Lit exam. I had a feeling Tamron and Alison would try to talk you into going there."

"Well, I'm not. I'm going to KSU with you." I jumped up, grabbed his face and kissed him. Then I turned around, snatched up my letter, and ran inside to tell my parents the good news.

CHAPTER 12

I Didn't See That Coming

Sam

O ur senior year of high school went by fast and, before we knew it, the school was taking orders for our caps and gowns for graduation. Alec and I would be starting Kennesaw State in the fall. We were supposed to start apartment hunting soon, but he'd been acting strange on and off for weeks. He was distant, and not only did it hurt, it had me really worried. I couldn't shake the feeling something was seriously wrong. Some days he was late for school, or he'd leave early. When I asked about it, he blew me off, told me something had come up. His brief explanation about the fender bender still seemed shady. We'd never kept secrets from each other before, at least not up until that point.

When he didn't show up at all one day, I'd had enough of his evasive answers. I was concerned and wanted to know what was going on. I heard his truck pull up to my house just after dinnertime, and I walked out to the front porch to meet him.

As soon as I saw him, I ran up and hugged him. But his body was stiff. He didn't mold himself to me the way he usually did.

He wasn't welcoming, and it felt unnatural, making my heart ache in my chest.

As he pulled away, his touch felt robotic. He took my hand and walked us over to sit on the porch swing, where we used to cuddle, look at the stars, and talk about our dreams. Only now it felt forced, distant, and cold.

Suddenly, I wanted to run inside and hide upstairs in my room. Instead, my body froze in place with the dread of what I feared was coming. My eyes filled with tears, as I felt powerless to stop it.

Alec cleared his throat. "Look, Samone, we need to talk. Things just aren't . . ."

I quickly put my hand over his mouth, wishing it could hold in the words. I let out a whimper as I shook my head. The word "no" was stuck in my throat, but I couldn't find the voice to say it. Then he shifted us on the swing so we were sitting on our own sides. My hand fell from his face to my lap. There was maybe half a foot between us, but it felt like half a mile.

"Really Samone, you have to listen to me . . . please. We need to talk and it just can't wait any longer. It'll only be harder on both of us, and it's better to just get it over with. A . . . clean break, you know, a fresh start," he said.

I just sat there. I didn't know how long it was until he continued. He must have taken my silence for acceptance, because he breathed what seemed like a sigh of relief and began again.

"Things just aren't working out between us, and I think we need to end it here and now while there's still hope of us being friends. Don't . . ." He rested his hand on my shoulder. "Please don't say we can't be friends, Samone. I know we can. We just have to want to. We were too young to think we would be together forever, grow old, and watch our grandchildren play some day. Those are young-love dreams. They're just not realistic. We graduate next month, and it's time to think about the future."

"I don't understand why you're doing this. Everything was perfect. Why are you ruining us? You *were* my future . . ." I whispered, choking on a sob as I hugged myself.

When he reached for my hand, I jerked it away.

"Don't touch me!" I screamed. "Just go, Alec. Leave me alone."

"I'm sorry, Samone. I really am."

He had the balls to look like he meant those last words, and that made me angrier than anything. As I sat there, hugging my knees to my chest, panic overwhelmed me, and my face felt flushed and numb. I watched him walk down the steps and along the path, get in his truck, and drive away. He never even looked back. Apparently, a fresh start for him was easy.

CHAPTER 13

Light Switch

Sam

School sucked. Even after school sucked. Alec wouldn't so much as look at me. I'd never felt so utterly sad in my life. The end of my senior year went from fun and happy to depressed and devastated. Mom and Dad were beside themselves with how to make me feel better. But how could they? I'd spent the better part of two years with a guy I thought I'd spend the rest of my life with. I gave him my virginity. I loved him, only to be crushed in the end.

I was on my way to the cafeteria when I saw Alec coming out of the office. He had a yellow slip of paper in his hand, a late pass. He was late—again. He turned in my direction. I continued on my path. When he was about to walk past me, I stepped in front of him.

"Hey. Just getting here?" I asked.

"Huh? Oh, yeah," he muttered.

"Alec, can we talk please?"

"What about?"

"I . . . I miss you," I whispered as my voice shook.

His face-hardened and he stepped to the side. "You can't say things like that, Samone."

I know he saw the hurt in my eyes, because for a split second, his showed regret.

"But you said you wanted us to be friends."

"I did, but . . . I don't think we can," he warned.

"Please Alec, we *can* be friends. You haven't even *tried!* Most of the time you won't even look at me."

"I guess I was wrong. I was stupid to think we could go from being what we were . . . to being just friends. It's too . . . confusing."

"That's because we love each other. We belong together. I don't know about you, but I can't just turn my feelings off like a damn light switch," I pleaded.

"I'm sorry, Samone, but . . . I don't love you anymore."

He said the words, but his face revealed the lie I knew it to be. I couldn't stop the hope that flooded my heart.

"You're lying. I know it. You know it," I hissed. "I don't know why you're doing this to us, but I hope you figure out whatever the hell it is, fast."

He didn't say another word, just roughed his hand through his hair, turned around, and walked away.

CHAPTER 14

Cold Depths of Crystal Blue

Sam

It was a Saturday night, two long months since Alec had broken up with me. Okay, I'll admit it. I sent him more than a few text messages, pleading with him to give us another chance. He never replied to any of them, not even the picture I sent of us from one of our hiking trips at Sweetwater Creek State Park.

Graduation came and went, I'd hoped, with the celebration of academic achievement and promise of a new life, that things would change, but they didn't, and he remained as aloof as ever.

My eighteenth birthday passed. It was supposed to be one of those landmark birthdays, filled with fun and celebration. I went through the typical eighteenth birthday motions, but my heart just wasn't in it. That night, I sat on the couch, staring at the season passes Alec had bought us for Six Flags Over Georgia. He hadn't been able to wait for my birthday to give them to me. I cried just looking at them, unable to even find a sliver of solace in a bowl of mint chocolate chip ice cream.

One summer evening, when Heather and I were getting

ready for a party at her boyfriend, Peter's house, she said it was time for me to suck it up and show Alec just what he'd thrown away. I knew it was dumb, but I couldn't give up on hope. Maybe, when he saw I was there too, things would just fall back into place. I hoped if he saw me looking my best and happy without him, even if it wasn't genuine, he might want to get back what he gave up . . . what he threw away, you know, the whole "stars aligned-happily ever after" kind of bullshit magic people talk about. But that wasn't realistic.

I hated that word—realistic. It rolled off my tongue like an expletive.

Heather was right. I decided to show him what he'd given up, hoping he would remember the feeling of our love. I always thought it was strong and real. It'd always felt that way. I couldn't reconcile our last months together, even the way he had become distant, with his actions at the end. No matter how much time passed, I couldn't understand or accept he ended us the way he did, that it was over with no hope of us getting back together. I, at least, needed some damn answers.

As we pulled up to Peter's house, I couldn't stop the swell of anticipation and hope at seeing him again. I knew he'd be there. His best friend, Heather's cousin, Marchello, said he would be. He also said, every time one of my text messages came through, Alec's face would go sad before he could stop it, and he'd turn his phone off. But he wasn't seeing anyone. At all. So that had to be a good sign. Right?

I didn't see him when I entered the house. I scanned the living room, but he wasn't there, just countless couples making out on every couch, chair and even the floor in the corner.

Good God, get a room already.

Shaking my head, I turned and grabbed Heather's hand to go get our drinks from Peter's makeshift bar in the kitchen. That's when I saw him.

No wonder I hadn't seen him right away. Some slutty, blonde skank was straddling his lap, grinding her herself into him. He was kissing her neck, and his hands were grabbing her ass, rocking along with the movement of her hips.

I stood frozen in place, my heart slowly breaking again.

How could he do this? I didn't think I could ever feel any worse than I did at that moment. But then, Alec's beautiful crystal blue eyes met mine. They looked cold, different, off somehow. Not like my Alec. But then again, he wasn't *my* Alec anymore.

Nobody else could have recognized the regret in his knitted brow, but I did. At least I thought I did, until he turned his head back to the slut's neck. He pulled her closer, and if they weren't clothed, they could have been having sex right then and there.

So much for "making love" being something you do only with someone who means the world to you, someone you love with your whole heart.

It was special for us the first time we'd made love, or at least I thought it had been. Every time we were together, it had felt special, like we were the only people who existed on the planet. But Alec wasn't making love with this slut. And I knew she wasn't anything special. I'd seen that tramp stamp rocking on guys' laps at parties enough to know that she was always hooking up with whomever would have her. I'd just never imagined my Alec would be one of them.

Flashes of our first time flooded my mind. He'd made it so special. Yeah, it hurt at first, but he was gentle and made me feel like I was his whole world. Watching him with her, I couldn't believe we were each other's first. From what he was doing with her now, I wondered if he'd really been a virgin our first time. He'd never done that with me before.

He slowly stood up as she wrapped her legs around him. When he walked past me, we locked eyes, for the first time ever, a chill ran through me as I looked into the cold depths of crystal blue. He looked like he was pissed at me for being there. He kept walking down the hall as the slut gyrated her overused asset against his waistline. I couldn't peel my eyes away from the scene before me. He set her down and pushed her up against the wall, grinding himself against her while she nuzzled his ear.

With one last angry look at me, he reached around her and opened the guest bedroom door. She grabbed his hand and yanked him in the room, slamming the door behind them, finally breaking his eye contact with me.

I couldn't stop my feet from moving. It was like some force was pulling me toward that bedroom. Finally standing in front of the door, my feet felt glued to the spot where her shrill laughter and slutty moans seeped from the room. Creaks and headboard thumping echoed in a steady rhythm of sex from the room, making my stomach churn.

I couldn't move. I couldn't tear my eyes from that damn bedroom doorknob.

I slid down the wall with my mind focused on the door that stood between me and my whole heart. I didn't think it was possible to hurt any more, but at that moment, my heart was well and truly shredded.

CHAPTER 15

Goodbye Atlanta, Hello Auburn

Sam

The next thing I remembered was waking up in my bed. I took a shower, got dressed, made a sesame bagel, and drank a hot cup of tea. Resolved to not wallow in my pain, or let it define me, I stomped off to my bedroom, threw my suitcase on my bed, and began shoving clothes and shoes into it. That was it. I had to get the hell out of there. After I finished packing, I left a note for my parents and one for Heather. I couldn't deal with talking to them face to face yet. I got in my car and headed to Auburn. Alison and Tamron would be able to get my mind off of Alec. And right then, there was nothing I needed more. When I arrived, though, I just sat in my car and stared at the locked door to their old style apartment building.

I felt like my world had shattered into a million pieces. The act of leaving, getting into my car, and driving away from Atlanta, somehow felt so final. While I waited for them to come home, I second-guessed every decision I'd made since seeing Alec with the slut. What had I done? Should I go back? Should I have confronted him, instead of leaving? How could he do that to me? We'd been making plans for our future together, and the next thing I knew, he was ripping my heart to shreds.

Was anything he'd ever said or done genuine? Did he do all of that just to have sex with me? Did he ever love me?

I knew if I didn't get out of my car, I'd end up driving back to Atlanta, certainly to more pain than I knew I could endure. I couldn't remember the damn door code to get in to their apartment building, so I just sat on the steps, my back against the column, and waited for my best friends to come home. I must have fallen asleep, because the next thing I knew, I heard their voices talking right beside me. I sat there with my eyes closed, still as a stone, as they discussed my unplanned visit.

"I wonder why she's here. Did she call or text that she was coming?" Tamron asked in a worried voice.

"I don't know. Maybe we missed a message. Tamron, check your phone. There're no messages from her on mine. Good Lord, look at her. She's a mess. Her cheeks are all splotchy red, and she's got bags under her eyes. It'll take a week of cucumber treatments to repair that damage," Alison whispered in a hushed tone.

"So help me, Alison, if Alec is the cause of this, I will castrate him myself!" Tamron's heated voice retorted. "We warned him not to hurt her."

I cracked open my eyes and sat up straight. I stretched my arms and looked from Alison to Tamron, then down at my hands clasped together in my lap. Tamron sat down on one of the steps below me and wrapped her arms around my legs in a strange kind of a hug, while Alison sat beside me, rubbing her hands up and down my back. For the first time since I'd known them, they were both silent. I knew they probably had a lot of burning questions, but neither seemed able to find her voice at that moment. They were waiting for my explanation. I was sure they'd be angry with me for not telling them what had happened earlier. It was Tamron who broke the silence first.

"What the ever-loving fuck did Alec do?" she asked.

And that was all it took for the floodgates to open and for me to become a sobbing mess on the front steps to their apartment building.

"Come on, let's go inside and get Sam settled in with a cup

of hot tea. We can talk about this in private," Alison urged, looking around us.

I'd been there once before, right after they first moved in and remembered their apartment being cozy, and even though I felt horrible, their place felt like home because they were there. For the first time since Alec broke my heart, I felt like I could breathe again.

Tamron made a cup of my favorite chai tea. As I drank it, I told them about Alec's strange behavior leading up to his breakup. I also shared the texts messages I'd sent that never got a response, as well as Alec's actions with the slut at Peter's house party, then my driving to Auburn to be with them.

Again, they were silent. It was unsettling and made me feel edgy. I tore off little pieces of my napkin, waiting for one of them to say something. Alison reached across the table and took my hands in hers. I looked up and saw Tamron standing there, too. Both of their eyes glistened with tears, their cheeks pink with the anger I knew they felt toward Alec.

"Sweetie, let's call it a night and get some rest. You've got to be tired," Tamron said.

Alison nodded her head.

"I'll make the sofa up while Tamron helps you get settled in. We can talk in the morning. You can also explain why we're just now hearing about this instead of months ago when Alec broke up with you."

I nodded my head and took a drink of my tea.

"I know you're wondering why we've been so quiet, but if we discuss it right now, I've a feeling Tamron and I would end up driving to Atlanta and kicking the hell out of that weasel fuck. While I can assure you it would give us both a great amount of satisfaction, we know it would only hurt you more."

They both hugged me goodnight and went to their bedrooms. Lying there quietly on the sofa bed, I felt lightheaded as the tears flowed freely down my face and into my ears.

I rolled over to my side, and pulled Alec's favorite Falcons t-shirt out of my bag on the floor. I knew it was stupid to hang on to it after all this time. I mean, it wasn't like it even smelled

like him anymore. I washed it like a normal person would. And yet, I continued to cuddle it every night as I slept.

The next morning, I decided it was time for *my* fresh start. I wasn't going to focus on Alec anymore. I folded and put his Falcons t-shirt in a bag and locked it away in the trunk of my car. When the girls got up, I had coffee ready and even made them French toast. It smelled like heaven to me, and by the looks on their faces, they thought so, too. I'd always loved cooking and baking. It was therapeutic for me. While we ate, I noticed, every so often, Tamron and Alison looking at each other and winking or a nodding their heads.

"Okay, what the hell is going on with you two?"

"Our boyfriends are having a frat party tonight, and we think you should come," Tamron blurted out.

"Don't say no, Sam, just say yes and go. It'll be fun and a way to start fresh and enjoy life again. Besides, you need to meet Tamron's Quinn and my Riley. It's been long overdue anyway," Alison said, all while not breaking eye contact with me, which meant saying no wasn't an option.

"Ugh, yes, fine, I'll go with y'all. I have my favorite jeans and t-shirt with me." I smiled up at them and noticed their Cheshire grins. "Ohhhh no. Absolutely not. You both have that 'let's play dress up with Sam' look on your faces. It's a frat party. I'm not dressin' to impress anyone. As a matter of fact, the absolute last thing I want is to have to deal with some drunk-off-his-ass, smokin'-hot-and-he-knows-it college guy trying to get into my pants. Not interested, so y'all can take your sexy clothes and wear them yourselves. It's just jeans and a t-shirt for me."

I knew I'd just dead-blocked their fun. But I really wasn't looking for someone, not even a one-night-stand rebound fling. I just wanted to cut loose and have a fun night, to forget my problems for a few hours. I wasn't into casual sex.

I'd only ever been with Alec, and just the thought of it made me have flashbacks of him at Peter's party with that blonde slut gyrating all over his lap. I still recalled his cold, accusing eyes staring at me with anger before he turned and buried himself back into her neck. Nope. I was not interested in even going there.

"Fine. Wear your boring jeans and t-shirt. But get dressed, because we're all going to get our belly buttons pierced." Tamron said.

My mouth hung open as I stared at her. "Are you crazy? That's insane! I'm not doing that!"

"Oh for Pete's sake, Sam. It's not gonna hurt . . . much," Alison taunted.

"Yeah, easy for you to say. Yours isn't done."

"Exactly why I said we're—all—going," Tamron huffed.

"Oh my God. Why do I always let y'all talk me into doing things? Fine. Let's go. A new day, a new life. May as well mark it with a little more pain," I deadpanned.

CHAPTER 16

In For a Penny, In For a Pound

Sam

We arrived at Riley and Quinn's house around nine, an hour and a half late, but the girls wanted to keep the guys waiting and watching the door. I guess they always showed up late so no one ever knew when to expect them. I couldn't stop laughing at their silly ritual. God, how I had missed them.

To say the party wasn't what I expected would be an understatement. There were no beer cans in the yard, no loud music blaring. These guys were pretty respectful of their neighbors. Well . . . brownie points for them. As we walked into the house it was packed with people, drinking, dancing, laughing, and kissing in heated embraces.

"Sam, this is John." Tamron motioned to the guy who'd answered the door. "He used to live here, too, but he abandoned us after graduation and moved up to Alaska."

"Hi John. I'm Sam."

"Hey, nice to meet ya." He winked.

Suddenly, the girls took off, and I was left standing by the stairs, alone. I watched as they ran up to who I figured must have been Riley and Quinn. They spread their arms wide and grabbed the girls by their waists. Tamron and Alison squealed in unison, then proceeded to kiss their boyfriends. I sighed, longing for that type of happiness again.

Their kisses held a tenderness that seemed oddly out of place, the type that made you feel like you were imposing on a private moment, only they couldn't care less about sharing it in front of anyone who happened to be in the room. It was almost as if they were in their own little worlds, and none of the fifty or so people partying around them even existed.

My heart ached for the loss of what I'd had with Alec. Unable to watch any longer, I turned to go upstairs and find a bathroom when I ran smack into a naked chest—a hard, tanned, muscular chest. I stopped and looked up at the body I'd collided with to see the sexiest lips on the cutest smirk, coupled with the most incredible blue eyes I'd ever seen.

His hair was jet black, in stark contrast with his mesmerizing eyes, and so sexy, I didn't realize I was staring at them, nor was I aware that my hands were still pushed up flat against his chest. He cleared his throat, and I regained my composure. He looked past me to where the girls and their boyfriends were still standing and shook his head with a laugh.

"I'm so sorry," I blurted out.

"Oh, no, it's okay darlin.' They've run me out of the room plenty of times." He chuckled. "Hey, would you like a beer? I was going to grab one and head outside for some fresh air. You're welcome to join me."

I smiled up at him. "Sure, a beer sounds good, and the fresh air sounds even better." *Don't stare, Sam, don't stare . . . don't be a creeper.*

"Cool, I'll grab them and meet you outside. The back door is down the hall through the back of the kitchen."

As I walked through the house, I could feel everyone's eyes staring at me. I knew it was the ridiculous outfit Tamron and Alison talked me into wearing. Jeans and a t-shirt, I'd declared. Well, I was wearing jeans and a t-shirt, all right, but the jeans were cut into barely-there shorts. If they had normal pockets, they would have been longer than the hem of the shorts. I guess the designer had planned it that way, because the front pockets were barely deep enough for my lip-gloss and car keys. Then there was the t-shirt . . . yes, I also got to wear a t-shirt, like I said, but it was about two sizes too small and clung to my chest like a second layer of skin, stopping just above my freshly-pierced belly button.

"Why have the piercing if you're going to hide it?" Tamron had asked.

"Show it off. It's adorable and sexy . . ." Alison added.

I was too frustrated to remind them they had coerced me into getting it in the first place, even though I had always loved the idea of getting one. So there I was, walking through the frat house half-full of drunken college guys, to go outside and hide from staring eyes. I could feel people looking at me and hated being so self-conscious.

I heard the French doors close behind me a moment after I walked outside and there he was, Mr. Hot Stuff, walking toward me with two beers. I couldn't tear my eyes away. He motioned for me to sit down on the lounge chairs as he set our beers on a table between them. He had that cute smirk on his face again and held his hand out toward me.

"So now we can really meet each other. Hi, I'm Emmett. I live here with Riley and Quinn."

"Hi, I'm Sam," I smiled softly. "Alison and Tamron have been my best friends for as long as I can remember. I'm in town visiting them for a while. It's nice to meet you."

He was staring into my eyes; it felt very intense, like he could see straight through me to my soul. But, at the same time, it was comfortable. It was so weird. I didn't understand it.

"Tell me about yourself. Do you have a boyfriend?"

"Well, I just had a bad breakup, so I'm not really looking for a relationship. He really hurt me," I said as I twisted at my bracelet.

"I'm sorry, Sam. Guys can be such dicks sometimes. It sounds like you're better off without him. Even in a breakup, things can be handled nicely, or at least respectfully."

"He was a good guy. I don't really know what happened. But anyway, this is an ex-boyfriend free zone. I don't want to think about him. Let's just talk and get to know each other a little. Tamron and Alison dragged me here. I may as well have fun," I said. "What about you? Do you have a girlfriend?"

I wasn't sure why I suddenly felt nervous about his answer. I just met him. But I was nervous of what he would say, just the same.

"No, I don't have a girlfriend. I don't really do the girlfriend thing."

I wasn't sure what that meant, but I used it as another nail in my box of *'I don't want another relationship anytime this millennia'* reminder.

"Okay, to each their own." I laughed. "What are you studying in school? Do you go to Auburn, as well?"

"Yeah, I'm a sophomore. Planning on going to med school after I graduate. I hope eventually to become a trauma surgeon."

"Oh, that's cool, I want to be a psychologist."

"Sweet, we have something in common then. We both care about the wellbeing of others," he said, smiling over at me.

"Yeah, I've always wanted to help people, and I think mental illness is one of the most misunderstood conditions people face. I just want to make a positive difference with my life."

We sat there for a couple hours, talking about our likes, hopes, and dreams, laughing at random girls being thrown into the pool, cracking up at the guys who got suckered into helping them get out, only to be jerked in with them at the last minute.

I didn't know how many beers we'd had before he came out with a couple glasses of ice water.

"Where's the beer?" I giggled.

He shook his head. "No more beer tonight," he said. "If I am lucky enough to spend the night with you, I want to remember it tomorrow. And I sure as hell want you to remember it, too."

It was a 'come fuck me line' if I'd ever heard one, and I'll admit, it's the best one I'd heard yet. I wasn't looking for a rebound fling, but even I could see he *was* sex on legs, so I decided, what the hell, in for a penny, in for a pound.

Maybe the beer was doing all my thinking, but I hoped this would help ease the hurt. At the very least, it would be a temporary Band-Aid on my heart. As Emmett sat down, I took a deep breath and stood up, smiling at the shocked but excited expression on his face as I pulled him back up to his feet. I led us to the French doors and walked inside.

I didn't even notice the girls as we walked through the house. Whatever. They were having fun, and I was happy for them. Emmett paused in the kitchen and traded our water for some sweet tea. Then we headed up the stairs to his bedroom. I wondered where my panicky feelings were. I'd only ever been with Alec. My heart was broken. Yet here I was, following a guy I'd just met upstairs into his bedroom.

Yup. Had to be the beer.

But I was comfortable. I wasn't scared, nervous or worried if I was making a mistake. It felt as if we'd known each other forever, as if it was natural to have this strong, sexual attraction.

He opened the door to his room and stood back so I could walk in first, closing and locking the door behind him. I spun around at the sound of the lock clicking into place.

"Just to be sure no one stumbles in here looking for the bathroom. The last thing I want is some drunken fool interrupting us. Make yourself comfortable. I'm gonna change," he said

I sat on the edge of his bed, not sure what to do with myself. He walked over to his dresser and pulled out a pair of shorts and tossed them on his bed. When I turned around, his back was to me as he pulled his jeans down. He had the finest ass I'd ever seen, hotter than Channing Tatum's, and that's really saying something.

But Emmett's ass, mother of God, I was practically drooling, and even checked to make sure. Thank God I wasn't, but holy hell, I wanted to get my hands on this guy. In less than a minute, the jeans were off and his shorts were on, and sadly, that beautiful, naked ass was out of sight.

Damn.

He reached into his top drawer and shuffled around, looking for something. As he closed the drawer I saw a foil packet in his hand. I was on the pill, but we couldn't be too careful.

Emmett had the naughtiest expression on his face as he walked around to the edge of his bed where I was sitting.

For a moment, I worried about getting hurt again, the way Alec had hurt me. But I pushed those thoughts away and decided to face that possibility another day. Emmett said he didn't really do the girlfriend thing, so maybe it was okay to get lost in him once. Or twice . . .

He stood over me, and I swallowed hard as my gaze traveled from the waist of his shorts, up his naked chest, to his intense blue eyes.

"Are you nervous?" he asked as he took my hand in his.

"No . . . yes." I choked out a laugh. "I guess it comes and goes. One minute I think this is crazy, and the next I feel like it's normal."

He pulled me up to him, lowered his mouth to mine, and kissed me softly. "It's normal to think that." His teeth tugged at my ear. "But let's not think tonight . . . let's just feel." He ran his hands through my hair, capturing my mouth with his and kissing me breathless.

I kissed him back just as frantically, losing myself in the feel of him. I stiffened as his hands settled on the small of my back.

"Don't worry." He laid kisses on my neck and inhaled deeply. "You can trust me."

I sighed with relief as his mouth closed over mine again and he tugged at the bottom of my shirt. Lifting it over my head, he stepped back and looked at my black lacey bra. He smiled as he brushed his hand lightly over my skin, leaving a tingling trail across my flesh. Emmett was a force of nature. His presence commanded my attention, and my body answered of its own accord.

Emboldened by his touch, I ran my hands up his chest and

over his shoulders, pulling him back to me, kissing him. He reached down and unbuttoned my shorts, never breaking eye contact with me. My body shook slightly as he lowered my zipper and pushed my shorts down to my ankles. I held onto his arms as I stepped out of them, and reached for the waistband of his shorts, tugging them off. As he lowered me to his bed, I had a flash of Alec and the blond. I locked that memory away and let Emmett make a new one in its place.

The next morning, I woke up with Emmett's arm around me and my head resting against his chest. I could feel his eyes on me. It was so quiet in the house, a stark contrast to the previous night. As I lay there, still as stone, and wondered what would happen next.

CHAPTER 17
The Aftermath

Emmett

I was out of my element. Way—the hell—out. As I lay there in bed, everything felt normal. But I was the farthest from normal as I'd ever been. My own breathing was distracting me. How could it not when every single breath I exhaled caused silky brown hair to float up in my face?

Sam.

Last night, we met at the frat party. We drank, talked, and fucked. That was normal for me. Yeah, I was a player. I knew it, and was totally cool with it. The abnormal part was waking up the next morning with the girl's head on my chest and my arm wrapped around her as she slept.

Her breathing was an even rhythm, combined with the faint flowery scent in her hair, and it was almost enough to lull me back to sleep. Almost—if I didn't have to pee. I slowly withdrew my arm and gently positioned her head on my pillow. I was fascinated by the way her hair draped along her bare back and shoulders.

I walked around to the end of my bed, grabbed my shorts off the floor, and pulled them on. I didn't want another traumatizing event if I ran into Tamron or Alison in the hallway on my way to the bathroom.

My damn door creaked as I opened it, and I glanced back at the girl asleep in my bed. She stirred a little, but only enough to roll over onto her other side, exposing a hint of her perfect breast. Flashes of how kissable it was flooded my mind, and I forced myself to walk out of my room before I acted on my urges.

After relieving myself, I stood in front of the mirror and stared at my reflection.

What the fuck am I doing? I never let them spend the night. And to make things even more complicated, she's the girls' best friend. I raked my hands down my face. They're gonna fuckin skin me alive. No—they'll just chop my dick off—even better.

I'd intended to walk past my room and keep going downstairs, but when I got to my bedroom door, I couldn't stop myself from peeking in at Sam. She was beautiful. Funny. Smart. Sexy as hell. But she'd been hurt, and hurt bad by the little glimpse I had of the pain in her eyes when she briefly mentioned her ex last night.

What a rat bastard.

And now, she had me to deal with. I didn't even know what I was doing. I just hoped I didn't mix up her life anymore than it already was. I quietly closed my door and headed downstairs. Just before I made it down, I heard a low whistle from the floor above me. I looked up to see Quinn standing at the top of the stairs, motioning me to come back up.

"What's up, man?" I asked when I reached him.

"Apparently you, as usual." He laughed.

I leaned back against the wall. "Yeah. You know how it is." I tried to act normal.

"So, who was she? Did she get all clingy when you told her she couldn't spend the night?"

"Uhh, well . . ." I groaned as I ran my hands through my hair.

Quinn's eyes opened wide. "Wait. No fucking way—you let last night's romp sleep over?"

I nodded. "It seems that way. I mean, we . . . well, you know, but then I woke up with her head on my chest and my arm around her."

"Holy shit, Emmett. What the hell are you gonna do now? She's bound to wanna come back for more. They always do."

I leaned over and put my hands on my knees. "Well, there's another complication."

He rested his hand on my shoulder. "Whatever it is, we'll deal with it."

"Yeah, but she's not just some girl from the party. She's Sam—as in Tamron and Alison's best friend—Sam."

"Oh, fuck, man." He looked up to the ceiling as he leaned back against the wall.

"Yeah. I know." I groaned. "They're gonna have my ass, aren't they?"

"Dude, you gotta get out of here. I'll just say you had to work early or something. At least until Riley and I can get them to calm down after they find out."

"No. I'm not running off. I . . . like her. I think that's why I let her stay over. There's just something about her, like she pulls me to her."

"For fuck's sake, now you just sound like a girl."

"Shut up, man. I don't want her to wake up with me gone and feel like she was just some piece of ass."

He stared at me, his eyes wide, then shook his head. With one last bewildered glance in my direction, he turned around and walked back to his room muttering, "And that folks, is how life, as we know it, changed forever."

I briefly considered mainlining the cup of coffee I'd just brewed when I heard soft footsteps on the kitchen tile. I turned around and saw her standing there, wearing a pair of my boxers and my AU t-shirt, which swam on her small frame. I was suddenly thankful I was wearing loose fitting shorts and not my damn jeans, although the jeans would have solved the damn tenting issue I was about to have.

"Morning." I smiled, holding the coffee I had just poured

for myself out to her.

Her eyes lit up when they settled on the steaming cup in my hand. "Good morning," she smiled as she took the cup from me.

"We, uh, have milk and sugar, if you want some. There isn't any of that foo-foo creamer here though."

"Milk and sugar is good. Thanks."

"So, you like coffee," I said as I poured myself a new cup.

She chuckled. "Yeah, you could say that."

"We don't really have much normal food in the house this morning. I might be able to scrounge up an English muffin or two."

"Those are good." Her voice was a little shaky.

"Look, Sam, this doesn't have to be weird. I mean, we're both consenting adults. This is just new territory for me. I've never had this kinda interaction with a girl the morning after."

She tilted her head to the side. "Well, just what kinda interaction do you usually have then?"

"None."

She gasped. "None? Like ever?"

"Nope, I've never let a girl stay overnight before."

"What? You just use 'em and toss 'em out the front door?"

I held up my hands. "No, that's not it. The girls I'm usually with just go back to the party or whatever when we're done, then go home when everyone else does. There've been a few who wanted to sleep over, but I was up front with them from the beginning. It's just not my thing . . . or, well it wasn't. Until you."

"Oh . . ." she began, but shouting from the living room suddenly interrupted us.

"What the fucking hell, Quinn? How did you let this happen?" Tamron yelled as she rushed into the kitchen.

As soon as I saw the angry look on Tamron's face, I leaned back against the counter and stared up at the ceiling.

"Babe, just wait a minute . . ." Quinn urged as he caught up with her.

"No. I will not wait a damn minute, Quinn." She swung her head in my direction. "And you!" she seethed. "What the hell do you think you're doing with her?"

Sam cleared her voice. "Tamron, stop. There's no need to be upset or yell. We spent the night together. Quite frankly, it's none of your business."

Tamron shook her head. "Sam, Emmett doesn't spend the night with girls. He fucks them and moves on," she said in an exasperated tone.

"Well, he spent the night with me," Sam replied as she motioned to herself and the clothes she was wearing. "And I enjoyed it—every minute."

Tamron's face blanched, but then she turned and walked right up to me, stopping only inches away. "You should have known better. She's too good for you. She's not one of your whores, Emmett. And it's not just me you have to worry about either . . ."

"What's going on in here?" Alison yawned as she shuffled into the kitchen with Riley on her heels.

"Speak of the devil," I muttered.

"Oh, nothing really. Apparently, Emmett fucked Sam last night and I'm in the process of chewing him a new asshole. He'll be lucky if I don't punch him in the junk."

Alison's mouth and bloodshot eyes opened wide as she glared daggers at me.

"For the love of God, will everyone just stop and relax a damn minute?" Sam said with her hands on her hips. She glanced from Tamron to Alison and back again. "I guess you two haven't noticed, but I am an adult. I can and will make my own freaking decisions. Most especially regarding who I'm going to sleep with."

"We know, Sam, it's just . . ."

"No!" she yelled. "This conversation is so not happening with everyone standing here! I'm mortified! I know you two don't have any filters, but this is beyond bullshit and way, way, way past the line of being okay," she huffed. "Now, if you have something to say, we can take this upstairs—away from the guys. Geez." She walked past me, set her cup down, and squeezed my hand. "Emmett, I'm so sorry about all of this."

"It's okay, darlin.' I figured it was gonna be bad when they found out."

Sam smiled up at me, lifted on to her tiptoes, and gave me a chaste kiss on the cheek before walking out of the kitchen.

The girls looked at me, Tamron finally silent in her anger.

"You shouldn't have done that, Emmett. You knew she was our friend," Alison scolded as they followed Sam into the living room.

I breathed a sigh of relief at their exit and turned toward Riley and Quinn, both of whom were failing miserably at holding in their laughter.

"Shut up, assholes. It's not funny."

Riley held up his hands. "Sorry . . . sorry."

I walked out and climbed the stairs. I needed to get ready for my shift at the lumberyard. I stopped when I heard voices from Riley's room.

"Sam, with what you just went through, we just don't want to see you get hurt again. That's all. And as I'm sure you've gathered, Emmett's not exactly the stick-around kind-of-guy," Alison finished in a frustrated sigh.

"I know he's not. He told me last night when we were hanging out at the party, he doesn't do the girlfriend thing. But did it ever occur to either of you . . . that that was exactly what I needed? To be able to feel something good without worrying about getting hurt again?"

That should've relieved me, but for some reason, it bothered me even more.

CHAPTER 18

Frustrated

Sam

I couldn't believe Tamron and Alison's audacity. As I tore off Emmett's clothes and yanked on my own from the party, I vowed to hold my grudge long enough for them to think about their actions. I took out my phone and Googled cab companies. I found one that looked good and called the number listed.

"Apple Taxi, how may I help you?"

"Hi, I need a cab."

"Okay, what's the pick-up address?"

Shit! I don't know. It's not like I freaking drove here or paid attention to the house number or street name for that matter.

"Umm, sorry, let me just look a minute."

I looked around Emmett's room and saw some papers lying on his dresser. Shuffling through them, I found a piece of mail from Auburn University.

"Okay, it's 332 Mason Road."

"All right, I have a driver about ten minutes from that area. I'll send him over."

"Thanks."

I hung up then tossed my phone onto Emmett's bed. As I glanced at the twisted sheets, my mind flashed back to us tangled up in them. Just the thought of it had me feeling warm and smiling. I'd never been with anyone but Alec. Surprisingly, it didn't bother me as much as I thought it would. My heart still ached at the thought of him at that party and his cruel behavior. But I was moving on. I deserved better.

I opened Emmett's door only to run smack into his chest . . . again. My gaze meandered up his body to his piercing blue eyes as his hands caught my shoulders, sending tingles down my arms.

He chuckled. "We really gotta stop meeting like this . . . then again, I love the feel of you."

"Oh," I gasped. "Sorry. I was just on my way downstairs to wait for a cab."

"What the hell? No. I'll take you wherever you want to go."

I looked down and leaned my forehead against his chest, wishing he were shirtless this time, too. "It's okay I don't want to inconvenience you, and I've already called them anyway."

"Really, it's no problem," he insisted.

Looking up at him again, I stepped back and to the side. "Thanks, but I'm good. I'll uh, see you around." I headed downstairs, but was stopped as I opened the front door.

"Sam, what are you doing?" Alison asked.

"Taking a cab back to your place, then getting my car," I hissed.

"Stop. We'll take you," Tamron urged.

"No. If I wanted a ride I would've asked. Just leave me alone for a bit."

"Don't be mad at us. We're sorry," Alison pleaded.

I sighed and looked up at the ceiling. "You two should have thought of that before you decided to make my business yours . . . in front of everyone here, no less." I stepped through the threshold, closing the heavy door behind me, and waited alone for my cab.

I used the key the girls had given me to get in their apartment. I stepped inside and looked around at the messy living room. I put the sofa bed back together, folded the blanket and left them a note.

Girls,
I'll be at the closest Starbucks. I'm fine. I just need some time alone. I'll be back in time for dinner.

~Sam

Fortunately, there was a Starbucks a couple miles from where they lived. I settled in the lounge area with a latte and stared at my kindle app, while thoughts of Emmett flooded my mind.

CHAPTER 19

Happy And Content

Emmett

A month had gone by, and I was really enjoying life. I pulled into the parking lot at Tamron and Alison's apartment building. Sam had been staying with me more and more, but still occasionally spent the night with her friends. I smiled when I saw her walk out the door to meet me. My life changed the night I met her. I felt more alive than I ever had in my life.

I hadn't been with anyone else since then either. I couldn't even think about being with any other girl but Sam. Turning them away was definitely out of the norm for me. The looks on their faces surprised me. It also made me stop and think about what a dick I must have seemed like. But I never led them on. They knew I wasn't looking for a relationship.

As Sam walked up to my car, I smiled in anticipation for the day ahead. We were going kayaking on the Tallapoosa River in Wetumpka, Alabama.

"Hey you," she said as she got into my Camaro. She slipped her hand in mine and smiled.

"Hey," I replied and pulled her in for a kiss.

"Mmm . . . well, that was a nice hello." She giggled then motioned to the small pack she'd set at her feet. "I can't wait to get out on the water. I brought some Gatorade and protein bars."

"Good idea." I pulled out onto the road.

"How'd you get today off from work anyway?" she asked.

"A guy I worked with switched days with me. When I saw how nice it was gonna be today, I knew it'd be perfect."

"Cool, I haven't gone kayaking in forever . . . I didn't realize how much I missed it. My sister, Tricia, and I used to kayak the Chattahoochee north of Atlanta as often as we could . . . before she went away for college."

I pulled in and parked. Getting out, I walked around and opened her door for her. My parents had taught me how to be gentleman, and I wanted her to feel special.

As we were putting our rental kayaks in the water, I watched in surprise as she took her shirt off, exposing the bikini top she wore underneath. She sat down in the kayak, and I pushed it off the bank into the water.

She smiled as I floated mine up to hers. "Ready?"

"Yup, the current's flowing good too. It'll be a relaxing float today."

We came up to some small rapids and she looked over at me and with a lopsided grin on her face. "Are ya scared?"

"Ha! Me? Scared? No, I can handle it. That's barely a ripple."

"Okay, I'll see ya on the other side." She grinned as she paddled up and rode the rapid.

"Oh! Look, there's a bigger one," I said, pointing as I caught up to her.

"Sweet! Let's go!" she squealed.

We floated easily with the current, and paddled over the rapids. It was an awesome feeling . . . to have easy, normal fun with someone. I found myself feeling happy, content, and excited to be with her.

It felt too good to be true, and I knew all too well that fate had a way of stepping in and screwing things up. But Sam was worth the risk. I'd worry about fate another day.

CHAPTER 20

The Time Of Our Lives

Sam

Time flew by quickly. I managed to transfer from Kennesaw State to Auburn University before the start of school. Thank God Tamron and Alison had talked me into applying to both schools. Even then, it never would have worked out in time, if it weren't for my dad being an Auburn alumni, and his connections to the Provost and Vice President of Academic Affairs.

I couldn't imagine attending Kennesaw State after what Alec had done. There were too many painful memories back home. Going to the school we'd dreamed of together, without him, or even worse, at the risk of seeing him with someone else, would have made me miserable.

I was moving on, spending time with the girls and Emmett. The parties at the frat house were fun. I even picked up a part-time job at Jackson's Reading Corner, a little bookstore ten-minutes from Emmett's house. I loved working there, and the owner, Mr. Jackson, didn't mind if I read occasionally to pass the time, as long as I had everything shelved for the day and was attentive to the customers.

Our days were busy with classes at Auburn. It helped that I didn't have to stay in a dorm because the out-of-state tuition fees were insanely high. I didn't even want to know what the room and board cost would be. I was lucky my parents had saved for college since I was born. I marked the application deadline date for financial aid for next year's tuition to help offset it.

Being with Emmett felt natural. It was easy. Before I knew it, I was staying with Emmett more than I was staying with the girls at their apartment near campus. Of course, at first, they were both very vocal about their concerns regarding my sudden relationship with him. But, luckily for me, he was their boyfriends' close friend and housemate, so they eventually accepted him, though they were somewhat guarded about my "almost" living with him. Emmett and I talked about that one morning while I was cooking breakfast.

"You know, Peach, I never expected to be in a relationship with anyone. But I love spending time with you. I'm really happy when you stay here with me."

I giggled at his nickname for me. He'd said I was his sweet Georgia peach and, afterwards, had taken to calling me Peach instead of darlin.'

"Yeah, I know what you mean," I replied. "I didn't think I would get close to a guy after the way my ex hurt me . . . but you and I just work. There's no drama. It feels right. It feels good to be happy and cared for again."

As he handed me my cup of coffee, he reached behind me for a piece of bacon I'd just cooked. I smacked his hand away.

"What are you doing? You'll burn your mouth! I just took that out of the pan."

I couldn't help but laugh at his guilty expression.

"But it smells so damn good. How can you expect me not to eat a piece?"

"Easy. Leave. It. Alone," I teased.

"Fine," he sulked.

"Oh geez, just give it a minute to cool off at least. Then you can have all you want."

I swear, you'd think I'd washed and waxed his Camaro with the smile that appeared on his face.

"Emmett, my parents are on their way into town to visit. They're going to stay at a hotel near Alison and Tamron's apartment. Tamron's mom and dad drove over with them to see the girls, too," I said. "I'd like for you to meet them."

"Sounds good, Peach," he said. "Just let me know when you want to go."

"They're almost there. If we head over now, we'll get there before they do," I said.

"All right, let me jump in the shower first. Okay?"

"Okay." I smiled. "You, umm, need any help with that?" I asked

"I always need your help with that," he said with that sexy smirk of his.

I joined him in the shower. He definitely needed me, in every way possible. He showed me how much, and I lost myself to his wet hands and wandering mouth.

We dressed again and drove over to the girl's apartment. I was excited to see my parents and have them meet Emmett. I loved him. I just hoped they would too. Pulling up to the girls' apartment, we saw Quinn's car parked out front. I released a shaky breath as Emmett took my hand in his.

"Looks like Quinn came to the *meet the parents* gathering, too," Emmett teased.

"Yeah, Tamron said she was going to have him come over to meet her parents, as well."

We got out of the car and heard laughing around the side of the apartment building. Walking around toward the back, we saw Tamron and Quinn in a frantic kiss. I grabbed Emmett's arm to turn us around and wait out front, but he beat me to it with a catcalling whistle that shocked the couple apart. Tamron, of course, cussed at him right away.

"For fuck's sake, Emmett! Was that necessary? We're busy here," she yelled.

Quinn just shook his head. "It's okay, babe. He's just getting me back for interrupting him and Sam yesterday morning. At least we were only kissing. Be glad of that," he said, shaking his head again.

"Better me than Tamron's dad, man. I'm sure that's not the first impression you want to give her parents, y'all nearly tearing each other's clothes off in an alley."

Tamron's face blanched and she smacked Quinn on the shoulder. "You heathen!"

We all busted up laughing just as we heard a car pull into the parking lot.

"I think they're here, y'all," I called.

We walked back out front and saw our parents getting out of my dad's car. Tamron's dad was in the front with my dad and, as usual, her mom rode in the back with my mom. They did that so they could chat away. I always kind of thought it was old-fashioned, but it made me smile.

I ran up to my parents and gave them both hugs. Tamron swapped with me when I was done, and we each hugged the other's parents, too.

Tamron stepped back and said, "Mom, Dad, this is Quinn. Quinn, this is my mom and dad."

Quinn stepped forward and shook both of their hands.

I stepped to the side of Emmett and said, "Mom and Dad, this is my Emmett. Emmett, meet my parents."

"It's nice to meet you, Mr. and Mrs. Lang," Emmett said, shaking my dad's hand and kissing the top of my mom's.

For a moment, my heart pierced with pain at the memory of Alec doing the same thing when he met my parents, but I pushed it out of my mind. It was over between us, and I wasn't about to stir up all those emotions. I was happy again.

"Please, Emmett, just Maggie and Vance is fine," Mom said.

"Well let's get to it. This old man is hungry," my dad said.

We all got in our cars and followed Tamron and Quinn to the restaurant. Getting out and walking in hand in hand with Emmett, I caught my mom whispering to my dad, then Dad looking back at us. I don't know why, but I felt the need to drop

Emmett's hand until my dad smiled at me.

"You're okay, Princess," he teased.

Emmett laughed, and I wanted to die. I mean, it's not like he didn't know we were serious or even intimate for that matter. They knew we were practically living together. But it's still not a subject I wanted to discuss at length with my parents.

"It's okay, Peach. He gets it," Emmett whispered.

"I know. He just likes to tease me." I sighed.

We ate dinner and Tamron's and my parents gave Emmett and Quinn the twenty questions ritual. We understood. They just needed to know we were with good guys. Fortunately for us, we were.

After dinner, we gathered in the parking lot to say our goodbyes.

"Come visit soon, sweetheart. We miss you," Mom said.

"We will, Mom. I miss y'all, too." I hugged her tight.

"Vance, Maggie, it was nice meeting you both. We'll come see you soon," Emmett said.

I waved to Tamron's parents as mine were waving goodbye to her.

CHAPTER 21

Lightly Salted Air

Sam

A few nights later, Emmett got home from work at the lumberyard, and found me outside by the pool, reading a book on my phone as I waited for him. I'd made us raspberry lemonade club sodas. His smile was so adorable, and made me want to get lost in kissing him. He didn't sit down in the lounge chair beside me, but instead sat down behind me in mine as I scooted forward. He pulled me back onto his lap, turning my head for kiss as he placed a manila envelope in my lap.

"What's this?" I asked.

"Just open it, Peach."

My heart raced with anticipation. He was so excited, so I knew it had to be good. I pulled out the contents and saw a reservation slip for The Summit Resort in Panama City Beach, Florida.

I squealed. "Holy crap, Emmett! Are we going to the beach? What about classes?"

He snorted a full belly laugh and nodded. "Yes, Peach, and don't worry about classes, we're going for Labor Day weekend. We need to get some supplies though. I'm fairly certain you'll need a few bathing suits, since I'm sure you won't want to be constantly putting on and taking off wet ones. That would just be soooo cold," he said with wink, as he trailed his fingers up the inside of my thigh.

Emmett requested I step out of the changing room and model each bathing suit. I hadn't thought he would want to sit there and wait while I went through the grueling process of bikini elimination. It didn't take long for his reasoning to become evident. I stepped out of the stall and peeked around the corner to the cushy waiting chair at the entrance to the fitting room.

His eyes lit with pleasure as I turned around in a slow spin, modeling the fourth garment. He wore a look of hunger as he tried to remain stoic for the store staff. The slight squirming in his seat gave away how much he approved of my selections.

"Well, which ones do you like?" I teased.

"Umm, I . . . I can't decide. I think you should try them on again."

I gave him a sideways glance.

"Okay, okay," he laughed. "Just get all of them. You look incredible."

I couldn't stop the smile as it spread wide across my face. It felt good to incite the reaction in him. He cleared his throat as I turned around one last time before slipping around the corner, back to the changing stall.

We made our purchases then stopped in a local superstore and bought some snorkeling gear and body boards, grabbing a few snacks and drinks for the drive.

We counted the states license plates as we made the almost four hour drive from Auburn to Panama City Beach, arriving at The Summit Resort just after lunchtime. After Emmett checked us in, we unloaded our bags and supplies onto a luggage cart and rode the elevator up to our room on the eleventh floor. I was surprised to see it wasn't so much a standard hotel room but rather more like a condo. It had a warm, home away from home feeling, with a coastal paradise twist.

It was almost dinnertime when Emmett suggested we try a restaurant he'd heard about called Hammerhead Fred's. The hostess seated us at a booth, and we ordered oysters as an appetizer, we were excited to see it was served on a slab of driftwood nearly as long as the table. As we ate, he told me about a trip his family had taken to the beach when he was ten.

"My little brother, Alby, was eight years old and had a bad ear infection, so he was cranky most of the drive here. I remember feeling so bad I couldn't help him feel better. I stayed in the room with him though, and didn't go to the beach until two days later when he was finally feeling better. We were really close, like best friends. He's my half-brother. My biological father died a couple months after I was born. Mom remarried, and had my brother a couple years later. It sucks not ever having the chance to know my birth father, but our dad was awesome and loved us very much. I'm thankful to have had him raise me, and ended up with the best little brother."

"Oh, Emmett, that sounds awful for him to have been so sick," I said, reaching for his hand.

"I always remembered that trip, and wanted to come back to the beach, but Dad's work was hectic and life was too busy. Then we lost our parents just a few years ago. I just never felt at ease about coming back here."

"Oh my God, I'm so sorry to hear that. I can't imagine losing my parents. I wondered why you never brought them up."

"Anyway, one morning I was lying in bed, playing with your hair, and the idea hit me. So I booked the trip."

"I'm happy you did. It means so much to me that you're willing to share this special place with me."

After we finished with dinner, we walked behind the resort along the beach, watched in awe as the sky began to fill with beautiful shades of yellow, red, and orange.

That night, the balcony door stood open, letting the lightly salted air breeze through the condo. I stood at the railing looking out over the horizon as the sun kissed the water's edge. He walked up behind me and wrapped me in his arms.

I rested my head back against his chest with a sigh. "It feels so good out here."

He ran his hands up and down my arms as his lips left a trail of kisses on my neck.

"Yes," he whispered in my ear. "It does."

As I turned around to face him, he dropped his arm down beneath me, picking me up in his strong embrace. He kissed me slowly, methodically, as he cradled me to his chest and walked us into the bedroom.

"You're so beautiful, my Peach. I want to make love to you all night," he said, then pulled at my bottom lip with his teeth.

I felt the heat in my cheeks, as he looked deep into my eyes.

He reached down and slowly lifted my shirt off. His hands brushing against my skin left a heated trail of tingles.

"Me, too," I breathed out while he gently laid me on the bed.

He unbuttoned the top of my denim skirt, pulling it down over my hips. As his fingers traced the contours of my leg to the back of my knee, a giggle slipped out.

My hands flew to my mouth as we both chuckled.

"I'm sorry. I know how ticklish you are, but I couldn't resist the temptation to feel your soft skin."

"It's ok." I whispered, running my fingers underneath the waistband of his shorts and tugging at them.

He lowered and stepped out of his shorts, and I smiled in anticipation at the sight of his tanned, muscular body.

He lay down next to me and kissed me softly, pulling me into his arms. But it soon turned heated and hungry as our passion consumed us. We were like an inferno setting our love ablaze in the night. Afterwards, I snuggled into him and rested my head on his chest.

"I love you, Emmett."

"I love you, too, Peach," he replied, kissing the top of my head.

"Thank you for bringing me here. It's beautiful."

"You're welcome. I couldn't wait to get you here and all to myself. I'm a greedy bastard and got sick of sharing your time with the girls." He laughed.

I smacked his shoulder. "You are not a bastard! Greedy with my time, maybe, but I love that, too."

We spent the weekend switching between drinks at the tiki-bar by the two Olympic-sized pools and hot tubs to the blue-shaded lounges on the beach. We body surfed and swam to cool off from the hot sun. Every night, we walked along the beach, picking up shells for me to use as charms.

As we lay in bed on the last night of our weekend getaway, wrapped in each other's arms, Emmett kissed the top of my head and twined his fingers with mine.

"I'm so happy you're in my life. I've never needed anyone this way before. I can't imagine going back to my cold existence before you," he whispered.

"Me, too. It scares me sometimes. I feel like I need you as much as my next breath."

"Don't worry, Peach. We'll always have each other."

I had a flash of pain at those last words. A deep-rooted fear surfaced, a remnant of my days with Alec when he had promised me the same thing, and that had ended in the worst pain of my life. Again, I pushed those thoughts and fears away. I had to live in the now, not the past. I refused to let his actions diminish the happiness I had in my life.

CHAPTER 22

It's A Small Awkward World

Sam

After returning home, we finished out the fall semester, and everything seemed to fall into step, until one morning, when I woke to caresses along my spine. Emmett was watching me sleep again. I tried to be still. I didn't want him to stop. The gentle care he took with me was mesmerizing, and the tingle his hands left behind prickled up the back of my neck.

Then a buzz sounded before the ringtone. I didn't want to move, but as soon as "Uptown Girl" sprang from the phone in my discarded jeans pocket, I knew Emmett would race to get it before it woke me up.

I shifted and reached to grab it, but he beat me to it. Oh God! I squeezed my eyes closed at the thought of him reading "My Lover" with Alec's contact picture. I really didn't want my boyfriend seeing my ex-boyfriend's face. I'd never had it in me to delete his contact information, or even look at it to change the name. Seeing his picture always threw me into a hard sadness and flashes of pain at that last memory of him. Why was Alec calling me? Why now, when everything with Emmett was so perfect?

"No fucking way this is happening."

I popped my eyes back open and froze at the pale expression on Emmett's face. He wasn't angry. No . . . it was . . . hurt. Utter disappointment and pain.

He turned the phone and showed me the picture.

"I'm so sorry, Emmett. I didn't think to take his number out of my phone."

He spiked his fingers through his hair on a heavy exhale. His hurtful expression morphed into resignation. He looked from my phone then across his bedroom at me with an awareness I knew wasn't good.

"Do you . . . know Alec?"

He nodded, slowly handing me my cell phone as it continued to play Alec's ringtone. I felt my world crashing in on me.

"Hello?" I answered, my voice hesitant and uncertain. I heard a sigh on the other end of the phone.

"Samone. I wasn't sure if you would answer."

"Yeah. I almost didn't."

"Well, I'm relieved you did. I want . . . no, wait, I *need* to see you. To talk to you. Please say you'll see me. I know I don't deserve it, that I hurt you. I'm so sorry for that."

I sat in silence and looked up to Emmett standing at the foot of his bed with a blank stare on his beautiful face.

"I'm sorry, Alec, but I'm with someone now. I've . . . I've moved on."

"Samone, please. I need to make this right," he pleaded. "Just meet me for lunch, or breakfast, or even a quick cup of coffee. Anything."

"I don't know, Alec. I mean, I would like to know why you hurt me, but I just don't think it's a good idea to see you."

I cringed as I saw Emmett in my peripheral vision slide down to a sitting position against the wall of his bedroom. I didn't know what their connection was, but I was filled with dread.

"Please, Samone. Please."

"You wrecked me! You know that, right?" I hissed.

"I know," he groaned. "I think about it all the time. You'll never know how much I regret that, Samone."

I sighed. "Fine, but just breakfast and you will explain yourself to me."

"Thank you, baby. I love you."

"You don't get to call me that, or say you love me anymore." I startled when I heard Emmett's head smack back against the wall. "Just breakfast and your complete honesty. That's it, Alec."

"Okay. Sorry. I know. See you at Reveille the day after tomorrow, eight a.m.?"

"Fine. Whatever. Eight a.m."

I hung up and dropped my phone onto Emmett's bed. When I looked up I saw he was sitting on the floor, leaning against the wall, with his hands at his sides. He wouldn't look at me.

"Emmett," I whispered.

He just shook his head and held his hand up.

I wanted to see his eyes. I needed to see them. My throat felt like it was closing up, and my chest was tightening with heartache the longer he hid them from me. "Emmett," I tried again.

"Just give me a damn minute Sam."

His clipped tone and use of my name instead of Peach tore at my heart. We sat in a stifling silence for what felt like an eternity.

"Did you know?" he asked.

"Know what?"

"That he was my fucking brother?" he seethed.

His words were like a slap to my face. I couldn't believe what I'd just heard. Alec and Emmett were brothers.

My stomach roiled and churned, weighed down by a ton of bricks. I nearly threw up as I ran to the bathroom down the hall. I grabbed the toilet seat and dry-heaved into the bowl as my gut twisted with pain.

I sank back onto the cold, tile floor. My mind was spinning as I attempted to rein in my thoughts. Why hadn't I noticed the striking resemblances? Was this why he'd always felt so comfortable to me? So many things clicked in my head and began to make sense.

Although the subject of exes had come up before, the pain of losing Alec, and what he'd done was so raw, I dismissed the subject immediately whenever Emmett brought it up. I never even referred to Alec by his real name, just referring to him as the asshat. Then the realization he might even consider that I knew they were brothers hit me, and the sting of tears ran from my eyes, burning me with anger and devastation.

I heard his feet shuffle into the bathroom and looked up as he leaned against the doorway. His eyes were as bloodshot as mine felt.

"Sam, I need to know if you knew that Alec was my brother," he demanded.

"Of course not! What kind of person do you think I am?"

His words cut at me.

"Damn it, I'm sorry! I just don't know what to fucking think right now!"

He turned around and punched a hole in the hallway wall, then leaned his head against it. He pulled his hand out of the wall and plaster stained with his blood fell to the floor. He walked away, and like a punch to my gut, I heard each step as he descended the stairs. The front door slammed and his car roared to life then sped away.

I stood in Emmett's room, packing my things into an overnight bag, when I heard the front door open and close hard. My heart pounded as the anticipation of the next moments swirled in my head. I looked up as Emmett walked into the doorway of his room. He leaned against the doorframe, staring at me.

"What are you doing?" he asked.

"I'm just packing a few things for the drive back to Atlanta. I'm . . . going to stay with my parents for a few days."

He huffed a breath. "And see Alby right?"

I looked at him in confusion.

"Alby . . . it's what I call him. Stands for his full name, Alec Byron Morris, and he calls me Emjay for Emmett James Walker. It's just something we did as kids, and it stuck.

"Oh, that explains a lot. Well, yes, I'm going. I need answers. That's all. He really hurt me, Emmett. I need to know why. I didn't realize how hurt I still was until I heard his voice. I'm sorry, but I need this closure, and I deserve an explanation."

"Yeah. I get it. But I don't fucking like it. I don't fucking like any of this! I hate that you and my brother were together. But I love you, Peach, and I need you with me. Just promise you'll come back to me."

I walked over and pulled his strong body into mine, wrapping my arms around him. I looked up into his eyes.

"Of course I'll come back to you. Always."

As he leaned down and kissed the top of my head, a small part of me wondered why I suddenly felt unsure of my answer.

I should have known Alec was too good of a person to leave things the way they were between us. I guess it was better in the long run, rather than running into him at some family gathering, and seeing him face-to-face.

As I drove away from Emmett's house, I saw him in my rear view mirror, standing in his doorway looking broken and sad. Driving back to Georgia, I was confused and upset. I tapped my phone screen and called the girls, grateful my parents had insisted on the hands-free Bluetooth. I was having a hard enough time driving.

"Sam?" Alison answered.

"Hey," I murmured.

"What's wrong? Are you okay?"

"Is Tamron with you? Could you put me on speakerphone? I, umm, need to talk to y'all."

"Yeah, she's here. Hang on." She muffled the phone or

pulled it away then yelled, "Tamron! Sam's on the phone, get in here. Something sounds really wrong with her." Then her voice rang clear once again. "Okay, I've got you on speaker and, Tamron's right here."

"What's going on, Sam?" Tamron asked.

"Alec called me," I whispered.

"What the ever-loving fuck does he think he's doing?" Tamron yelled.

"Sam, sweetie." Alison paused. "Don't worry about it. His guilty conscience is probably finally showing its worthless ass. I hope you told him to get bent."

I didn't answer. I couldn't find the words. They were going to flip when they found out was going on, not to mention what I was doing.

"Sam. Why aren't you saying anything? Come on. Tell us how you told him to fuck himself. It'll be therapeutic for all of us." I cringed at Tamron's urging.

"Was that a horn honking? Are you in your car? Where are you going? Are you on your way over? Tamron, turn the coffee pot on. No, wait. It's after four. Grab a bottle of merlot instead. We can celebrate her being able to tell his no-good ass off."

They were making it hard to think. I took the next exit and pulled into a gas station. After putting my car in park, I leaned my head back against the headrest, and ran my hands down my face.

"I'm not on my way over, Alison. I'm on my way back to Atlanta."

"What did she say?" Tamron screeched in the background.

"You heard me, Tam, I'm going back to Atlanta. And before you ask, yes, I'm going to see Alec."

"Sam. Sam, Sam, Sam, Sam. Are you insane? You're thinking crazy. Just get your ass back to Emmett's house. He's your future, not that shameless, heartless prick," Alison fumed.

The tears streamed down my face. What was I doing? They were right. Emmett was my future. I loved him. I was happy with him. I sighed. "I just need answers. I deserve to know why

Alec hurt me."

"Oh, Sam. We know how bad he hurt you. But sometimes, you just gotta say screw it and don't look back," Tamron said.

"You can't just leave Emmett, sweetie. He loves you, and you love him. How do you think this is making him feel? Y'all are all happy, then the prick calls you, and you just up and leave? Even if it is just for answers, you have to think about how that would make you feel, if it were reversed," Alison added.

"Oh God, it's even worse than all of that," I cried.

"What on earth could even come close to making this situation worse?" Tamron sighed.

My head fell forward into my hands. "They're brothers. Alec and Emmett. They're brothers."

"Oh my God," they said in unison.

CHAPTER 23

Putting The Pieces Back Together

Sam

I pulled into my parents' driveway and put my car in park. I sat there for a few minutes before going inside. I wanted to see Mom and Dad, but I wasn't sure how they would feel about me coming back to talk to Alec. The abrupt way I'd left after that party had worried them, and even though I never told them how Alec had stomped on my heart, they knew it had gone down badly.

Tamron and Alison didn't understand. They tried, but their anger at Alec clouded their judgment. Or maybe it was my judgment being clouded by my own broken heart. I went inside and saw Mom and Dad sitting on the couch, cuddled into each other's arms. Their love always seemed easy and perfect. I suddenly thought of Emmett and felt my smile broaden at our love. That thought, however, was ruined by a flash of him sitting against the wall in his bedroom after I hung up from talking to Alec.

"Hey, Princess," Dad said.

Mom gasped. "Oh my gosh, sweetheart. We didn't know you were coming! I would have put a lasagna in the oven and made a streusel."

"It's okay. It was a last minute trip. No worries."

"Well, do you want some coffee? Your mom got one of those fandangled espresso machines."

I smiled at my dad; he was a regular cup of black coffee—plain, no foo foo stuff type of guy.

"No, thank you. I'm really tired, Dad. If it's okay, I'm . . . just going to head upstairs, take a shower, and go to bed."

Dad looked at me with a scrunched brow.

"Okay, Princess," he muttered hesitantly. "We'll see you in the morning. I have to be in to the office early, but your mom will be here."

"Goodnight, sweetheart," Mom said as she got up to give me a hug and kiss.

"Are you sure you're okay?" Dad asked.

"Yeah. Just tired. We'll talk in the morning."

I headed up stairs and into my room. As I stripped my clothes off, I decided I was too exhausted for a shower and would take it in the morning. I dropped onto my bed, falling fast asleep as my head nestled into my pillow.

The next morning I called my boss, Mr. Jackson, and apologized for leaving without any kind of notice. I explained that something had happened and I had to come back home to Georgia. He was as sweet as ever and wished me well, said he would hold my job for me as long as he could. He even said if my stay ended up being longer and I needed a job reference, he would be happy to help me. I made a mental note to send him a thank you card with a couple fancy bookmarks I'd made. I really loved working there.

Alec called to confirm we were still on for breakfast at Reveille Café in the morning. The drive wasn't far from my parents' house, so I arrived early and ordered my favorite, white elephant latte, while I waited for Alec to arrive.

I was looking down when I sensed him walk in, and I immediately flashed back to the last time I'd seen him, walking into that bedroom with the slutty skank. My chest tightened, and I felt flushed. I wasn't sure I could do this.

I couldn't breathe. I stood with my hand held over my mouth and grabbed my purse to leave. I couldn't go through with it. This was too hard, too much had happened, and I didn't think I could handle sitting across from him without losing it.

Before I could step away from the table, his warm hand wrapped around my elbow. He pulled me close, and as much as I wanted to resist, as much as I wanted to fight his hold on me, I couldn't. His embrace stole what little breath I had left.

"Samone, it's okay. Please don't go. Just give me a chance to apologize, a chance to explain," he pleaded.

Looking up at him, I nodded. It was all I could do. As always in our relationship, I was mesmerized by his intense stare, those crystal blue eyes piercing my heart.

"Okay, Alec, okay," I murmured.

We sat across from each other in silence. I was anxious and uncomfortable being near him and just wanted to get it over with, so I decided to break the silence.

"Okay, Alec. Let's talk."

"Hi." He smiled. "How are you?"

"Well, I'm here and clearly you can tell this isn't easy for me, so can we skip the pleasantries and get right into your explanation, please?"

Alec cleared his throat. "I'm sorry, Samone. I'm so sorry. You'll never know how deeply sorry I am. There isn't any excuse in the world for what I did at that party, for how badly I hurt you."

I felt an instant pain in my heart and tightness in my throat as unbidden images of that night flashed through my mind. I must have worn that pain clear as day across my face, because Alec reached across the table and tried to take my hands, but I pulled back as if his touch had burned me, and laid my hands clenched together in my lap. Looking up, I saw pain skitter across his face, as well.

"All I can say right now is, something happened . . . or,

changed for me, and I had to break up with you. We just couldn't be together. I needed time alone to process it all. I know I ignored the multitude of text messages you sent me, but you have to know how each one pierced my heart."

I let out a sarcastic laugh. "Really? I have to know that, huh? Well, actually no, Alec, I didn't realize my unanswered texts and ignored phone calls had any effect on you whatsoever. I've never been hurt by anyone in my life, as deeply as I was by you."

"If I'd known you were going to move away and go to Auburn, I can assure you, it would've gone down differently."

"Really? How could you have even expected me to stay here? You put me through hell, Alec! There was no way I could stay and go to Kennesaw State," my voice shook.

"I was so devastated, I couldn't even take a steady breath until I crossed over the state line into Alabama."

"Hurting you that night at Peter's party was the hardest thing I've ever done. But that was the only way to make you stop hoping we could get back together."

I felt like I was going to puke. "It sure didn't look hard," I seethed then chuckled as I glared daggers at him. "Well, I'm pretty sure *it was* hard."

At the very least, he had the good grace to look ashamed.

"Samone, tell me now, if I hadn't done that, would you have walked away?" He shook his head. "It doesn't matter. What's done is done, and I can't take it back. Believe me, if I could, I would erase all the pain I have caused you. Please, just tell me it's not too late for us. Please say we can start over."

I laughed. I tried not to, I really did, but I laughed. "Alec, we can never start over and forget what happened. You broke my heart and shattered my soul. About the only thing we can do is talk about it, so tell me what happened. Why did you feel you had to go to such extremes to hurt me and push me away? Then . . . *maybe* we can move forward, but we can never start over. What you did will always be a part of our history . . . a part of who we are as friends. But, God help me, a part of me still loves you, and I'm willing to try and forgive you. I just need to know why."

"I can't explain everything right now. I'm still sorting some things out, but I was wrong to exclude you. Please, on our love, I beg you, Samone, to let me have the time I need before telling you."

I'm sure, the look on my face told him I was way more than a little reluctant.

"Please, just one more chance. It's all I ask, and I know I don't deserve it, but I love you so much. It hurt every day—every damn minute we were apart—it hurt my heart. I promise to never hurt you again, that I will explain everything as soon as I can. If you'll let me, if you can try to understand what I am going through, I'll spend every waking minute showing you how sorry I am."

I knew I didn't owe him anything, but my heart longed for an explanation, and a part of me did still love him, just not the way he hoped for. They say your first love always stays in a special place in your heart. Thoughts of Emmett standing in his doorway as I drove away crossed my mind again, and I felt a different kind of pain. Alec must have mistook my sad expression for an answer because he started to get up to leave.

"It's okay, I see I went too far. I knew it. I've lost you," he said.

I reached across the table and grabbed his hand. "No, Alec, it's not that. Look, I've something important to tell you."

He looked puzzled. "Okay. What is it?"

"Now, please, don't react. Just listen until I'm done."

He motioned for me to continue.

"After the party and you . . . you know, put on your cruel show—"

"Samone, I said I'm sorry. I don't know what else to say, but I'll say it forever if I have to."

"No. Just listen. Please don't interrupt. After the party at Peter's house, I went to Auburn to spend some time with the girls. They took me to their boyfriends' frat party, and I met someone, and we've been together ever since. Practically live together really." I took a deep breath as Alec stared intently at me. "His name is Emmett, Alec—Emmett Walker."

He flinched and yanked his hand away.

"Wait, please. I didn't know that he was your brother. He didn't know who I was until you called my cell and your picture popped up on the screen. Your actions crushed me so badly, I could never speak of you. But you need to understand, I'm with Emmett now. We can try to be friends, Alec, but don't make me wait forever for an explanation. I'm willing to forgive, but I need to know why you did and said the things you did in order to do that."

His expression transformed from devastation to resignation, as he seemed to accept all I was willing to offer him.

"Okay. Thank you, Samone. You won't regret it. I promise," he said.

With all the difficult parts now out in the open, we each ordered a bagel and talked of easier things, like our plans for the upcoming spring semester of college.

It felt remarkably easy to talk to him again. He even mentioned he wanted us to go to our old park where we'd spent so much time under the old oak tree. He said we would talk about everything, and he would answer all my questions. Although it had been a special place for us, I felt it may be easier for him there to talk about whatever issues he had. It was a familiar place where we had shared many deep conversations. We bared our souls beneath the leaves of that tree. I agreed to go, as friends. I just hoped that Emmett would understand.

"I'm not moving back here. I'm staying in Auburn. I like the university there, and Emmett and I have a good thing between us."

The look of pain that crossed his face was hard to witness, but I forced myself to sit there. He'd caused me more pain than he would ever feel. Truthfully, a small part of me savored the justice of it all. In that fleeting moment, I felt like the villain in our sordid tale.

CHAPTER 24

Torn

Sam

I needed to decide what I was going to do. I wasn't sure about leaving Atlanta and going back to Auburn just yet. A part of me felt like I needed to stick around for a while. Thankfully, we were on break between fall and spring semesters. I could feel that Alec needed me. My mind grated at why I should even care after what he'd done to me. But something was really wrong, whatever this mystery problem of his was being the pivotal factor in the equation.

But the other part of me was pulled back to Emmett. I loved him and longed for the feel of him holding me in his arms. I missed his smile. But a piece of my heart died a little each time I thought of his expression as he stood in the doorway of his room, watching me pack to come back here. The resigned tone of his voice, as the realization struck him that I'd be seeing Alec.

I retrieved my cell and checked my recent calls list. Emmett's name was usually at the top, but now it was five contacts down. I looked at the date of our last call. It was three days ago. Tapping his name, my head hung in shame. I should have called him earlier.

The phone rang and rang. Just as I thought it would go to voicemail, he answered.

"Peach."

"Hi Emmett."

Silence filled my ears.

"I'm sorry I haven't called. I, umm, got so wrapped up in things here."

"It's okay, though a text message would've been nice, if nothing else, to know that you made the drive safely," he snapped.

"I know. I don't know what to say. I'm sorry. I love you."

"Ahh damn it. I love you too, Peach. I didn't mean to be an ass. I just worry, you know. This whole thing sucks."

"Yeah. It does," I answered.

"So, have you seen him?" he asked in a strained voice.

"Yes," I whispered. "We met for breakfast the morning after I got back here."

"I see."

"Emmett, something is really wrong. I just don't know what it is. He still won't tell me why he broke up with me."

"Or why he acted like the biggest douche on the planet?" he seethed.

I gasped.

"Yeah, I know about what happened at that party, Peach. I called the girls after you left, and they told me what he did, and how he hurt you. I really get it now, why you never talked about it before. I just can't believe my little brother pulled some asshat shit like that on the girl he supposedly loved. And for fuck's sake, I'm still pissed-off that your ex is my brother!"

I couldn't talk. I just listened as he ranted on.

"I'm sorry, Peach. It's just hard to deal with all this."

"I know," I whispered. "It's okay."

"It'll be okay when you come home to me. When are you leaving Atlanta?"

"Umm, about that . . ."

"Oh, hell no! Don't you dare say you're not coming home! I'll drive down there and throw your ass over my shoulder and walk back to fucking Auburn if I have to!"

"Emmett, please, listen to me for a minute. There really is something wrong here. Alec has some big secret he won't tell me about yet. I have a really bad feeling. I think I need to stay here for a while and at least make sure he's okay."

He didn't say anything. I could hear him breathing. His silence was deafening.

"Emmett?"

"Peach, I don't know what to say. On one hand, I'm seriously pissed-off and shocked and hurt and pissed-off some more. But, on the other hand, you're freaking me out with all of this 'something's really wrong, big secret of his' shit, and I'm really worried about my brother. This whole thing is a clusterfuck. We're all gonna need to see a shrink after this is all said and done."

"I want to come home, babe, I really do, but I just can't yet. I have to be sure he's okay, and I'm not. The way he loved me . . ."

Emmett's sharp intake of breath startled me, but I continued.

" . . . there has to be something God-awful for him to have hurt me the way he did. I'm scared of what it could be. I'm really afraid for him. I need to stay for a bit. I'll come home to you, I promise."

"Okay, Peach. Stay, but keep in contact with me, ya hear? A text message takes less than a minute and gives me relief of which you have no idea. I worry about you when you're not with me. And please, let me know if you find anything out about whatever he's hiding. I know I'm pissed, but he's still my little brother, and I'm worried about him too. As soon as I can wrap my head around this shit, I'm gonna call him. We have to talk about this. I can't go the rest of my life feeling like I wanna throat punch him. Yeah, we're definitely gonna need a damn shrink."

"I'll keep in contact and let you know as soon as I know anything. I love and miss you."

"Okay. I love and miss you, too, Peach."

There was a little over a month before the start of spring semester at Auburn. I wasn't about to stay with my parents while I stuck around to sort out Alec's bizarre issues. Since I'd changed my original plans and moved to Auburn, Heather had already found an alternate housemate for her freshman year at college here. I could bunk with them, but I wasn't keen on sleeping on a futon for a month.

Luckily, I found a small, furnished condo for rent on a month-to-month lease. The strange part was, in a way, it reminded me of the place where Emmett and I had stayed in Panama City Beach. It was oddly comforting, like he was with me instead of being a state away.

I went back out to my car and brought all my stuff inside. Then I curled up with spoonful of mint chocolate chip ice cream. It was either that or go raid my parents' liquor cabinet, and I didn't feel up to the twenty questions that would go with that visit. Satisfied for the time being, I pulled out my iPad and read. That's what I needed, to get lost in a book and someone else's world.

Thoughts of Emmett surfaced in my mind. I missed him. I knew he was feeling all kinds of mixed emotions, and I felt a deep ache in my chest.

CHAPTER 25

I Wish I Was Selfish

Emmett

I was beginning to think, when I told Sam we were all gonna need a shrink after this was over, that I was more on point than I first believed. I certainly felt like I was losing my mind. I loved her and wanted her with me, but I loved my little brother, too. I was worried about him. He was cryptic with her about this damn secret of his. I hated that they had been together. Hated it. But I loved them both and wanted them to be happy.

I woke up and called John. I needed to talk this out with my best friend and clear my head.

"Hey, man," he answered. "It's a bit early isn't it?"

"Yeah, sorry. I always forget about the time zone." I replied.

"S'okay, man. What's up?"

"It's just Peach. And Alec. And every damn thing."

"What do you mean? What's wrong with them?"

As I told him the whole sordid tale, there was a mixture of expletives and silence on the other end of the line. When I finished, he let out a long, low whistle.

"Wow. That's some seriously fucked-up shit."

"Yeah, tell me about it," I said.

"Well, what are you going to do?"

"I don't know. Well, I do. I just don't know what to do afterwards." I sighed. "I'll probably lose my damn mind without her. But I love them both and want them to be happy. He was her first love, you know, and that love never leaves you. I know she'll never leave my heart. I've never been in love with a girl before her. But I know my Peach; she has to make sure that he's okay. I'm worried about Alec, too. Whatever he's hiding has to be bad. But she's also going to be with him on a daily basis, and her feelings are bound to be confused. I just keep thinking maybe I need to take a step back."

"Are you out of your fucking mind?" John yelled.

"No, man, listen. I've thought about this a lot. It's a shitty situation, and no matter how you spin it, someone gets hurt and left alone. I don't want Alec to be left again. When our parents died . . . it was hard on both of us, but, because he was younger, I think he felt abandoned. He went through a really dark time for a while, and I wasn't sure he would come back from that. Especially socially."

"Damn, I know that's rough, man. But that doesn't mean you should just walk away from the love of *your* life," John said.

"No, I know. But it's eating at me. It's the right thing to do for both of them."

"But it's *not* the right thing to do for you. And I don't think it's the right thing for Sam either. You said he broke things off with her and pulled that crazy shit after, to push her away. I'd say he gave up any rights to her a long time ago. What if he breaks her heart again?"

"Yeah, but Peach thinks there's a reason behind it. This secret he's keeping. I just feel like this is the way it needs to go. I don't believe he would ever hurt her again."

"Shit. Well, if you need to get away, you know you can always come chill with me here. I can hook you up with some Grade A Alaskan sweethearts."

I shook my head. "Thanks, man. I may head out your way eventually, but I don't need or want anyone else, Alaskan or otherwise. For now, I need to stick around here, for as long as I can handle it anyway."

"Well good luck, Emmett. You're gonna need a truck load of it."

"Thanks. Later, man."

"Later," he said before hanging up.

I dropped my phone on my dresser, walked into the bathroom down the hall, and stared at my reflection in the mirror. I wasn't sure of how this day would end, but I made a mental note to check the whiskey in the liquor cabinet to be sure I could drown my sorrows later on should I need to.

As lame as it is to break up with someone over the phone, it's how I decided I should do it. I knew if I saw her, I'd never go through with it. I'd cave in a split second. The scent of her perfume wafted through my mind, and I nearly threw my phone across the room. Instead, I dialed her number.

"Hey, babe," she answered.

"Hey, Sam," I murmured.

She gasped. "Is . . . everything okay? Is something wrong?" she asked.

"Everything's fine. Well, it will be. Listen, we need to talk."

"Okay. What's up? Miss me? I miss you! Maybe we can meet somewhere in the middle and see a movie, have dinner. That would work," she urged.

"Peach. No. I can't."

"Okay, maybe tomorrow?"

"No, not tomorrow either. Listen to me for a minute, okay?"

"Sorry, babe. I just miss you. All right, I'm listening. Go ahead."

"Just let me say everything I have to say before you respond, okay?"

"Emmett, stop, you're freaking me out!"

"Fuck! There's no easy way to say this. It's over, Sam. I, uh, can't deal with this shit right now. You should just be with Alec."

"What? No, absolutely not, Emmett! You're not throwing me away like he did! I love you. You love me. We can work through this. I told you, I'm only staying to make sure he's okay, and to find out what he's hiding. I'm just worried about him. I'm not staying to get back together with him. I love *you*."

"Sam, just stop. It's over."

She started crying, but I had to keep going. I had to end it.

"It was—fun while it lasted." I punched my hand into the mattress, where she used to sleep by my side.

"What? Are you telling me I was just a piece of ass to you? Now, that there's a complication, you're wiping your hands of me?" she retorted.

"God, Sam, we . . . we just weren't meant to be together. Look, I'm sorry. Hope you're both okay. I gotta go."

I hung up the phone before she could say anything else and shoved it in my back pocket. Grabbing my keys, I went for a drive and tried to purge the images of her from my head.

CHAPTER 26

Some Things You Can't Take Back

Emmett

A s the weeks went by, I hated myself for breaking up with Sam. The whole thing sucked. So I got in my car and drove to Atlanta. I didn't want to hurt him, but I had to call Alec, and tell him. I couldn't just sit there and give up on Sam. Damn it. I tried to do the "*right*" thing. But I wanted her. I needed her. Most of all, I fucking loved her. I was empty without her. I was a shell.

But I'm a greedy bastard. I knew Alec loved her. I remembered how he talked about her that day at Aunt Robin's. Before I knew who she was. Before he destroyed her spirit.

He had that whole she's-The-One, Emmett, kind of love in his eyes. Don't get me wrong. I love my little brother, but Sam had consumed me, including the part that used to think rationally . . . selflessly. Without her, those parts were gone, leaving behind nothing but need and greed.

Fuck it, I should just go to Hartsfield-Atlanta airport, buy a one-way ticket across the pond, and never look back.

But it was too late for that. I knew Sam loved me, too. Needed me. Wanted me. I could see the way my presence affected her when she thought I wasn't looking. I know because it's the same way she affected me.

How could she think I didn't care, that she was just another piece of ass to me? As if Samone Lang could ever just be someone's fling. For fuck's sake, she could lift my life up or destroy it with one breath.

No. I couldn't just sit idle and let her go. If Alec thought he could just pop back into her life, apologize, and win her back, he was sorely mistaken. Little brother would survive. His broken heart would heal; he'd move on and live a long, happy life . . . but not with my peach.

He should've never let her go in the first place. When he broke her heart, he threw their love away. He threw *her* away. Whether any of us knew it then or not, he pushed her to me. And now she was mine. I'd be damned if I was gonna let her go. I just had to convince her to give me another chance after breaking up with her.

Just deciding to fight for Sam made me feel like I could finally breathe again. I had to call him before things progressed any further. Before she found the strength to open her heart up to him again. God, I hated to hurt Alec, but I might as well have been dead, than go on like I was, living without her.

I scrolled through my contacts in my phone and called him.

"Hello." The word was clipped.

"Hey Alby."

Silence. It made my stomach drop.

"What's up Emmett?" he retorted.

I flinched at his use of my name. "Can we talk? In person, I mean."

"I don't have the time to drive to Auburn."

"You don't have to. I'm here, in Atlanta."

"Fucking hell. Of course you are."

I sighed. "Just meet me at my hotel. We can have a beer in the lounge here and talk."

"Yeah. Fine. What time?"

"When can you be here? I'm staying at the Atlanta Marriott Suites in Midtown."

"Okay, I'll uh, see you in about an hour."

He hung up. I groaned. I knew it wasn't going to go well. The thing was, we both loved Sam. Alec didn't know I loved her yet. I was sure he thought she was just a piece of ass to me, one among many.

I'll admit, I used to be a player. I liked to have fun. I wasn't the "different girl every night" kind of guy though. College was for learning *and* having fun. So . . . I had some friends with benefits. But how the hell could Alec think I could even look at Sam that way? I can't imagine *anyone* ever thinking that of Sam. Especially not if they knew her. And, man, did I know her. She practically lived with me for months.

I was already there and waiting when Alec walked in. God, we used to be so close. It really hurt to see his expression when he saw me sitting there. I could feel the giant chasm between us as he walked toward my table.

"Mind if I sit?" Alec asked, his tone stiff.

"Please do. How are you?" I asked. He looked haggard. My once-carefree brother had the weight of pain and sadness on his shoulders, and it was palpable. The tormented expression on his face was almost enough to change my plans. But I reminded myself how he'd treated her, the way she would close up at the mention of her ex. I loved Sam, and I needed her in my life.

"Look, Emmett, this isn't a social call, so let's skip the bullshit. Obviously, if you cared how I was, you never would've tried to steal Samone from me."

I almost came out of my chair. "Alec, that's not what happened! How many times do I have to tell you? I didn't know *my* Sam was *your* Samone! She lives here in Atlanta. I live in fucking Auburn. That's a two-hour drive." I grabbed my glass and tossed the whiskey back. "How the hell was I supposed to know you were going to throw her away, or that she and I would end up at the same frat party? What are even the chances of that happening? She told me she was running from a bad break up, but I had no idea *you* were the person who'd broken her heart."

Running my hands through my hair, I remembered the shattered expression on her face when she told me she was getting over a break up. I never asked her about it, because I couldn't stand to see that look in her eyes.

"I swear, Alec, I didn't know who she was. We were just drawn to each other."

"Yeah, yeah, Emmett, I've heard all of this before. Whatever. Doesn't change the fact you were practically living with her for months. It doesn't change fact that, even though you're gone and she's back here, where she belongs, things just still aren't even close to being back to how they should be." He slumped down in his seat. "Even though you left her, you're still there, an unspoken part of everything. She won't even give me a chance to win her love back. You know what? Fuck this shit . . . I didn't even want to come down here, but you insisted it was so important we talk face-to-face. So, brother, tell me . . . what is so important? Samone and I are supposed to have dinner tonight. I'm hoping to rekindle her feelings."

My head rested in my hands, and I scrubbed them over my face as I looked up at him. "All right then, fine . . . I'm in love with her."

At first, there was a genuinely shocked expression on his face, but then he erupted in crazed laughter.

"Oh, isn't this rich? Extra, extra, read all about it! My brother, Emmett Walker, playboy extraordinaire, is *in love* and *off the market!* Better watch out, bro, half of the teaching assistants at Auburn will be positively jilted!"

"Alec, seriously? Look, I'm sorry. I'll never be able to express how hard this is, how hard it's been for me."

He let out an irritated grunt. "You? Ha! You have no idea, what can be hard to deal with in life."

"The fuck I don't! You think you're the only one to deal with hard things in life? You think you're the only one fate took people you love away from you? We both have suffered unbelievable loss when Mom and Dad died!"

"Whatever, man." He slammed the beer I'd ordered him down. "I'm not talking about that. I'm talking about Samone."

I shook my head. "Yeah, I know it's been hell for you, too. But Sam makes me feel alive and happy. I can't bear the thought of not being hers, or her not being mine. Just the possibility makes it hard to fucking breathe. I'm all mixed up. I can't eat, sleep, nothing. It's like half of my soul is missing with her gone, and I can't . . . I *won't* let that slip away. I can't live without her."

Alec stood abruptly. "You know what, Emjay? Why don't you go throw your poetic bullshit on someone else's door? I love Samone, and I'm not about to let your dick get in the way of our happiness."

I slammed my hand down on the table. "That's weak bullshit!"

He ignored my outburst.

"I'm going to win her back. I'll do everything in my power to earn her forgiveness. But tell me something, brother, does she know about your past relationships? Does she know you slept with nearly half the TAs at Auburn your freshman year? Now you listen to me carefully, Samone isn't just another piece of ass for you or anyone. She's the type of woman to spend your life with and cherish. I love her and want her happiness . . . above my own. She's not just someone to screw when the mood hits then toss aside!"

"Me? Toss her aside?" I was outraged. "Are you even hearing yourself right now? You. Threw. Her. Away. You did that! You broke her heart. You have no idea how bad you hurt her. I was the one who picked up the pieces. So don't even start your holier-than-thou bullshit with me! You. Will. Lose."

As angry as I was, I could see, when he'd said her name and piece of ass in the same sentence, how it made his teeth clench. But I didn't need that, to know he loved her. I knew he did. The problem was that I did, too.

"I don't think of Sam like that at all. I love her. She's inside my heart. I feel nothing but pain when she's gone. And I think you should know . . . she's in love with me, too."

His face blanched and twisted with pain, but I had to press on. He had to know the truth. I owed him that much.

"She's told me time and again. We always made sure the

last thing we said was that we loved each other. I'm going to fight for her whole heart, brother. I can't just let her go. I love you, and I'm sorry, but fate screwed us both. I'm going to do my best to be happy again, and that means being with Sam."

"Over my dead body, will I let you have her. She deserves better than you, Emjay. Damn it, she deserves better than me too, but I know I can give her what she wants and needs to make her happy."

I'd had enough of his bullshit. "Fine, little brother, if that's how you want it."

Alec shook his head and ran his hands through his hair. A bad sign for either of us to do. He'd reached the end of what he could handle, and I felt a good brotherly brawling coming on. Instead, he just looked at me sitting there, a sad, regretful expression on his face. Not saying one more word, he threw some cash on the table to pay for our drinks then walked out of the hotel lounge and, at the time, what felt like my life.

I went to the bathroom and was washing my hands when I caught my reflection in the mirror. Damn that face. Damn this fucking day. I just stood there. I couldn't pull my eyes away from my reflection staring back at me. I was troubled and uncertain, while my heart pounded like a tattoo gun in my chest. What the hell had I been thinking? How could I have said that? When it was all said and done, and I looked back into the mirror, I just hoped I could live with what I saw.

That was the first black mark on my soul . . .

CHAPTER 27

Some Things Are Better Left Unsaid

Sam

After Emmett ended our relationship, I cursed love and fate and every thing to do with soul mates and happiness. But I never even entertained the idea of rekindling my relationship with Alec. I couldn't. I was in love with Emmett.

I knew that Alec was hoping we could reconcile. He made no secret that he desperately wanted to get back what we'd had. But I didn't feel that way about him anymore. My heart and love belonged to Emmett.

I let Alec stay over periodically, on the nights he would get antsy about leaving late after watching movies, but never in my room. He always slept on the couch.

Christmas was just a week away, and Alec wanted us to spend it together, but I needed to make sure he knew where we stood first. I didn't want to lead him on in any way. He made mistakes, but I still didn't know why he'd hurt me. He hinted about a special gift, and I didn't want any blurred lines between us.

After thinking about it for days, I decided there would never be a good or right time to remind him of the truth, and what I'd said in the café the day we talked. After Emmett broke up with me, Alec tried not to make it obvious, but he definitely turned up his efforts to win me back. So I decided to "rip the Band-Aid off" and get it over with. Because, no matter what I said, the longer I put it off, the more his hope would grow and the worse it was going to hurt him.

"Alec, I think we need to talk again," I said as he helped me carry bags of groceries upstairs to my condo.

"All right. What about?" His voice sounded nervous. I guess he could tell by the tone of mine that he wasn't going to like what I had to say.

As I fumbled for the keys in my purse, I turned around and leaned against the front door.

"You know that I love you—I'll always love you, Alec. But, it's not in the same *way* you love me. I want us to remain friends. I just need you to understand that I'm *in love* with Emmett."

His eyes grew wide at my words, his mouth dropped open before his brow scrunched down in anger. "You can't love him, Samone. He's not capable of loving you. He's a player, not the type to settle down."

"That's not true," I whispered. "He settled down with me."

"Yeah, and look how far that got you. He left you when the going got tough. Did he fight for you? No. He knows you're here . . . with me. I may not have you back yet, but you can damn well bet he knows I'm trying. Only a fool wouldn't."

I sighed as I set my purse down on the doormat.

He set the groceries on the floor and roughed his hands through his hair and down his face. "Damn it, Samone, he hurt you! I saw it!"

"Well, I guess it runs in the family, because you hurt me too, only worse—you were cruel."

His face blanched. "I said I was sorry. I had my reasons."

"Yeah, so you've said. But you still haven't told me!"

"I'm going explain everything tomorrow, when we have

lunch by our tree. Please don't love him. Don't waste you heart on him."

"It's too late. I love and need him."

The words were like a hot piece of coal burning in my heart. My chest hurt as I watched the light leave Alec's eyes.

Until then, I think he had thought and hoped my time with Emmett was nothing but a rebound fling, an infatuation he hoped to extinguish.

After that, everything was a blur. It had all happened so fast, and I was frozen where I stood. He stepped back to lean on the railing, like he was trying to gather his thoughts.

The damn wood railing broke, causing Alec to fall backwards. His arms flew up and his feet flew out. I watched in helpless horror as he tumbled, head over feet, down the stairs.

I screamed out in terror and ran down the stairs. When I reached the bottom, I knelt by his side, as he lay there, unmoving. I fumbled in my purse for my phone and dialed 911. I wasn't sure if I would ever see his eyes again, whether alight with happiness, or devoid of joy. I'd take either as long as it meant he was okay.

That was the last time I saw his crystal blue eyes, and they were devoid of their usual light, because I couldn't give his love a chance. Because I loved two men, and couldn't leave well enough alone. I should have walked away from both of them.

I wish I'd never told him that I loved Emmett, too. Emmett had ended things between us. His words, *"It was fun while it lasted,"* had resonated in my head, but it just felt so dishonest to keep it from Alec. I didn't want him living under false pretenses and hope for us. I wanted his understanding. Instead, I only gave him more pain.

"Excuse me, Ms. Lang, we've had to move Mr. Morris to the ICU," Dr. Shaw said, pulling me from my thoughts.

"What are you talking about? I thought Alec's injuries weren't life threatening. He's not shaking as much anymore. Why has he been moved to the ICU?" I asked.

"Are you a member of his family?"

"No. I'm his . . . friend."

"I'm sorry, but I need to talk to a member of his family."

"Umm . . . well, it's really just us. Now. I mean, he has his Aunt Robin, but she's on a trek across Europe with her boyfriend. And he has his brother, Emmett. But he's not here. Can you check his file please? I know he put me as an emergency contact before his Aunt left for Europe."

Dr. Shaw flipped through Alec's chart to the last page.

"Ahh. Here it is. Samone Lang, right?"

"Yes, that's right," I answered, relieved.

"Well, Ms. Lang, the test results are conclusive. The EEG shows significant seizure activity. Mr. Morris has epilepsy."

"No, you must be mistaken," I said. "Alec doesn't have epilepsy. I mean, I think I would know. We dated for nearly two years in high school. Your damn tests are wrong. Alec has never said anything to me about having epilepsy, and that's not something he would hide from me."

"I'm sorry, Ms. Lang, from the best my colleagues and I can tell, since his fall, Mr. Morris has been in *Convulsive Status Epilepticus.*"

I must have had a confused look on my face, because Dr. Shaw smiled apologetically and walked me over to a chair in the ICU waiting room. When we sat down he continued.

"It's a condition that occurs in epileptic patients who are in a state of continuous seizure activity that lasts more than five minutes, or if they have frequent recurrent seizures without regaining full consciousness in between them."

It was like white noise in my ears as I tried to focus on what he was saying.

"Patients with *Convulsive Status Epilepticus* have an increased risk of permanent brain damage and death."

I gasped as my hands flew to my mouth.

"As you can see, Mr. Morris has yet to regain consciousness, and he's having frequent tonic-clonic seizures. In between those tonic clonic, or convulsions, he's still registering significant seizure activity that isn't showing physically. I really need to know what anti-epileptic medications he takes. Does Mr. Morris have any immediate family I can call and discuss his medical care with? I need to know his complete medical history. I need a list of his current medications before moving forward with treatment options," Dr. Shaw said.

"Alec isn't taking any prescription medications . . . that I know of. He doesn't even take vitamins," I said as I shook my head.

Dr. Shaw let out a frustrated sigh. "Would you mind calling his brother, please? At the moment, he's in stable condition, but that could change at any time. I can assure you, the issues between Mr. Morris and his brother aren't as important as his current state of health."

I nodded. "Yes, of course. I think I'll take a walk for this call, if you don't mind."

"That's fine." Pointing to a sign on the wall, he stated, "We prefer no cell phone usage in the ICU anyway. Remember, Ms. Lang, time is of the essence."

Right. Time is of the essence. Please, Emmett, pick up the phone.

Ever since he broke up with me, he wouldn't answer his phone or respond to my text messages.

Oh God, he's never going to even listen to my message.

"Hi Emmett, it's me. It's urgent. This isn't about us. Please listen and don't delete this. Look, something's happened. Alec's in the hospital. This neurologist, Dr. Shaw, is saying that his test results show seizure activity and that he has epilepsy. The doctor needs to know his complete medical history, and what medications he takes for his seizures. I mean . . . this is crazy. Alec doesn't have epilepsy. We'd have known if he were having seizures. I never would've called unless it was something important. But none of this is Alec's fault. It's my fault. I'm sorry, Emmett, more sorry than you'll ever know. Anyway, this doesn't matter right now. Please, just call Kennestone Hospital and ask to speak with Dr. Shaw. You don't even have to call me back. I lov . . . I'm sorry."

Auburn's about an hour behind us, so he was probably still

at work. I scrolled through my contacts for the Lumberyard.

A chipper voice answered. "Auburn Lumber Mill, how may I direct your call?"

My mind grated on her upbeat tone. I reminded myself, this girl was doing her job and had no idea, the nature of my call. I swallowed hard after a quick breath.

"Hi, I'm trying to reach Emmett Walker."

"One moment please."

I stood leaning against a bench outside the hospital, my leg shaking as I waited. I listened to her tap-tap-tapping the keys on her computer, and I wanted to scream at her to just pick up a phone or radio and call for him.

"I'm sorry, miss, but Mr. Walker isn't on schedule for today."

"What? Are you sure?"

"I just looked. He hasn't been here all week, and he's not on the schedule again for another week after this."

"Oh. Can I leave a message, in case he calls in?"

"Sure. What's your name?"

"Sam. Please ask him to call my cellphone. It's urgent."

"All right, did you want to leave a number?"

"No, he has it. Thanks for your time."

Walking back into Alec's room in the ICU, I felt my heart sink in my chest. He was just lying there, his eyes closed. He looked peaceful. They had him hooked up to monitors and a blood pressure machine. There were IV lines in his arms and one was connected to a bag of blood.

What the hell?

They weren't giving him blood when I left to call Emmett. I decided to wait there and ask Dr. Shaw why they had started a blood transfusion. Something had changed. I needed to know what it was. God, I hoped Emmett would call back.

CHAPTER 28

2230

Sam

As I sat in the cold, hard chair at Alec's bedside, my mind raced back to the morning. I didn't want to remember it. I didn't want to think those thoughts again. What the hell was wrong with me?

Why couldn't I just have left well enough alone? He didn't have to know. He didn't have to hurt . . . his eyes never would've held the stark realization, the torment of true pain and misconceived betrayal. It didn't matter that it was unintentional, that Alec and I weren't together when it happened. Because it didn't change the fact that it was with Emmett. But most of all, it didn't change the fact that I loved them both, and nothing was gained, but everything could be lost from those words I spoke this morning. My selfish attempt to clear my conscience, for not being able to love Alec the way he needed me to, and not being able to let Emmett go.

Neither of us knew who the other was. We were just two lonely strangers at a damn college frat party. Being with Emmett felt so right, more right than I'd ever felt in my entire life. I felt whole when I was with him. If I'm honest with myself, the thought of being without Emmett feels so wrong, it causes physical pain in my chest.

The months following that frat party were like heaven. We fit into each other's lives so well. Until that last Sunday morning Emmett and I were together. When Alec called, our worlds turned upside down, our lives shattered with one cruel twist of fate—they were brothers.

Sitting there, I held his hand. It was the only sense of warmth I felt. Everything else was so cold. Everything and everyone. God, why hadn't Alec told me he had epilepsy? How could he have kept something like that from me? What if Emmett didn't listen to my message or never returned my call? I decided to send him a text. Maybe he'd at least see it before deleting it. He hadn't replied to any I'd sent after he ended our relationship.

Me: Emergency with Alec!

@ Kennestone Hosp. I left you a msg.

pls listen to it & call for Dr. Shaw

Please reply . . . please please please . . .

E: Don't leave. I'm on my way.

Before I realized something was happening, several nurses rushed into the room. Alarms sounded, and I was pushed out of the way.

Oh no! Alec!

"Ms. Lang, we need you to step outside," a nurse said.

"Wait, what happened? What's wrong with him? Alec!" I screamed as I backed out of the door.

There was so much going on in that cold room, I couldn't see Alec anymore, only the people crammed around his bed, frantically working on him. I focused on the backs of their heads. I don't know why, but I did. Some of them were shaking their heads, others nodding, some were turning in different directions . . . looking around, I guessed, but for what?

"Please, help him, please, make him better," I prayed.

I couldn't tell what they were doing. There was so much yelling and noise. I kept my hands over my ears to shut out the pandemonium. Silence . . . oh, thank God, it finally got quiet again. I was relieved that Alec would be okay. Thank God," I whispered. I didn't know what I would do if I lost him.

I looked up and saw the doctor's head had stopped moving, his eyes downcast. I strained to see what the hell he was looking at on the floor. Why was he just standing there? I stepped closer. I wanted to yell at him to move and call out orders.

But another voice stopped me cold. It was a doctor I'd seen Dr. Shaw talking to earlier. "Dr. Shaw, you need to call it. We did everything we could do," he said.

Dr. Shaw's head jerked up as he looked to him, then at the ceiling. "Damn it!" he swore. "Time of death . . . 2230 hours."

What?

My head was pounding, my hands and feet suddenly felt heavy. My attention snapped to Alec's bed. I couldn't tear my eyes away from him. He looked so peaceful lying there. As a nurse drew the sheet up over his head, it jolted me out of my moment of peace.

"Oh my God! Alec! No, stop! Don't do that! He's not dead. He can't be!" I cried. "No! Alec! Please, don't go! Please!" I begged.

My knees were suddenly weak. I felt familiar strong arms surround me, and they held me tight. God, I had never thought I'd feel them again, but then, at that time, and for that reason, I wished so badly that I hadn't.

"Sam, I'm here," he whispered in my ear. His hands were warm as they rubbed my arms, a stark contrast to the cold I'd endured all day.

How had he gotten there so fast? He should've still been driving. It had only been a short while since I called him. He lowered me to a chair in the hall across from Alec's room.

"What's . . . what the hell's going on in there?" He turned around toward the door of Alec's room. He looked back at me, "Why were you in there? Is that . . . shit, please, please say no . . . Is that Alec's room?"

I nodded as I wiped at my tears. I just couldn't find my voice.

"Why the fuck is there a sheet over his head?" He looked at me with desperate, disbelieving eyes before turning back toward Alec's room. "Oh fuck—no!"

He threw his hands up in the air, roughed them through his hair and slowly walked into the room. He stopped halfway between the door and Alec's bed, and looked back at me with panic in his eyes.

He made it to the bed and sat on the edge, just staring at the floor. His hand switched from a fist to resting flatly on Alec's chest like a broken lifeline. When he turned to look at Alec's lifeless form lying under the sheet, I could see his lips were moving. I just couldn't hear what he was saying. But every few words or so, he cried harder and harder.

As I watched the one-sided exchange, his body wracked with sobs, inadvertently pulled the sheet from Alec's face. Emmett gasped and nearly fell off the bed, holding one hand over his mouth as the other was frozen in a sheet-clinched fist on Alec's chest, and I cried even harder than before. I jumped up and ran down the hall, barely grabbing a mop bucket in time to throw up. A nurse ran out of another room and clutched me by my elbow, holding me steady.

"Miss, are you all right?"

I shook my head and pointed back down the hall where Alec's room was. She helped me walk back to the doorway of his room. When she looked inside and saw Emmett sobbing as he held Alec in his arms, she slung her arm over my shoulder and pulled me closer.

"I'm so sorry for your loss." She stepped back and dug in the pocket of her scrubs for a Kleenex. "But he really shouldn't be in there."

"Oh God, please give him a minute. Please, we just need some time," I said, wiping tears from my face.

"All right then, let me see if the chaplain is here," she said as she walked away.

I leaned against the doorframe and tried to compose myself before walking back into Alec's room.

"Please, Alby, please be okay. I can't lose you. Please," he begged as he rocked Alec's body in his arms.

As I stepped inside, Emmett turned and looked at me. His eyes were bloodshot, tears and snot running down his face.

Neither of us could speak. We just stared at each other as I walked over to Alec's bedside. I finally looked down at Alec's face as Emmett gently laid his head back down on the pillow. I couldn't breathe. I started gasping for air as my tears began to flow down my cheeks again.

Emmett rushed around to the other side of Alec's bed and sat down pulling me onto his lap in the visitor chair, he brushed one of his hands down my back. His other hand caressed my face. I couldn't help but meet his eyes, and I was lost. The strong set of his jaw was angled down toward me, and his brows were knit tight with the pain of his loss.

But it was his compassionate, tear-strained eyes that broke the last of my strength. My own eyes pooled over again, and the tears streamed down both of our faces. Seeing his messy black hair, a darker match to Alec's calico brown, ripped a strangled cry from my chest.

Emmett's soothing voice both eased me and sliced through my heart at the same time. After weeks of nothing but coldness from him, of his total avoidance, hearing my name on his lips, and being comforted in his embrace, was just too much for me to bear. Not there. Not then. Alec was lying there dead. His light was out forever. We never even got to say goodbye.

My heart ached for fear that the last conscious memories or thoughts that Alec had were of torment because he knew I loved Emmett, too. Did he feel despair at the whole situation? Was epilepsy the big secret he was hiding? Why didn't he think he could tell me? He wouldn't have had to go through all of it alone.

I hated myself right then, because I knew I needed Emmett. I hated that he'd been pushing me away for weeks. But I loved Emmett with every ounce of my being. Alec had just died. I couldn't breathe. It was too much. Everything felt tight. *Alec, oh God, no.* I couldn't believe he was gone.

"No, please, no . . . Emmett, what have we done? Oh, Alec, I'm so sorry," I cried the words.

"Sam, stop. You have to calm down. We didn't do anything wrong." His voice cracked as he turned his head back toward Alec.

147

I couldn't stop the tears. I felt like I was going to hyperventilate.

"Breathe with me now, easy, Peach," he whispered.

His choked endearment was my undoing.

CHAPTER 29

Emptiness

Emmett

A part of me died the night we lost him. I was acutely aware of Sam's presence as soon as my feet stepped off the elevator in the hospital. I ran up behind her as she was screaming and wrapped my arms around her. In that instant, I knew only that I wanted to console her, whatever it was that had her so beside herself. But when I turned and saw the body—his body—lying covered by a sheet, that's when a part of me died.

Our lives were irrevocably changed from that moment on.

The hospital had given us Alec's belongings the day after he died, but Sam wasn't able to even look at the bag. She just started crying about how he wasn't there anymore. She didn't want to look at his empty clothes and empty shoes. She was distraught . . . we both were. But I knew I had to hold on to that bag. I knew we'd both want and need to see it later. It was the last, vibrant piece of Alec we had left.

About a month after Alec died, I opened it and took out his shoes, socks, jeans, shirt, and jacket, either the hospital had thrown out his boxers, or he went commando. Either option was fine by me. It was when I picked up his jacket, that I found it, a little black velvet box. My heart sank down into my stomach. I didn't even make it to the bathroom before I threw my guts up.

God, it was a good thing Sam hadn't wanted to see that bag. She would have lost it. I sat on my couch and stared at that little black box. Probably for hours. I wanted to open it and see what he'd chosen for her. I wanted a glimpse of the hope he held in his heart for getting Sam back. I deserved the pain of seeing that token of hope, since I'd basically spat on it when we last talked. But I just couldn't bring myself to open it. I kept staring at it and thinking. Thinking and staring. Staring and remembering . . .

I thought about the last time I talked to him. What we both said to each other, the harsh words and callousness between us. The last words he'd spoken to me ran on an endless loop through my mind.

'Over my dead body, will I let you have her.'

I stood up, walked in the bathroom, and looked at my reflection. I knew the answer to my question when I looked in the mirror that night after he stormed off.

And now that it was all said and done, and I stood looking back into the mirror, I couldn't live with what I fucking saw. The black mark on my soul grew as the tears ran down my face. His sad, regretful expression after I spoke the wretched words *"Fine, little brother, if that's how you want it"* haunted my mind.

I turned around and punched Aunt Robin's bathroom wall.

Fuck!

I washed my hand off in the sink, avoiding that damned reflective glass.

As I walked past the wet-bar, I stopped and grabbed a rocks-glass and poured myself two fingers of whiskey. When I slumped back down on the couch I groaned aloud again at the sight of that damn little black velvet box.

CHAPTER 30
Can't Be Together

Sam

Two months after Alec died, our lives finally started to fall back into place. We'd both taken a leave of absence for the spring semester at Auburn, planning to return for a class or two in the summer. Thankfully, the admissions office said we could do that. It was just too soon after Alec's death for us to even consider trying to concentrate on classes.

I was still on a month-to-month lease in my condo. Emmett had stayed over again, and we were having coffee at the breakfast bar in the kitchen. I knew it was a perilous line we were walking, falling so easily into the patterns of the past, when it felt okay for us to be together and love each other. Before we knew of our mutual connection with Alec. But then fate had to have her cosmic laugh and torment our hearts, and with one phone call, ruined three lives.

I knew it was coming, but it didn't prepare me for the physical pain my heart felt as the argument unfolded. We would be going back to Auburn at end of the month when my lease had been fulfilled. Emmett wanted us to move in together. He didn't want to stay at the frat house with Riley and Quinn. He said we needed our own space.

But that morning in the bathroom, as I took my shower and

looked at his products sitting next to mine, I suddenly felt like I couldn't breathe.

I stepped out of the shower and wrapped a towel around myself, then walked over to the vanity where I saw his toothbrush next to mine, and in the drawer laid his comb and razor. The urge to run hit me with such force, I felt like I'd lost my breath. I remembered the few times that Alec stayed over, his things in all the same places. However irrational, it felt like Emmett and I being back together somehow erased the importance of Alec in our lives.

With a shake of my head, I pulled myself together, dressed, and joined Emmett in the kitchen. He immediately cleared his throat, and I knew that was it. He was going to ruin everything, because I wasn't ready. He pushed his laptop away, and of course, the screen was on the Auburn Apartment Guide's website. God, I couldn't breathe.

Please don't do this, Emmett, I thought. Alec's dead. He's gone, yet I can still see where his things used to sit, and now are holding yours instead. The memory is like a flash beacon of the hope he had for us to get back together, and it's hurting my heart. It's making me feel like we're doing something wrong. I know we aren't, but my guilt is overwhelming, and in my mind, I can still see that tormented look in Alec's wary eyes, right before he fell.

"Peach, I want to start looking at apartments in Auburn. I need to get everything out of my old room at the frat house, so it's open for the new guy Riley said wanted to move in, if I wasn't coming back before the summer session starts. I've only actually slept at my Aunt's house a handful of times these last few months." He pointed to his laptop. "Looking at these listings, I just can't see us both paying money for separate apartments when we know we'll always be staying with each other. Why don't we just do it . . . let's move in together. I can pay for the rent, or, if you'd rather, we can split the cost. We could get a place somewhere close to campus."

I was flustered and searched for the right words. "Well . . . that just, it just doesn't make any sense at all. Why would we do that?" I asked. "I mean, you have to have your own place, Emmett," I said with a snarky undertone I didn't actually mean.

"Sam, what the hell are you talking about? It makes perfect sense!"

"No, Emmett, it doesn't!" I continued. "No, I'm sorry, please . . . I've been thinking a lot lately, and we can't *be* together, let alone *live* together," I choked out as tears began to roll down my cheeks. I looked up at Emmett and his tormented, lost expression will forever be burned in my memory, an expression I put on his face yet again. I hated myself for it.

"You know what?" he asked as he slammed the screen on his laptop closed. "I can't do this. I love you, and damn it I *know* you love me, too. But I get it. You're hurting and mourning Alec's death. Well, guess what Sam? He was *my* brother, and I'm hurting, too! He's gone, and I'll never be able to talk to him again! The last time we talked was the night before he died, and—"

"Wait, what? I thought you guys hadn't talked for weeks?"

"Peach, haven't you even wondered how I was able to get to the hospital so fast that night?" he asked with a frustrated sigh.

"Well yeah, but so much was happening. Alec had just died, and when you were holding me, I felt so lost. I had so many conflicting emotions, but I do remember asking myself how you got there so fast."

"I was already in town."

His words shocked me silent.

"Look I wasn't planning on coming to Atlanta. But I just couldn't stop thinking about you. It had been nearly a month since you left, and I hadn't slept well in over a week. I stayed away, Peach. Damn it, I didn't even call, and I wanted to, so much. I needed to hear your voice, even if it was only one word. I needed that connection. But if I had answered your calls or replied to your text messages, I knew I would lose my mind, and I was trying to respect you and Alec being together."

"But *you* pushed *me* away! *You* told me to be with *him*— and I wasn't—by the way. We were keeping it just friends. As much as he wanted us to, I just couldn't be with him like that again . . . not while I was in love with you."

Emmett stood and leaned against the counter. He roughed his hands through his hair and sighed. "I was so tired, Sam. The mornings were the worst. I always reached over to pull you into my chest and watch you sleep. God, I loved watching you sleep. The way your chest would rise and fall with your breaths, your hair laying around your face. But you weren't there. And it punched my gut every damn morning."

I stood and walked over to him, pulling him close and wrapping my arms around his waist. "Emmett, it was hard for me too," I whispered.

"I just wanted to see you. I *needed* to see you. So I got in my car and went for a drive, you know . . . to think. I didn't have a plan or know where I was going. I just drove until I went past the first sign for Atlanta, and then I knew what I had to do. I thought, if I saw you with Alec, if I knew you were happy with him, maybe it would convince me you were where you needed to be, and it wouldn't hurt so much anymore."

"Emmett . . . I'm sorry," I whispered. "I missed you, too. And we weren't together like that. But you never came to see me. You never called. I had no idea you were in town. How could I have known?"

"I got a hotel room, and I just sat there. After I got there, I couldn't stand the thought of seeing you with him, seeing his arms around you, holding your hand, or kissing you. I know I pushed you to be with him. I didn't know you decided not to give him a chance. I drove all that way, thinking that seeing it would fucking fix it for me, but once I was there, I realized it would be too much. So I went down to the hotel lounge to have a beer, and just sat there thinking. I decided it was no kind of life the way I was living, and I was going to fight for you. I called Alec, and he finally agreed to meet. We talked, and I told him that I loved you and I wasn't going to give you up without a fight. Looking back, I'm sure he was thrilled to keep my presence a secret."

"Oh, Emmett . . ." I whispered.

"Yeah well, dear brother didn't exactly take kindly to any of it, especially when I told him I knew you loved me, too."

"What? Why would you say that?"

"Because it's the truth Sam!"

"He had a right to know what we had was more than just a rebound fling for you. And that you weren't just another random hook-up for me. He deserved better than our deceit. I know, we didn't know about each other then, and y'all were broken up when we were together, but I couldn't sit there and lie to myself anymore . . . or to him."

I dropped to my knees, sobbing with my head in my hands. And, of course, he was right there, picking me up and carrying me to the couch.

"Peach, stop. Breathe. Just relax."

"Oh God, Emmett." I grabbed a Kleenex and wiped the snot from my nose. "That morning, before Alec fell . . . I told him I was in love with you—that I loved both of you—but I couldn't be with him the way he wanted. It was selfish to tell him. He didn't need to know. You had left me, I didn't think we would ever get back together. But I felt like I owed him the truth. I didn't want him to think that he could win me back or lead him on. I watched the light leave his eyes, Emmett, like my disclosure broke his spirit. You told him the night before, and I . . . I confirmed it that morning. He was so devastated. Dear God, what did we do?"

"Sam, the railing broke. Alec fell. It was an accident. We didn't do anything. We both loved him. Just, please, Peach, please . . . don't push me away. I can't lose you again. Don't throw away what we have. We can be together and try to live a happy life. I feel like Alec would have wanted us to heal and move on, together. He wouldn't have wanted this pain for us."

"Are you *crazy?* We can't be together! It's not right. You have to go," I ordered with a sniffle. "I can't even think about this. How can we even consider going on like nothing happened, being together when Alec is dead? God, Emmett, he looked so sad, thinking God only knows what. He looked like he was empty. I'll never forget that tormented look in his eyes, his pain."

I reached for Emmett then, but he jerked his hand back away from me so fast, he knocked the vase off the coffee table, and it crashed on the tile floor, sending shards of green glass everywhere. He didn't stop though. He just walked over to the kitchen counter and grabbed his sunglasses and car keys. I jumped up and ran to him.

"Emmett, please, stay. Where are you going?"

"Sam, don't. If this is it, then just fucking say it. I can't do this. I have to go. Guess it didn't matter in the end, did it? I have no brother, no girlfriend . . . I have nothing."

"Emmett, please . . . I love you."

"*No, Sam!* You said it's done. *Clearly* we're done. Don't say we have to walk away from each other, that it's not *right* for us to be together, and then in the same breath tell me you love me. You need to sort this shit out in your head."

"But I do love you . . . that hasn't changed." I whispered.

"Don't you dare say you love me. *Never* again."

He opened my condo door and walked out, never once looking back.

Oh God, what have I done?

I curled up on the couch and lost myself to my sobs, to what could've been, but never would be. I cried until there was nothing left inside, so barren and lost, all I could do was fall asleep, still mourning for our three broken hearts, two broken lives, and the one we lost forever.

CHAPTER 31

Emmett's Letter

Sam

A little over two weeks later, I received a letter from Emmett. It was beautifully written, yet heartbreaking at the same time. I must have read it over and over a hundred times.

Peach,

     I'll never understand what happened, what set the things in motion for my life to be what and where it is today. All I know is, these mistakes have brought me closer to you. My heart...my soul...my one true love. I would do anything for you, help you, nurture you, and protect you...I would die for you. I need you to understand the depth of my love. You need to know why I do the things I do and what they mean. I need you to know and believe you're my priority.

I remember the early hours when I would be awake and you were still sleeping. Those were the best hours of my day. You're were so peaceful then. There weren't any looks for me to decipher. Everything was clear. I lived to see your smile and hear your laugh. I need that again, to hold you in my arms, and feel your breath across my lips, to make love to you.

It's all of those moments, Sam, the things that make my miserable life worth living. You're my phoenix, my salvation from the darkness inside my black soul. If you can love and forgive me for abandoning you when you just wanted to be sure Alec was okay, I swear to you, together, we will make the best of it. I'll make myself better. Learn to be a better man. Be the man that you deserve. Peach, this is my promise to you. My deepest love, my life is yours forever.

Emmett

I set his letter down on the coffee table, sunk back into the couch, and stared at his beautiful face on my phone. It was a picture I'd snapped while we were kayaking the Tallapoosa River, what now felt like a lifetime ago.

I wanted to call him. But I didn't know what to say, the way we left things . . . was volatile. I loved Emmett. Not having him in my life—was like trying to have a beginning without an end—my heart rebelled at the possibility that this was our end.

CHAPTER 32

Hope

Emmett

I t had only been a couple of weeks since Sam and I had our big fight. They were some of the longest weeks of my life. I missed her every day. I missed my little brother. I hated the way fate had interfered in our lives. I didn't think Sam would even answer the phone when I called her. But the idea of us going to Hawaii, to celebrate Alec's life and say our goodbyes, felt like the perfect place to send him off to peace. We talked about it and both realized that we needed closure. I was happy, relieved, and shocked when Sam hesitantly agreed to go with me. I hoped the trip and closure would help start healing the aching holes left in both of our hearts from Alec's death, and I wanted to fix the problems between us. I needed her in my life.

I hadn't shown or told Sam about the little black jewelry box. It still sat in the dresser drawer in my room at Aunt Robin's house, where I put it after finding it among his belongings from the hospital. I hadn't even looked inside. It wasn't meant for me. I'd been waiting for the right time to give his token of devotion and love to her. But I never found the *right* moment. I thought maybe during our trip to Hawaii would be that *right* time for her.

We'd decided to celebrate his life by saying goodbye in the

Toro Nagashi way, a Japanese tradition of lantern offerings on the water. Sam thought it would beautiful, peaceful, and I had to admit, it looked pretty awesome. We would release a floating memorial, a little lantern sitting on top of floating boards with written messages of things we wanted to say, our goodbyes and prayers for a peaceful afterlife.

CHAPTER 33

New Beginnings

Sam

A week later we left for Hawaii. Bittersweet. That's what the trip was going to be. Painfully beautiful. The seatbelt signs were on, and we were getting ready for takeoff. I'd flown a lot in my life, so why I was white-knuckling it was beyond me. I was relieved to have the man I loved at my side again. I prayed we could fix our problems and reunite for good. The last couple weeks without him had felt unbearably empty. But maybe it was letting go of Alec that was weighing so heavily on my heart. It should have been a relief to pay him our last respects . . . but I feared it wouldn't be. Alec would always be in my heart—in both of our hearts, but I wasn't sure we'd ever truly heal.

"Peach, are you okay?" Emmett asked, gently squeezing my hand.

"Yeah, I'm fine. Well no, actually, I'm not, but I will be," I assured him, even to my own ears they sounded like hollow words. I saw his eyes sadden with the pain and guilt that always lingered there.

"Maybe, when we get settled in the cottage, we can see if we can find a local craft shop and pick up a few supplies for you to make some jewelry pieces. They'd be great gifts for Tamron and Alison. Much better than buying something made somewhere else anyway. I love watching you design," he said.

I could feel my cheeks flame just from the look on his face—pure adoration. I didn't know what I'd done to deserve him, but he was always able to heal my broken heart, and being with him again already made me feel a little better. He had a connection to my heart and eased the pain there.

I smiled up at him and replied, "That's a good idea. I haven't made anything in a while. It'll be nice to get back into it again when we get home."

Emmett

As the seatbelt lights turned off, Sam visibly relaxed. I wasn't sure why she was so wound up about the flight. Maybe it was just the trip itself. I knew we'd both been looking forward to it, yet also dreading it at the same time.

Holding her hand in mine, I closed my eyes and thought about Alec. I didn't know how I was going to say goodbye to him. For so long, he and Aunt Robin were all I had. After Mom and Dad's accident, nothing was ever the same. It was always just us. Now that he was gone, I just didn't know. I didn't feel as empty as I thought I would. I was sure that was because of Sam. She made everything easier. Brighter . . . lighter.

When she designed her pieces, she got this focused happy look about her. It was mesmerizing. When she'd finish and bring it over to show me, a look of pride would take over. It was simple. Her intense concentration and sense of accomplishment was beautiful.

Those were some of the few moments when my soul felt clean and my heart felt lighter. I felt like she could heal the brokenness of my heart and soul. My sanity was in her little hands. She had no idea how powerful a hold she had on me.

I leaned back on the headrest, and let my thoughts drift to

Alec. I thought of all the times we'd spent together growing up and the mischief we caused. We'd gotten into a decent amount of trouble when we were young. Spent a lot of time grounded, but we'd communicate through our made-up Morse code by tapping on the bedroom wall between us. We had a lot of good times, but also our fair share of fights, too. None, however, were as deeply hurtful, nor had created as wide a chasm between us, as our fight over Sam.

We never had a chance to heal the damage over that one, and our last words continued to haunt me. I would never be able to share them with Sam. I didn't want her to know how selfish and desperate I'd been. I didn't want her to know how black my soul had become.

CHAPTER 34

Saying Goodbye

Emmett

A s we made our final descent and the jet circled for landing in Honolulu, Sam reached over and laced her fingers through mine. It felt like a lifeline, and I exhaled with relief. She squeezed once before rubbing her thumb back and forth along my wrist. It was a small gesture, but the implication was significant. She was ready, and so was I.

As we made our way through the airport, I couldn't help but look at all the travelers and wonder if it was as hard for them to take each step as it was for me. Were any of them taking a step closer to saying goodbye forever, to someone they'd loved their entire lives? My throat felt tight, and I had to fight back the tears as we made our way to baggage claim. There was an empty spot in my heart where Alec used to dwell.

Sam squeezed my hand and looked up at me, and I could see a similar sadness in her watery eyes. I feared this was going to be much harder than expected. I wasn't prepared to say goodbye to my little brother, and I knew then, that I never would be.

After grabbing our bags, we walked outside and hailed a cab to take us to the cottage I'd reserved. As Sam and I sat in the back, she kept her fingers laced through mine and peeked up at me periodically. It felt good to be together again. I began to feel whole.

Those couple weeks after our fight were even worse than when we realized her ex was my little brother, because I thought we were truly over, that there was no hope of us overcoming Alec's death and being together again. I cursed fate for ruining our lives and for making my brother and I fall in love with the same girl, no matter how innocently it had happened. But most of all, I cursed fate for taking Alec from us.

As we settled in the cottage, I began to think about the *Toro Nagashi* and what I wanted to say to Alec in my messages on the lantern. Sam and I both agreed to keep our last memories confidential, and not talk about what we would write. Each would be private, something we could at last share with him to say our final goodbyes.

I'd written mine in a notebook and was ready to put them on Alec's lantern, messages of how much I loved him and how sorry I was for the way things had turned out, and for what I'd said the last time I saw him. I promised to take care of Sam, and spend the rest of my life making her feel loved and cherished. I wished him peace, and told him he would always be my little brother, and that I would always love him.

When Sam walked around the corner and came into the sitting room, she had a white sundress on, and looked like my very own angel. Her beauty stopped my breath, and I felt compelled to hold her, touch her, and feel her in my arms. I stood and hugged her close, her body melted into mine. Taking a deep breath, I could smell her flowery shampoo and it made me smile. Who would have ever thought that such a thing could make me so happy? But it did, and I loved it.

"Peach, let's talk a minute."

"All right," she said, looking up at me.

We sat down on the couch.

"I'm sorry I tried to push you into us living together. I understand now that you weren't ready, and that's okay. Can we just agree to take things day-to-day until we're both comfortable with where we are?"

"Yes. I want that, too. I love you so much, Emmett, and I'm

sorry I blew up at you. I was afraid to admit I wanted the same things, because I was having so many mixed feelings . . . and the guilt of Alec being gone while we were still alive—playing house—It was too much, too soon. When you said you wanted to live together, it was hard to accept we were moving on without him," she smiled softly.

"Peach, I know this is going to be an emotional trip for both of us, but I also think Alec would want us to witness the beauty of this place, as well. Where I had expected constant anxiety, I now feel at peace about this trip. It's much better than I had thought it would be. I know we've waited a long time to say our goodbyes. It's been a burden on both of us, dreading and knowing that, eventually, the day would come, but needing that closure at the same time. I hope and believe we'll find the peace we need."

She looked relieved and sank back against my chest. "Thank you. That's exactly what I needed to hear. I'm so happy to be here, happier than I thought I'd be. You're right. I do have a kind of relief. This trip was the best idea, and I'm so relieved about coming."

"Let's go for that walk."

We walked along the beach and down to a few shops. Sam found quite a lot of supplies and was excited about what she was going to make. I could practically see the ideas flowing through her mind. Once again, it felt like she was cleansing my black soul. How I was ever lucky enough to have her in my life, I'll never know, but I'd spend the rest of it trying to show her just how happy she made me.

Sam

It was finally the day, the day to celebrate Alec's life and to say our goodbyes. We'd gotten the things we needed to make our floating lantern and had written our messages to him on the panels. It felt cathartic to say all the things I'd been thinking, how I would always love and remember him, how sorry I was for being selfish, but he deserved to know how I felt about Emmett, that telling him had been the right thing to do in order for us all to move forward, how I hoped he'd be happy Emmett and I had found each other again, how I was sorry if he felt betrayed in his last moments, and that I wished him nothing but peace.

With tiki torches lighting our path to the beach, we headed down to the water and lit our candles in the lantern. The sun was setting in orange and red hues. Emmett's messages were on the opposite side of mine, and it was as if we wrapped Alec's lantern in a cocoon of our love. That, in and of itself, was truly peaceful.

Emmett and I held hands and kissed the top of the lantern before setting it into the water. Just the feel of his hand in mine gave me the strength I needed to say goodbye. Setting it afloat, we watched Alec's lantern leave the shore, it was beautiful and serene. We watched until we couldn't see it anymore.

We spent that night on the beach and slept under the stars, cuddled in one another's arms, cherishing that we still had each other, and had overcome the odds against us. After all that time, finally saying our goodbyes had lifted a tremendous weight from our souls, and we at last felt a measure of peace.

CHAPTER 35

Fun In The Sun

Sam

W e spent the rest of our trip playing on the beach and swimming in the ocean. We snorkeled in the reefs and saw all the beautiful, amazing fish and corals. Their colors were vivid. I loved the sea turtles. They were majestic and graceful old souls.

I couldn't stop myself from peeking up at Emmett's sexy body as he swam ahead of me. The way his muscles flexed made me hunger for him. He would catch me looking, and the cutest smirk would cross his face. I knew he was thinking the same as I was. It was a good thing we were of like minds, as our nights grew hotter and steamier.

Emmett longed to surf, so I read in the sun while he rode the waves. It wasn't something on my bucket list, but I enjoyed watching him from afar. Sometimes he would catch one just right and smile all the way in, filling me with pride and joy. That night after dinner, we returned to the beach and splashed each other like children, running through the water. I tackled him, and we ended up in a heated kiss as I lay across his chest, and the warm waves flowed around us like a scene out of *From Here to Eternity*.

It was surreal being there in Emmett's arms. I vowed to myself, never to push him away again. What we had was real and special, and for the first time since finding out that Emmett and Alec were brothers, I finally felt peace about us being together. I knew I could move forward with him, and felt ready to take that next step.

"Emmett, I want to tell you something."

He tensed, staring into my eyes. "What is it, Peach?"

I snuggled into his chest and smiled up at him as the waves washed up from the shoreline. "I'm ready for us to spend more time together. I missed you so badly following our fight, and after being here together, I know I can't go back to the way it was without you. It would break me. I love you so much. Let's try again."

He smiled the biggest smile I'd ever seen. "That's the best news I've heard in a long time, Peach. I love you too, more than I'll ever be able to show you, but I'll damn well try."

CHAPTER 36

Emmett's Gift

Emmett

"Hey, Riley. Come on in. The beer's in the fridge," I said.

"What's up, Emmett? Haven't seen you since you got back from Hawaii. How'd it go? That floating lantern thing sounded like a cool idea," Riley said, leaning against the counter with the beer in his hand.

"It was unreal. I mean, my little brother, man. I just, God . . . sometimes it's hard to believe it's true, but then setting Alec's lantern afloat made it so damn real. I didn't think anything could hurt as bad as when I stood in the hallway in that hospital and realized it was him, lying underneath that sheet. But I was wrong, Riley. So damn wrong. Sam was great though. The service was amazing. She found this song to play while we said our goodbyes, 'In Loving Memory' by Alter Bridge. Play it sometime, man, and just listen to the words."

"Yeah, I'll Google it."

"It was perfect. It felt like he was there with us. It was the most peaceful I've felt in a long time. I just couldn't get our last words out of my mind. But now I feel better about Alec, and I think everything will be okay."

Riley took a swig of his beer and stretched out on my couch.

"Oh, man, I know it's been hard for you. At least you and Sam are finally together again and working things out. Y'all are the real deal, ya know. You two have that whole soul-mate shit going on. Everyone can see it."

"Listen, man, I know this is going to make me sound like a girl, but I don't care. I'm so damn excited. I thought of the best gift for Sam."

"What—" Riley began.

"I was planning to tell Peach about Alec's engagement ring while we were in Hawaii, but the time never felt right. She's never seen it. I thought it would be too hard for her. I'm taking it to a jeweler in the morning to have the diamond set in an infinity symbol pendant. I hope giving it to her in this form will make it easier to accept. It won't be such a blow, like seeing the actual engagement ring he'd picked out for her."

"Yeah, man, that's—"

"I know what you're thinking, and that's fine dude. I don't care. I am so damn happy and in love. Someday, Riley, you just wait and see. You'll be in love and know exactly what I'm talking about."

"Dude, you *are* a girl! I tried like two different times to say how fucking cool I thought that was, but you just kept going on and on and on. I couldn't have gotten a word in even if I was using a damn megaphone! And Emmett, dude. I know already, man. Alison is it for me. I am so in love with that girl, she makes me feel all sorts of weird happy shit. Sometimes, I worry about my manliness, but I chalk it up to being in love, and I feel better again."

I laughed at Riley, but was happy for my friend. I always knew if anyone could calm that boy down it would be Alison, and she'd done a damn good job.

"So, Ry, Sam and I are going to take our relationship to the next level. I'm just waiting for her to get home from seeing Alison and Tamron. She gave them the bracelets she made."

A knock sounded on my door. Riley answered it and let Marchello, Alec's old housemate, in. He had an old-style storage chest with him and looked a haggard mess.

"What's up, Marchello, are you all right, man?" I asked.

"Hey, Emmett, Riley. Uh, no, man. I got something you need to see. I don't know if you should show Sam, too, but I think you need to see it and figured, when you were ready, you could call her."

"Okay, what is it?"

"I think we finally have the answers to Alec's behavior. I was going through the attic at our place and found this old storage chest, so I opened it up, figuring it was Alec's. It has some stuff in it and a bunch of letters he wrote to your mom. I don't know, maybe, like . . . a way of writing things down in a journal or something, but . . . not. Anyway, you need to read these letters. Then I think you need to call Sam and let her read them, too," he finished as he dropped down onto my couch.

I sat down next to him and stared at the old chest. It was one he'd had when we were kids. My hands felt heavy as I reached forward to flip open the latch on the front. I held my breath, and I pulled his precious items out, and then set them on the coffee table.

There was the miniature dolphin water globe he'd gotten when he was eight years old on our family trip to Panama City Beach. I turned it upside down and watched as the glitter floated around the two dolphins. Remembering when he'd seen it in the gift shop, and the pure look of wonder on his face.

After setting it back on the table, I picked up his Swiss army knife that Dad gave him when he'd turned thirteen. It matched the one Dad had given me. With a shaky hand, I set it back down and picked up the stack of folded letters.

I read them, and as I took in his tear-stained words, my heart died. I needed a drink, so I poured two fingers of whiskey into a glass and sat down on my couch. We now had the answers to Alec's strange and cruel behavior toward Sam. Marchello was right. I had to call her. She had to know.

She came over, and after Riley and Marchello left, we sat down and read Alec's letters to my mom together. I held her hand and stroked her back as the tears flowed down both of our faces.

Alec's letters:

January 12th

Hey Mom,

I know you're gone, but I still need to talk to you. I need to talk to someone about this, but I can't talk to anyone here, at least not until I know what it all means, and there's no way I'm going to keep a diary like a girl. So I figured maybe, if I wrote some letters to you, I could pretend that you're still around.

Anyway, here's the thing. I've been having some weird things happening lately so I went to the doctor, and he sent me to a neurologist. The neurologist ran some tests and diagnosed me with a type of epilepsy. So I'm really scared now. Samone and I have our whole lives ahead of us, and we're about to graduate from high school. Then we're going to Kennesaw State and get an apartment together.

But Mom, I just can't do this. I love her so much. God, Mom, I wish you had a chance to meet her. She's amazing and full of life and love. But how can I continue with our plans when I have this new diagnosis? I don't fully understand any of it yet. I just know I have some type of seizures now and that there are a lot of medications out there that treat it. It's just a matter of finding the right medication that works for me.

But Samone ... Mom, she's so young and has so much going for her. I just feel like I'm bringing her down if I stay with her. I've been dodging her at school. She keeps looking at me for answers because she sees me coming to school late or leaving early for doctor appointments. I can't tell her why though, so I just brush her off, and it's hurting her, which breaks my heart.

I'm acting like a total bastard, Mom. She deserves so much better than me. She deserves the truth, and I just can't give that to her. Not yet. I have to know more about what is happening with me. I don't want to be a burden on her. My future is so unclear. She needs someone who can give her everything that she wants and needs.

I guess that's it for now. I have to decide what to do next. I know I'm not being fair to her.

Love you always,
Alec

February 19th

Hey Mom,

They tried a new medicine and it didn't work for me. I took it but the side effects made me sleepy. On the way to school I ran into a median with my truck. Of course, Samone saw the damage and asked about it. I didn't tell her why I hit the median, but I know she thinks there is something more going on.

I'm not sure what to do. Wish you were here.

Love you always,

Alec

March 8th

Hey Mom,

   I did it . . . I broke up with Samone.
God, it was the hardest thing I've ever done.
I honestly don't know how I was able to do it.
She was so broken sitting on her front porch
swing, hugging her knees to her chest. Her tears
were streaming down her face. I just said it
all fast, and when I left, I never looked
back. If I would've looked back at her, I
know I would've run back and wrapped her up
into my arms and never let her go.

   It was the right thing to do for Samone.
I had to stay strong for her. She probably
thinks I'm horrible now. But I had to shut down
my emotions just to get through it.

   I have another appointment with my
neurologist in a few weeks. Going to see what
he says.

   Love you always,
   Alec

April 18th

Hey Mom,

So we're trying a new medicine. That last one didn't work. I had another EEG and the seizure activity is still pretty bad. God, I wish I knew why this was happening.

Oh and Samone keeps texting me. She won't stop. My resolve is faltering. I can feel it. Every time she sends a message, I think about answering her, but I know I shouldn't, so I turn my phone off and fall into whatever I'm doing at the time. Once again, I feel like a bastard. I wish you were here.

I know you'd know what to do.

Love you always,

Alec

June 21st

Hey Mom,

Well, I graduated high school last month. I should be happy, this should be the time of my life. But I'm miserable. On top of that, Samone just won't give up on us. Peter is having a party and Marchello said she will be there. I have a plan to get her to back off. It'll make her finally give up all hope on us. I have to do this to protect her.

She needs to be angry at me so she'll never look back. It's going to be the hardest thing I've ever done, even harder than when I broke up with her. God, if she would just give up, I wouldn't have to hurt her again. I wouldn't have to do this, but she won't, so I have to do what I have to do, so I can ensure she goes on with her future.

I'm sorry, Mom, because you're not going to be very proud of me when you're looking down on me tonight.

Love you always,
Alec

June 22nd
Hey Mom,

I did it again. I hurt Samone. And it was the deepest, cruelest hurt and it killed me to do it. I can't even talk about what I had to do at that party in order to push her away. I can't even talk anymore right now. I'm so ashamed. I hate myself. Please don't be disappointed in me.

Love you always,
Alec

December 12th

Hey Mom,

I know it's been a while. I broke down and called Samone. You'll never believe this. She was with EmJay in Auburn. She went to see her best friends, Alison and Tamron, and EmJay is their boyfriends' housemate. They hooked up at a party, and she's been practically living with him for months.

She didn't know he was my brother, and he didn't she was my Samone, but it doesn't change the pain and betrayal I feel, even if unintended. I can't even think straight right now. I just have to tell Samone the truth about what's happened to me.

She came back and met with me at our old cafe. I know she wants answers, but I hope she can wait just a little longer. I'll tell her everything. I want to tell her. I hate keeping this from her and that I hurt her.

Wish me luck, Mom. I know I'm going to need it.

Love you always,
Alec

January 3rd
Hey Mom,
    So my test results came back. In addition
to this damn epilepsy I have a brain tumor, the
doctors are saying it's what caused the
seizures. I'm really scared Mom, I don't know
what's gonna happen. I have an appointment
with my doctor in two weeks to go over
treatment options.
    I'm not even sure about trying to get
Samone back now. I just don't know what to do.
I know I never want to hurt her like I did
before again.
    God, I wish you were here.
    Love you always,
    Alec

Her hands shook as she sat gripping Alec's letters tightly. "Oh Emmett," she sobbed as I took Alec's letters, and set them back into his storage chest. She curled into my arms, and I held her tight.

"I know, Peach . . . I know." I ran my hand up and down her back and kissed the top of her head.

"We have to look at these letters for what they are, an answer to a lot of our unanswered questions. We can't move forward if we dwell on our guilt. We still didn't do anything wrong, but now we know why Alec did and said things he did. Thankfully, we finally have answers, and now, some closure."

Sam and I held each other for hours while she had fits of crying, and when she finally fell asleep that night, I carried her to the bed and let her rest. The next morning when I woke up, I just lay there and watched her sleep. She was so peaceful. I couldn't bear the thought of seeing that brokenness on her face again when she woke up, so I stayed silent and let her sleep for as long as possible.

As she lay there sleeping, I found myself thinking about Alec's letters. I couldn't believe he'd gone through all of that alone. Why didn't he tell me about it?

The next day, while Sam was having lunch and another spa day with her sister, Tricia, I called Aunt Robin, and she said she'd never heard anything from Alec about his condition. Since he was already eighteen before the date of the first letter, we guessed he decided he should go to the doctor on his own.

I read the letters to her over the phone so she could understand what had happened to him, as well. But somehow, reading his words out loud and saying it made it so much more real to me.

I broke down, and Aunt Robin and I cried together on the phone.

"I wish I could've taken Alec's letters over to your house. We could have read them together in person."

"Sweetie, do you want me to come home?"

"No. It's fine. Y'all saved a long time for this trip. It's not like you can go back anytime soon."

"Really, it's okay. Kent and I can cut the trip short. We only extended because he had work over here, and I thought I'd stay a while since he had a hotel and had to be here anyway."

"Nah, stay and have some fun. There's no use in both of us sitting here grieving. We both need to focus on the positive things in life."

"All right. If you change your mind, just call, and I'll be on the first flight back to the states."

"Thanks, Aunt Robin."

"Anytime. So how was the trip to Hawaii? Was the *Toro Nagashi* ceremony nice?"

"It couldn't have been more perfect. It was peaceful. Sometimes I feel like shit for thinking this, but it felt good to say goodbye to him."

"No, don't feel bad, Emmett. It's a natural part of grieving. So, are you and Sam back together? How is she holding up?"

"Yeah, we're back together. Gonna see how it goes. I found an engagement ring in Alec's jacket from his hospital belongings."

"Oh my God."

"Yup."

"Did you tell Sam about it?"

"No. It would've upset her too much. But I'll tell her eventually. I had the diamond set in an infinity pendant for her, so she can always remember him."

"That's an amazingly thoughtful gift. She's lucky to have you."

"It's me who's lucky to have her."

"I'm sure she'll cherish it."

"Thanks. I gotta go. She's waking up, and I want to have coffee on before she gets out of the shower. I love you, Aunt Robin."

"I love you, too, sweetie."

When Sam woke up, we had breakfast. Even though she said she was ready to take our relationship to the next level, I was nervous about even bringing the subject of living together up. I decided to look through the apartment rentals on an Auburn apartment guide site just in case she said yes, and saved a few ads for us to call on and set appointments to look at. I felt it was finally time for us to move in together.

CHAPTER 37

Healing Hearts

Emmett

A week had gone by, and I picked up Sam's pendant from the jeweler. I turned on the Keurig and started toasting a couple English muffins while she was in the shower. I could hardly wait for us to get through with breakfast so I could give it to her. She walked into the kitchen dressed in a pair of jeans and one of her baby doll shirts and was the prettiest girl I'd ever seen. She joined me at the breakfast bar and wrapped her arms around me, hugging me tight. Our bodies melted together. I leaned down and kissed her. I couldn't resist. With a passion that quickly heated, I picked her up, carried her back to her bedroom, and made love to her.

"Hmmm, that was the best breakfast detour I've ever had." She giggled, batting my hand away from her thigh when I reached for her again.

I laughed. "I'm hungry," I told her. "And now our English muffins are going to be cold."

We got dressed . . . again . . . and walked back to the kitchen. She took the English muffins and sprinkled a little water on each one then popped them in the microwave for five seconds. They were just as if I'd taken them out of the toaster. After we finished eating, I decided I couldn't wait any longer.

"Peach, I have something for you."

She looked up at me from the table with a coy smile. "What is it?"

"Please, come here and sit with me on the couch, so I can show you."

Once settled, I took her hand in mine, set the long velvet box in her palm, and let her open it.

"Emmett, this is breathtaking. I love it," she replied.

"There's an interesting story behind this gift." I took a deep breath. "Six months after Alec died, I felt ready to go through his personal things from the hospital. I found a velvet jewelry box in his jacket pocket."

She looked up at me, her beautiful brown eyes wide with shock.

"It was a diamond engagement ring."

She gasped as she placed a hand over her mouth. I lightly rubbed my hand up and down her back while giving her a moment to process what I'd just said.

"I wanted to give it to you right away, but I knew you weren't in a place to see it yet. So after we got back from our trip, and Marchello brought over Alec's letters, I took it to a jeweler. I just picked it up yesterday."

Her breath hitched as she held the velvet box in her hand and stared at the pendant inside.

"I had Alec's diamond set inside this infinity pendant so you could always keep his token of love close to your heart. I thought you would like a memento to represent the importance of him in your life."

She looked up at me and smiled one of the sweetest smiles I'd ever seen. The way it met her eyes, and the slight quiver to her upturned lips, showed me just how happy she was.

"That's amazing, Emmett. It's absolutely beautiful, and I love what it means, and that you thought of this. It makes me feel so special, like I have a piece of his heart with me. Thank you, I love you so much, Emmett."

"I love you too, Peach."

It was exactly what I had hoped for and more. She would now have this with her to remember him, and hopefully look toward a happy life in the future. She could feel good about those memories, and not sad for all the misunderstandings.

$\mathcal{S}am$

After breakfast, Emmett sat on the counter, flipping through the newspaper and drinking his coffee. I was sitting on the couch reading when a paper airplane flew over and landed in my lap. I jumped then laughed and looked up at his adorable smirk.

"Unfold it, Peach."

I did as he asked and saw his message inside, four little words . . .

Move in with me?

I smiled up at him and nodded. It was such a sweet gesture, and I couldn't help but appreciate his creativity. The last time he asked me to move in with him, resulted in the loneliest two weeks of my life.

We drove back to Auburn and spent the day going from apartment to apartment until we found the right one. It was a large, ground level unit near a dog park where we could walk Gage. It was also much closer to campus than Riley and Quinn's. Thankfully, I'd signed a month-to-month lease on my condo in Atlanta, so we could move into our new apartment soon.

There wasn't a lot to pack since my condo came fully furnished, and Emmett had all of his stuff ready to go from his Aunt's house. We planned to pack up his room at the frat house, as well as see the girls, Riley, and Quinn. We would also have to shop for more furniture. The first purchase would be a bed and some bar stools. Everything else we could take a little longer to decide on.

I occasionally found myself touching Emmett's infinity pendant with Alec's diamond. It made me smile and feel whole. I couldn't think of what I had done to deserve Emmett in my life, but I thanked God for him every day. He always knew exactly what I needed.

CHAPTER 38

Packing Up

Sam

As we pulled up to Riley and Quinn's house, the street was vacant of cars. Emmett parked his Camaro in the driveway, and we went inside. They were already up and sitting in their gaming chairs, playing some combat game on the big screen TV. They waved us inside with quick hellos.

Emmett and I each grabbed a cup of coffee in the kitchen before heading upstairs to his old bedroom. When we walked in, I flashbacked to my first time there, and I giggled as I sat on the end of his bed. He walked over and stood between my legs, running his hands through my hair.

"Penny for your thoughts, Peach."

"I was just remembering the first time I followed you in here," I replied, looking up at him.

"Really?" he smirked. "Well, maybe we should do a replay," he replied then pushed me back onto his bed.

"Yes, we should," I said, pulling his head down for a kiss.

He lay down beside me and gathered my body into his. Reaching down, he twined his fingers with mine and lifted my arm up above our heads.

"I love you, Peach," he said, kissing me lightly on the inside of my elbow.

I giggled at the soft touch. "I love you, too."

He trailed kisses from my neck to my cheek before capturing my mouth with his and slowly entangling his tongue with mine. I let out a whimper as he lifted himself up and sat back on his knees, looking down at me with a glint in his eyes.

"What're you doing?" I whispered.

A sexy smile spread wide across his face as he lifted my foot to his chest. "Trust me?"

"Of course," I whispered.

He ran his fingers up to my knee, and back down the top of my leg. Then he started massaging my foot.

"Oh my God, Emmett, that feels so . . . good." I sighed, leaning my head back into the mattress and closing my eyes.

"Does this feel good, too?" he asked, placing warm kisses on the top of my ankle before setting it down on the bed.

"Yes, it does."

He lifted my other foot up against his chest and massaged it, gently lowering it to the bed, and trailed kisses up my leg. I arched my back as he ran his fingers up under the hem of my shirt and lifted it over my head, tossing it on the floor.

I needed to feel his skin against mine. I reached up and ran my hands over his strong muscles, feeling them move as he pulled his shirt off. He hovered over me, and I wrapped my arms around his neck and pulled his body down to mine, reveling in every touch of his body as we made love. Afterwards, I snuggled into his chest, his heartbeat a steady rhythm in my ear.

"That was amazing, Peach," he said, kissing the top of my head.

"Mmmm, yes it was, babe. We should forget packing and do that again," I said.

"The sooner we pack and get through the barbeque, the sooner we can drive home and make love in our own bed."

I laughed. He was so matter-of-fact about it, like all that really mattered was us getting home, when I knew he damn well he was as excited about the barbeque as I was.

I heard the doorbell ring and hoped it was the girls. I really missed Tamron and Alison. I ran downstairs, past the guys still gaming in the living room with their headsets on. They probably hadn't even heard the doorbell.

When I opened the door, I was surprised to see John standing there. Usually he only came down from Alaska in the winter months.

John had gone to college with the guys and graduated last year. He and Emmett were best friends from their days back in Georgia right after Emmett and Alec moved up from Florida. I think Emmett chose Auburn in part because John had chosen to go there. I couldn't blame him. John was a nice guy, and who wouldn't want to go to a college where you already had a best friend?

After giving him a hug, I invited him in. This would be a real surprise for Emmett. As we walked back to the living room, Emmett came down the stairs. The look on his face was adorable. He was surprised, all right.

"John?" Emmett called.

"Hey, Emmett, what's up, man?" He looked at me with a devilish glint in his eye. "Hi Peachy," he added, earning himself a smack on the back of his head from Emmett at the use of his version of Emmett's pet name for me.

"When did you get in?" Emmett asked.

John shook his head. "About five minutes ago. I drove straight here from the car rental place at the airport."

"Holy shit, man! I had no idea you were coming. Great to see ya. Damn . . . it's been too long," Emmett said, pulling him into one of those back-slapping guy hugs.

"Yeah, long-ass flight, too, but it's all good man, I got to sit by a hottie. For the first time, I was happy to be by a chatty person. Even got her number. She lives here in Auburn. Girl like that could tempt me from Alaska. Tempt, not convince," John added after seeing Emmett's and my surprised expressions.

We laughed, both of us knowing there was absolutely no way John would ever move away from Alaska.

We sat out back and caught up with him over a few beers while I waited anxiously for the girls to get there. Wondering where they were, I sent a quick group text.

Me: Where the hell are y'all?

T: A bit snarky aren't ya?

A: We're coming . . . soon.

T: Don't tell her. Make her wait.

Me: What the hell is that supposed to mean?

A: Don't worry about Tamron. She's just pissy because, in order to see you, she has to see Quinn, and they had a fight.

T: Great. I didn't want to get Sam involved too, Alison.

Me: A fight? No way. I'm here, and Quinn isn't acting like there's a problem. He's playing some video game with Riley like he always does.

T: Fucker.

A: Relax, Tamron.

Me: Wow, I really need to get caught up on this.

T: We'll be there in a few.

A: We're leaving the apartment now.

Me: Awesome. See y'all soon.

It was rapid-fire texting at its best and we had perfected it. We had an entire conversation in less than three minutes. When the doorbell rang again, I excused myself and rushed inside to intervene between Tamron and Quinn. I wondered what their fight was about, because they always seemed so happy together.

I opened the door and threw my arms around my best

friends, each of us squealing our hellos. It wasn't until I let them inside that I felt the air thicken, and knew it had to be the fight between Tamron and Quinn. I would talk to Tamron about that, and soon. Alison walked over to Riley and gave him a kiss, but let out a shriek when he grabbed her ass as she spun back toward me. On our way to the kitchen, Tamron walked by Quinn without saying a word or even glancing in his direction.

I grabbed us glasses of lemonade then set chips and salsa on the counter for an afternoon snack.

"So, umm, what exactly was this fight about, Tamron? Why are you being so cold toward him?" I asked her in a hushed tone.

"Sam, I really don't want to talk about it. Okay? I just want to hang with you. We've missed you so much," she replied.

"Tamron. You can't expect her to accept that answer. First of all, and you know this is true, we wouldn't let her get away with shrugging us off like that if she and Emmett were fighting."

"All right. Fine. Damn it. He wants us to move in together," she explained.

I gasped and brought my hand up to my mouth. She shook her head and continued.

"See, this is exactly why I didn't want to tell you. I can hear it already. First of all, you're gonna be just like Alison and get all excited, and want us to move in together. I can see it already starting in your composure, you're all happy and bouncy. I am not in the mood for it. Second of all, you aren't one to talk about who should move in with who, since you have had your own issues with whether or not to move in with Emmett."

I gasped. "But Tamron, that's diff . . ."

"Yeah, it's different. I realize that, but it doesn't change the significance on my situation. I'll tell you like I told him; I'm not ready to move in with him," she sighed. "Why the ever-loving fuck did he have to ask me? He's got a good thing here with Riley. I have a good thing at home with Alison. I don't want to rock that relationship boat. I mean I love him, which is why I can't move in with him."

"Okay, but that's really the best reason to move in with

him." I said softly.

She shook her head. "We've been dating for almost two years, and I do miss him when he's not with me, but what if it doesn't work out? I'll lose him! I can't take that chance. So, I told him no, that it was ridiculous for him to even ask." She breathed a huge sigh, and laid her head in her hands."

"Wow, Tamron. Quinn didn't understand that?" I asked.

Alison huffed. "He would *if* she'd have just told him that. But no. All she told him was that last part about it being ridiculous. So to be honest, I can't blame him, and that pisses Tamron off even more."

I smiled at Tamron. She looked up at me between her fingers, like hiding from a scene in a movie you don't want to see but can't keep from looking.

"Tamron, it'll be all right. I'm sure it'll all work out in the end, as long as you keep your heart open to Quinn. And you know Alison and I are always here for you."

I walked around the counter to give her a hug, noticing the tears in her eyes. She wiped them away and hugged me back. I hoped she might be ready to talk to Quinn, but as we pulled apart, he walked through the kitchen to get a beer and didn't even look at her.

He made a point to say hi to Alison and me though, and I could tell some real damage had been done. I felt the chasm between them as stark as if I were standing in one for real. Quinn grabbed two beers then made his way back into the living room.

Tamron leaned back against the counter with a sigh. "It's probably too late to fix it now. I can't tell him all of that anyway. He won't understand. It's just . . . God, I can't lose him."

"You're going to lose him, if you don't explain it to him, Tamron. You have to at least try," I told her with Alison nodding in agreement.

She closed her eyes and shook her head. I knew she probably wasn't ready to talk to Quinn, but she looked like she was getting there, and I hoped she would be soon.

We spent the afternoon talking about all we had missed while away from each other. I told the girls about my trip to Hawaii with Emmett. They listened intently as I told them about Alec's memorial. I grabbed my phone and showed them pictures of Alec's lantern. Neither one asked me what I had written on my panels. They knew it was something just between Alec and me. But they each squeezed my hands as I spoke about Emmett and I drawing strength from each other, as we set his lantern afloat in the ocean. I'm sure they were relieved we'd been able to finally say goodbye and get some closure.

Emmett walked into the kitchen and grabbed two more beers then went back outside. I wanted to join him so I could catch up with John, too.

"So, guess who's here." I said, smiling.

"Well, don't keep us waiting. Who?" Tamron asked.

But Alison was already up and walking to the back doors. "It's John!" she squealed.

"Here? Now? Really?" Tamron asked as she followed Alison outside.

Emmett and John were sitting on the brick wall surrounding the back yard. I walked up to Emmett and nestled between his legs, while the girls ambled up to John. He had enough time to jump down before they threw their arms around him and hugged him tight.

"Tamron, Alison . . ." he said, laughing. "It's good to see you."

They started into twenty questions—when did he get there, why didn't he say he was coming? Did he have a girlfriend up there in Alaska, and if so, they wanted all the details about her, and they would need to make sure she knew the consequences of hurting him.

I smiled up at Emmett as he looked down at me with a glint in his eye.

"Those girls never change," he said and we both chuckled.

"Hey Emmett," Alison and Tamron said in unison, still standing with John's arms around them.

"No, there's no girlfriend," he finally answered. "But there are girls," he continued at their surprised expressions. "I do date, for fuck's sake. I just haven't found one that I want to have around on a regular basis. That's all."

Emmett cleared his throat. "There're lots of fine, southern girls down here in Alabama and Georgia, you know."

I motioned around at all of us. "Plus, we're all here. If you'd just stay down here permanently." I added.

"Never gonna happen, my friends," John answered. "I love Alaska. I'll keep coming down here for the heavy winter months, but Alaska is my home, and if I were to find a fine, southern girl, she would have to travel with me between here and Alaska."

We all laughed as Riley and Quinn walked through the back door. Riley walked up to Alison, and Quinn fired up the grill. I could sense Tamron's tension from across the yard. Man, I understood her hesitation, but I knew first hand it was better to be honest about your feelings, rather than keep it in, no matter what happened.

I went inside to grab a couple sodas. Tamron followed me in with a look of panic I'd never seen before. She shook her head when I started to ask what was wrong, and I realized she likely just needed a breather.

As the afternoon crept on, Quinn had slowly inched his way closer and closer to Tamron. I had a feeling he wasn't going to let things stay the way they were between them for long. Tamron was going to have to talk to him, and soon. Trouble was, she was nowhere near ready. I handed her the tray of hamburgers and hot dogs, and she grew more panicked than ever.

"Tamron, this is the best way to break the ice between you two. He has the grill ready. Just hand this to him and say 'hi' or 'here ya go.' You don't have to engage in real conversation yet. He still has to cook. But you'll at least have something other than silence to step you two closer to actually hashing out your problems. Remember, this all started because he wanted y'all to move in together. He loves you. It'll all work out."

She nodded and, in normal Tamron fashion, stood tall and walked out the back door, looking confident and ready. I smiled, hoping they'd be okay. Their relationship was one of the most rock-solid that I knew, and it made me feel very uneasy, for them to be in turmoil.

I gathered more drinks into a cooler and carried it outside. Emmett watched me with that same look he had upstairs in his old room. A chill ran through me as I thought of his arms wrapped around my body and his mouth kissing mine, softly at first, then turning hungry and greedy. With a shake of my head, I snapped myself from the sexy daydream. Man, just a look from him had me all hot and bothered. If it hadn't been for the company we were in, I would have rushed that barbeque along, too.

Tamron stood up and said, "I'm going to get some more chips and salsa. The guys look ready for another round. Alison would you help me with the beer?"

Alison started to rise from Riley's lap when Quinn stood up.

"I've got it, Alison," he said.

Tamron's panicked expression returned, but neither Alison nor I were able to help her at that point. And it needed to happen anyway, so we nodded at each other as Quinn followed Tamron inside. A few minutes later, I joined Alison.

"Maybe we should go get the chips and beer, because I doubt they'll be out anytime soon."

She nodded. "Good idea."

When we walked inside, muffled voices sounded from Quinn's bedroom. I grabbed the food while Alison snagged the drinks, and we walked back outside.

Riley looked up at us as we set the food and drinks down. "Well . . . are they talking?"

Alison tsked at him. "It's not like we eavesdropped, Riley." She looked around and smiled back at him. "But we did hear muffled voices."

Everyone exhaled a sigh of relief, and it was then I realized just how much Tamron and Quinn's situation had affected all of us.

After about an hour, Tamron and Quinn walked back outside, smiling, holding hands, and looking quite relieved. It gave me hope to see a strong relationship make it through a difficult and trying time.

Quinn sat down in a lounge chair and pulled Tamron onto his lap. When Riley handed him a beer he looked over at me and smiled sincerely and I nodded my head back at him.

It was late when everyone started to crash, we were exhausted, and a little buzzed, so we decided to stay one last night in Emmett's room upstairs. I fell asleep in Emmett's arms as his fingers played with my hair.

CHAPTER 39

Getting Settled

Sam

We got home to our new apartment in the morning. The thought of *home and Emmett* brought a warm, happy feeling to my heart. I smiled as we brought his things inside from his room at Riley and Quinn's. I was surprised how many of my clothes had been left in his bedroom. Emmett laughed and said he'd been planning to hold it all ransom if I hadn't taken him back. I smacked him on his fine, mouth-watering ass and ran past him into our apartment.

As Emmett unpacked in our bedroom, I was excited and felt such peace about us officially living together. He felt like my home.

Passing by in the hallway, I peeked into the bathroom to find Emmett stashing his things away. I remembered the last time he'd done so, and the fight we'd had because I couldn't handle seeing his things where Alec's had once been. The memory I had with Alec's things was painful, because it was a stark reminder of his hope for me to take him back. Alec's memorial had changed everything. I was happier, more understanding, and excited about my future with Emmett.

I walked up to him and wrapped my arms around his waist

from behind. He looked up at the mirror, the corners of his mouth lifting up in a smile. I relaxed into him when he turned around in my arms and leaned his head down to kiss me. It started out so softly, almost reverently, but, like everything with Emmett, soon turned heated and electrifying.

He walked me backwards out of the bathroom, toward our bed and leaned his body into mine, nibbling on my ear as he lowered me down. I smoothed my hands down his back, settling my fingers in his waistband and pulling him in to me. I opened myself up to him, to the passion that consumed us both.

We fell asleep after making love and woke up to hungry stomachs. I prepared sandwiches, and we ate in comfortable silence, stealing glances and smiles.

When we were done eating we drove back to Atlanta, and my parents' house to pick Gage up and bring him home with us. I couldn't wait to see them. As we pulled into their driveway, I saw Gage lying on the front porch. I chuckled as he yawned, lifting his head to see who interrupted his nap. He jumped up and wagged his tail with such enthusiasm, his entire back end wiggled back and forth. Emmett parked and walked around to open my door, but Gage was already there, greeting me with slobbery doggy kisses. Emmett laughed when he received his own Gage kiss.

Mom stood on the porch with a glass of tea, and as I climbed the steps, I could smell dinner roasting in the oven. My mouth watered just thinking about the meal she'd prepared for us. I hugged her close and kissed her on the cheek.

"Hey, Mom."

"Hello, Mrs. Lang," Emmett said, pulling her in for a hug.

My mom giggled. "Emmett, how many times do I have to tell you to call me Maggie? You're practically family now."

Emmett smiled as he held the front door open for us. "Okay, Maggie, it's great to see you. Is Vance around? I've been meaning to catch up with him. There's a car show in Atlanta next week. I wanted to see if he'd like to check it out with me."

"Yes, dear, he's just finishing for the day, in his office upstairs."

"Good deal, ladies, I'm going to go have a chat with him."

I watched as he climbed the stairs and shook my head, wondering if he was up to something. But I'd seen the ad for the car show in the paper, so I let it go.

"Well, are you excited to be moving in with Emmett?" Mom asked.

"Oh my God, yes. It's awesome!" I looked up and saw her soft smile. We giggled like young schoolgirls until her face turned serious.

"Now, Samone," she started.

I tensed, knowing something important was on her mind.

"I hope you and Emmett are being careful," she finished.

I sighed. "Yes, we're always careful. I did actually pay attention when you had 'the talk' with me."

"Oh thank God." She exhaled a deep breath as she wiped her hands down the sides of her apron.

"Mom, do you need any help with dinner?" I asked as she walked to the oven.

"No, honey, I have it all taken care of. It should be ready soon. Why don't you take Gage for a quick walk? He's been itching to go for the last hour, but with your Dad working upstairs and my cooking dinner, I haven't been able to get him out," she replied.

"Okay."

I grabbed Gage's leash and harness and went out to the front porch to get him ready to go. As I walked the neighborhood with Gage, I thought about him being a part of my home with Emmett. Something about it gave me a sense of completion, like having my own little family all in one place. It felt good to feel the burn in my legs, as we jogged up the hills. We walked back to my parent's house, and I heard hushed voices as I walked up the front steps.

When I walked inside, everyone was downstairs, and the curious side of me couldn't help but wonder what they'd all been talking about. They were laughing about something, and it just felt off. As I turned the corner and tip-toed into the kitchen, my parents, each in turn, peered at me with content smiles. Emmett looked like the cat that ate the canary. I planned to ask him about that later. He always found ways to distract me from things like that.

"So, are you kids all moved in and set up?" Dad asked as Emmett was packing up Gage's supplies.

"Yes Sir, we are," Emmett answered. "Maggie, dinner was delicious, as always."

"Thank you, dear." She grinned. "And let me know if you two need anything for your kitchen. I have so many pots and pans and other stuff, I could probably stock at least half of yours."

"I think we're good, Mom. But thanks," I said as I cleared the dished from the table.

"Well, let us know if there's anything we can help with," Dad said, handing me Gage's leash.

"We will. Thanks, Dad."

As the sun was setting on the drive back home to Auburn, Emmett was quiet. I thought it the perfect opportunity to ask a few lingering questions.

"Babe?"

"Yeah, Peach?"

"What were y'all laughing about when I came back in from walking Gage? Y'all looked happy, but you looked like you were up to something. It kinda seemed, I don't know. Just weird. What was that all about?"

"Oh, nothing really. I was telling them a joke I'd heard on the radio. So are you happy to have Gage coming home with us?"

"Yeah, I really missed him."

He changed the subject, so I let it drop. But something still felt off.

We got home and took everything inside. Emmett walked Gage outside around the apartment. I was so tired and couldn't wait to go to bed. Emmett brought Gage into our bedroom and he settled in nicely on the floor at the foot of our bed.

CHAPTER 40
Life Isn't Always Black And White

Emmett

I woke up before Sam and just lay there watching her sleep. She was so peaceful. Sometimes I was still surprised we'd finally moved in together. But we were finally ready, and I was more than ready for the next step, as well. I hoped she was, too. Just thinking about it made me feel complete. I couldn't wait to ask her. But I knew I had to make it special. I wanted it to be memorable, something she would forever look back on with happiness.

The night before, at her parents' house, I'd gone upstairs to talk to her dad, and ask him for his blessing to marry Sam. He said of course and was very happy and excited for us.

When we went downstairs to tell Maggie, she couldn't contain her happiness. We heard Sam and Gage coming back from their walk and changed the subject quickly. I wasn't sure when I was going to ask her, but I knew the right time would come, and I would know. I wanted to have the ring ready for whenever that may be.

I left a note for Sam by the Keurig that I needed something from Aunt Robin's house then drove to the jeweler's with a light heart. I wished we'd stayed over at her parents' house so

I didn't have to drive back to Atlanta, but I'd seen some engagement rings there while waiting to pick up the pendant I'd had made for Sam. There was one that would be perfect for her. I knew what I wanted . I just wanted to get there already. I stopped at another red light, irritated at hitting every one. Maybe I looked both ways once it turned green. The again, maybe not. Who knows. Either way, I don't remember anything after that.

I regained consciousness on a bed in a room divided by curtains, hanging from a beaded chain attached to the ceiling. It slowly dawned on me that I was in a hospital room. I blinked, looked around, and saw a beautiful young woman brush the curtains aside and step up to my bed. With tears streaking down her face, she placed her hands to my jaw and kissed my cheeks.

"Oh my God, Emmett. Are you okay? Are you in pain? What happened? I got a call from a nurse here that you were in a car accident," she said.

It was then I realized I probably knew her. She obviously knew me. I tried not to frighten her, but my expression must have shown my confusion. The only thing I knew then was that my name must be Emmett. Not so bad as far as names went. Better than it could have been.

Her expression was tight as her eyebrows knit in thought. Then her eyes grew wide with panic. "Emmett? Babe? Do you recognize me?" she asked.

I studied her at length, then shook my head. I couldn't get the word no to come out of my uncooperative mouth.

Her eyes filled up with tears again. "It's Sam . . . Peach. Remember? Oh my God. I have to find a doctor. I'll be right back. Don't worry. I am sure you'll be okay." She glanced back at me as she wiped her eyes with the back of her hand again and disappeared through the curtains.

I wasn't sure just what in this situation would pass for okay. Something bad must have happened. I must have some kind of relationship with her. She was beautiful, which made me smile. I was clearly doing all right with my unknown life. If I could only remember.

"Damn it," I muttered.

I was feeling empty with so many questions and unknowns floating around my head. I took a few minutes to gather my thoughts while waiting for the young woman to return with a doctor and assess my injuries.

My arm hurt, and I had a splint around my right wrist. There was pain in my lower left leg, I looked down and saw a cast around it. I reached up and felt a gauzy wrap around the top of my head. No wonder I felt like I had a migraine from hell. There was also a finger splint on my left hand. I guessed that wasn't bad as far as injuries went, but whatever happened had stolen my memory, too, and that *was* bad. *Very* bad.

I was looking all around the room when I saw a pair of sandals, adorable red painted toenails, and the slender ankles of very sexy legs stop next to a larger pair of black shoes and baggy sea-green pants on the other side of my curtain wall.

I could hear faint whispering and some sniffling, which, I assumed, must have been my doctor and this Sam woman. I couldn't make out everything, but heard the words *trauma, lucky it was only memory,* and *scans were clear.*

The doctor spread the curtain, and I saw I was in a larger room with windows and an automatic sliding door. The look on the young woman's face was heartbreaking, and frankly, rather disconcerting. I felt a weird connection to her, but I couldn't quite put my finger on that connection. Clearly, my heart knew she was important. My head just needed to figure out why.

"Mr. Walker, I'm Dr. Pace. I've been overseeing your care since you arrived here via ambulance."

The beautiful, young woman, Sam, watched me closely as the doctor went over my list of injuries. She looked at each part of my body as he referenced them, her brow furrowed and mouth turned down as she chewed at her bottom lip with worry.

But when he started to inquire about my memory, she hiccupped in a broken way, and I looked over and saw her wipe at a tear.

"I'd like to ask you a few questions. Do you know your name?"

"Well . . . she called me Emmett and you just called me Mr. Walker, so . . . Emmett Walker, I assume?"

"Do you know what year it is?"

I immediately looked around the room, subconsciously looking for clues. "No. I'm not sure."

"It's okay," he reassured. "What color is your blanket?"

I looked down at it and smiled, I knew that answer. It was a small thing, but it felt reassuring still. "Blue."

"Very good. Do you know what country we live in?"

"Yes, the United States."

"All right, good. Well, there's no way to be sure of the exact cause of your memory loss. But given the extent of your injuries, there's a high probability of head trauma. However, your scans came back clear. So there doesn't appear to be any medical reason, although it has been known to happen."

I groaned as he continued.

"Most people regain their memory after a period of time, by simply being back in their normal living environment. We'll run a few more tests to be sure there aren't any unseen complications. I wouldn't worry at this point, you really need to just relax. I've requested an evaluation consult with Dr. Shaw, one of the hospital's on-call neurologists."

Sam's breath hitched, and her hand flew up to cover her mouth. I wondered what that was about. With a nod, Dr. Pace left us alone to check on another patient.

"Umm, Sam? Are you okay?"

"Oh, do you remember me now?" Her eyes lit up with hope. "You just called me Sam."

"No, I'm so sorry. I still don't remember you. I just remembered you said your name was Sam."

"Oh." She nodded and twisted at the bracelet she wore. "It's okay. I just got a little hopeful, that's all. Well, is there anything that you need?"

"Yeah, in my cell phone, wherever that is, I have a list of

contacts. Could you call my brother, Alec, for me? I'm sure he must be worried."

She gasped and her hand flew back to her mouth as tears started filling her eyes. She shook her head, mumbling something unintelligible, then turned around, brushed the curtains aside, and ran from my room.

CHAPTER 41

Reality Sucks

Emmett

I lay there wondering what it was I'd said that could have upset Sam so badly. Did she know Alec? I guessed, by the way she was acting when she first saw me, so familiar and loving, that she must know my family, Alec and Aunt Robin. They were both good people, so I didn't understand what could have caused her reaction.

I looked around for my phone and saw my clothes in a bag on the bottom shelf of the stand next to my bed. On top laid a pitcher of water with a straw coming out the top. Then I saw my phone. It managed to survive the accident and still had a charge.

I opened my contacts and scrolled down to Alec's name then called, but it didn't even ring. It went straight to an out of service message.

What the ever-loving hell is going on?

I redialed his number from memory; at least I still remembered my family. I got the same message. I called Aunt Robin, but it went to voicemail. This was getting weirder and weirder. I clenched my fists as I wished so badly I could just remember.

Later, when Sam came back in, she looked much better. Dr.

Pace followed her in, along with another physician, Dr. Shaw, according to his nametag. He had his hand on Sam's shoulder, which seemed kind of odd, like he was familiar with her. I figured maybe they knew each other somehow. I didn't know what Sam did, but it was possible she worked at the hospital. I had all kinds of questions, but simply had no answers.

There were so many things I didn't know. I couldn't get ahold of Aunt Robin, and God only knew what the hell was wrong with Alec's phone.

"Mr. Walker, this is Dr. Shaw. He's the neurologist I spoke with you about earlier," Dr. Pace said.

I looked at Dr. Shaw and had a strange sense of déjà vu, but, as with everything else, I couldn't place it. My stomach tightened with nausea when I met his eyes.

"Dr. Shaw will run a few tests so we can rule out some possibilities regarding your memory loss," Dr. Pace finished.

"Okay, whatever we need to do," I replied.

I kept looking at Sam while Dr. Pace and Dr. Shaw talked in the corner of the room. She kept glancing from Dr. Shaw back to me. I began to ask her what the deal was between them, but she retreated through the curtain, followed closely behind by both doctors.

"A nurse's aide will be in shortly to take you down for an MRI," Dr. Shaw said on his way out.

About an hour later, a man wearing blue scrubs came in with a wheelchair.

He helped me into the wheelchair and propped my leg up on a metal flap that folded out near my calf. As we approached the elevator, Sam stepped out with a woman garbed in a dressy, knee-length skirt and a long, white lab coat.

The awkwardness of the moment gave me time to read her nametag. Melody Kisner, Grief Counselor. What was Sam doing with this woman? Was it just coincidence they were on the elevator together? I breathed a sigh of relief and squeezed Sam's hand when she reached out for me.

"I'll see you when you're done downstairs," she said.

The physical contact felt odd, like we knew each other

intimately. If only I could remember. I roughed my hands through my hair, getting more and more frustrated by the minute. The nurse's aide left me in a room with the technician who'd be running my MRI. It was cold in there, even more so than my room.

I laid down in the machine for the test while the technician wrapped me in another thin blanket, more like a heavy cotton sheet for all the warmth it provided. Even with three, I still felt a slight chill.

When the test finished, I went back up to my room, only to find Sam sitting by my bedside with the woman from the elevator. She stood up and wiped the tears from her face, as she cleared space for the nurse's aid to help me back into bed.

"Emmett, this is Ms. Kisner. She's the hospital's grief counselor. I . . . I umm, asked her to speak with you."

"What the hell? Why do I need a grief counselor? I just lost my memory. Where's my brother? I don't understand what the fuck is going on here!" I flinched from the pain in my splinted finger, when I reflexively tried to run my hand through my hair.

"Mr. Walker, please try to calm down. Ms. Lang and I need to talk to you. With your memory loss, you're forgetting some very important events. I'd like to discuss these with you," Ms. Kisner stated.

"Yes, I know I don't remember Sam, but that doesn't explain why I'd need to speak with a grief counselor." I regretted throwing my head back against the bed when instant pain shot through my skull.

"Emmett, please just let Ms. Kisner continue. This is hard enough as it is," Sam pleaded.

"Okay, I'm sorry. Look, I'm just so frustrated that I can't remember you. I feel a connection, but I just can't place it."

Sam squeezed her eyes shut.

Ms. Kisner cleared her throat and continued as if I hadn't interrupted her at all. "Mr. Walker, we need to talk about your brother, Alec." She paused . . . and let that information sink in.

"What about him? I've been trying to call him, but it goes

directly to a message that says his number is no longer in service."

The tears were filling Sam's eyes again, and a dark foreboding set in.

"Mr. Walker, Alec was in an accident about a year ago. He had an epileptic event as a result, and died here, in the hospital later that night," Ms. Kisner explained.

"Bull shit! You're lying. Get the hell out of my room!" I screamed at the lady, but my eyes were locked onto Sam, and I saw the cold, painful truth of it, in her bloodshot eyes.

A boulder settled heavily into the pit of my stomach. The nausea I'd felt earlier crawled up my throat. I snatched the bowl off the table and threw up. My entire body convulsed painfully, my leg twitching and head pounding as I retched.

Sam cried freely then, and I could feel the tears running down my face, as well. This couldn't be true. They were wrong. There was abso-fucking-lutely no way my little brother was dead. No fucking way!

Sam jumped to my side and slipped her small, soft hand into mine, while I reached up with the other and bit my knuckles. I couldn't breathe. I wretched again, but only green bile came up.

The next thing I knew, a nurse was running into my room.

"Get the fuck away from me!" I tried to lean away from the nurse as she pulled a syringe from her pocket, and inserted the needle into my IV line. After a moment, my body felt weirdly over-relaxed. My eyelids grew heavy, and everything turned black.

CHAPTER 42

Adjusting

Sam

Bringing Emmett home was hard. It was devastating that he still couldn't remember me. As expected, he wasn't handling Alec's death well either. Seeing the pain he went through as he tried to accept the reality, shredded my soul. I don't know what I would have done without Ms. Kisner. It was both surreal and unnerving, having Dr. Shaw as Emmett's neurologist, hitting a little too close to home since he was the same doctor who'd been there when Alec died.

Thankfully, Emmett's injuries weren't life threatening, and the only major thing we had to contend with was his memory loss. With his Aunt Robin still in Europe, he had little choice but to come home with me. He said he wanted to go back to his normal life and routine. The doctors said it should help bring his memory back. I hoped so.

However irrational, there was a small part of me that was hurt that Emmett couldn't remember me, almost as if his mind was trying to protect him from more pain and heartache considering he didn't remember Alec's death either, yet remembered other random things.

I worried he subconsciously wanted to forget me, and the pain I'd brought into his life. The girls said that was crazy, and

I was just stressed out, that Emmett loved me, and had fought for our relationship after all that had happened. I knew it all already, but it didn't make it any easier to deal with. I was overwhelmed with heartache. I tried to keep everyday things as normal as possible for Emmett, hoping something would spark his memory.

The first week, he slept on the couch every night, and it was near impossible to fall asleep with him so close, but so far away. Then one morning, I woke up wrapped in his arms, and he was awake, just watching me sleep. It was such a welcomed feeling, I began to cry silent tears.

"Good morning," I said as I stretched out on the bed and snuggled back into his chest. I relished in the familiar feel of his arms around me. The faint smell of his cologne that lingered on his skin.

"Good morning Peach," he whispered.

My heart leapt with joy when he called me Peach. "Oh my God, Emmett . . . you remembered?"

He looked sheepish and shook his head. "No. I'm sorry. I was just trying it out to see if it would spark a memory, but it didn't." As he saw my sad expression, he followed up saying, "But it feels right. Every morning, when I wake up on the couch without you, it feels wrong, so I crawled into bed with you. I promise I didn't do anything. I just held you and watched you sleep for a while. I like the normal feeling it gives me."

"That's because you used to do this every morning. It was kind of our routine, since you always woke up before me."

His eyes softened, as his brow relaxed, and he ran his fingers through my hair. "This feels familiar, too. Did I play with your hair like this?"

"Mmm hmm, you did. It's how you'd wake me up most mornings. That . . . and a kiss." I blushed.

"Hmm, maybe I should try that out, too. If you don't mind of course—it could spark a memory—you know," he said with his sexy smirk.

I slowly nodded my head, his gaze locked on my eyes, then down to my mouth, as I bit at my bottom lip.

He leaned his head down and gently pressed his lips to mine. He was tentative at first, and it took every ounce of my strength to not kiss him back with the heated passion I felt for him. But I knew we had to go slow. I couldn't rush this. It was when he opened his mouth to mine, that I lost my resolve and rolled over, straddling his waist. I ran my fingers down his strong arms and brought my hands to rest in the center of his abs, stopping just beneath the waistband of his shorts. His breath hitched, as I glided my fingers along his skin around to his sides. When he looked up at me, I saw he was as lost as I was in our passion.

He slid the strap of my nightshirt off my shoulder, and pulled me down to him, so I was lying on his chest. He followed the touch of his fingers on my shoulder and neck, with kisses leaving tingles behind.

He rolled us over, so I lay on my back beneath his strong body. I sighed as his lips made their way up my neck. "Now this . . ." he kissed just underneath my ear, "feels familiar." He turned my face to the side, and captured my mouth with his, leaving coolness on my lips, as his minty breath mixed with mine.

His mind might not have remembered me, but his body did, and at that moment, it was all we needed.

CHAPTER 43

Friends Are Amazing

Emmett

S am decided we should go to over to Riley and Quinn's to see all of our friends, so we took off in her little car. Mine was totaled, and I can't even begin to say how pissed off I was when I saw it. I mean, damn, it was a red 1969 Chevy Camaro in mint condition.

Sometimes I was angrier about my car than I was about my memory loss, at least until Sam walked into the room, and I was reminded of this beautiful, young woman I clearly had an intimate relationship with, but couldn't remember. I felt all kinds of familiarities, which made me comfortable being there in her—our apartment. But I constantly felt like a complete and utter dick for not remembering her. Her pain and sadness was a daily reminder. I dreamed of Alec every night, plagued by memories I wished I could forget, and those I couldn't hold on to.

Her dog, Gage, was awesome. Everywhere I went, he lay at my feet or tried to body block me from leaving the apartment. The only time he was happy about me walking toward the door was when I had his leash in my hand. Guess he was more perceptive than I realized.

We arrived at Riley and Quinn's house that afternoon, and there was a rental car in the driveway. I don't know how I was able to remember some things, but not Sam or that Alec had died.

Motherfucker. I just couldn't believe my little brother was dead.

Every morning, I woke up unsure how I would make it through another day without falling apart. I was off the pain meds, healing at a good rate, and only occasionally needed ibuprofen—so I began drinking more. But instead of a beer at the end of the day, I'd have whiskey. I wasn't drinking a lot, but it was becoming a regular enough of a habit. I started to regret it, before tossing it back, leaving an empty glass behind. I wasn't proud of it, but hitting the hard stuff helped calm my mind, and face the terrors of my dreams at night, where Alec was alive, but always just out of my reach.

It was a cruel thing what my memory was doing. Sometimes I wished I could forget Alec and remember Sam. It would have been easier than dealing with the pain of losing my little brother all over again each morning.

Sam reached over and grabbed my hand. "Are you okay, babe? Ready to go inside and see everyone?"

"Yeah, I was just thinking about Alec."

Her breath hitched and she squeezed my hand.

"I'll be okay. Let's go inside and say hi to everyone," I said as I kissed the top of her hand.

"Okay."

We rang the doorbell, and John answered with a smile. "Hey Emmett, Peachy."

It grated on me that he called her Peachy. I wasn't sure why. He was my best friend after all.

"I'm surprised you're here, John, you're down earlier than usual."

"Actually, I never left after our last barbeque. I was supposed to fly back the day after your accident. But, I wanted to be sure you were going to be okay. Then Sam called and said you'd lost some of your memory, and I just wanted to be here for you, man."

God, I was a dick. I'm sure it was something we probably

joked about, him calling Sam Peachy, especially with the smartass expression he sent my way as he said it. He looked like he genuinely cared for her, but in a friend way, I was sure.

"Well thanks, man. It's been a hard few weeks," I said with a nod.

"Yeah, let's save the heavy talk for after a few beers."

"Sounds good. Got any of the hard stuff? I've been more of a whiskey kind of guy lately."

I didn't miss the stiffness that crept into Sam's shoulders. I guessed she noticed more than I realized.

John gave me a sideways glance and nodded.

"You know Riley and Quinn, always have stock of everything. Or maybe you don't remember. I'm sorry man," he quickly finished.

"Nah, it's okay. I remember that," I murmured, looking over at where Sam was talking with Tamron and Alison.

It was well after lunch, but I decided it would be better to start off with a beer rather than going straight for the whiskey, even though it was calling my name. I had a moment of pause, when I realized I was craving its sweet oblivion. But I shook it off, and tried to listen to the conversation around me.

John walked outside with two beers and hopped up on the top of the brick wall that surrounded the back yard. I followed his lead.

He cleared his throat as he handed me my beer. "So, uh, you remember everything except Sam?" he asked.

I couldn't look at him, just kept kicking the brick wall with my heels. "Yeah, that about sums it up," I murmured. "The doctors call it selective amnesia. Sometimes I act like I don't remember things so Sam won't think it's only her I've forgotten, but I'm pretty sure she's figured it out. It must show on my face. She hasn't questioned me about it, but I can tell she knows. It sucks to see the pain in her eyes."

"Damn, man, that's harsh," John said.

"Yeah, tell me about it. The only other thing I forgot, was that Alec died." My throat hurt, and was so dry I took a long swig of my beer, nearly drinking the whole thing.

"Wow, dude, you gonna suck that shit down in one gulp, or enjoy the hops?" he asked with a shocked look on his face.

"Sorry, man, I just . . . I can't get over that Alec is gone. Fuck. He was my little brother! How the ever loving fuck can he be dead?"

John looked down at his feet. "I know, Emmett. I know. I remember, and it's still hard to accept."

"You know, at first, I didn't even remember my name. Once I'd heard it a few times, it felt normal. It feels natural for me to be with Sam, too, but I still don't remember her. I mean, my body clearly remembers hers, and that has been nothing short of amazing."

"Well see then, at least y'all have that," John replied. "I don't know what I would do if I forgot the love of my life, and before you say anything, let me tell you that is exactly what she is to you. She. Is. The. Love. Of. Your. Life. You guys were made for each other. Soul mates. I hope to find that kind of love someday."

"Let me ask you something," I said. "I know I call her Peach. But why do you call her Peachy, and why did I wanna knock your lights out when you said it after you answered the door?"

John laughed. "Because I do it to mess with you, but mostly because I adore that little girl like a sister," he added quickly. "You're just greedy about it, but it fits her perfectly, and I can't help it, because when I say it, she gets this lit up, happy expression on her face and giggles every time you start shit with me about it. It's worth a punch or two in the arm," he said and we both laughed.

Sam walked through the French doors carrying a tray of sandwiches and iced tea. She set it down on the picnic table and walked over to John and me.

"Hey, guys, can I get you anything?" she asked with an adorable smile.

"I'm good," I replied "John, do you want anything?"

"Nah, Peachy, I'm okay. Thanks anyway," he replied.

"Okay. We'll be eating soon, but I brought out a couple mini sandwiches in case you guys were hungry," she said as she pecked me on the cheek with a chaste kiss and walked back into the house.

"Damn it, man, I need a whiskey," I said.

"Sure, but . . . why don't we save the hard stuff for after dinner, okay?" John asked.

"Sure, good idea," I answered.

As I watched Sam and the girls bringing everything outside it became clearer what I had to do. I wasn't remembering, and I felt I needed an extreme change to figure it all out. We ate dinner, and as I sat across from Sam, I caught her looking at me with a subtle attempt at a smile. Her eyes were mostly down cast while she moved her food around her plate, only taking an occasional bite of her meal. I knew each day that I didn't remember her, only caused her more pain. It was killing a piece of my soul each time I witnessed it.

We were sitting around the fire pit when Sam walked outside with a glass of whiskey and handed it to me. There was a slight tremble to her fingers as I took the glass from her hand. It wasn't cold outside, so I knew it was me, and it made my stomach feel like there was a concrete block in it. I was losing my mind with all these emotions and trying to remember, yet not being able to. I tossed the whiskey back and stood up to get more. When I got inside the house, Tamron was waiting for me.

"Emmett, what the hell are you doing?" she seethed.

"Getting a drink," I replied.

She smacked me on the shoulder. "I know what you're doing. What I want to know is why. We always saved that shit for when we ran out of beer and were too blitzed to care. So why're you drinking it like it's going out of style?"

"Uh, I'm not. This was my first glass," I retorted.

"That's not what I am talking about. Sam said you've been drinking whiskey every night at home. That's not like you. I don't think you should keep doing that, Emmett. It's not going to help you remember her," she said.

"I know it won't, Tamron! But it helps me fucking forget that I can't remember her, or that my brother died! I can't fucking sleep at night without dreaming of Alec. It's tearing me apart. And I can't stand the constant look of disappointment on Sam's face! I can't keep doing this. I just can't." My hands dropped to my sides, and I hung my head down in shame. I could not pretend that Sam hadn't noticed.

"What do you mean, you can't keep doing this?" she asked in a hushed but strained voice.

"I mean . . . damn it, I can't keep living with Sam. I need my own place away from her and the constant turmoil. It's killing both of us. I need to deal with Alec's death before I can face not remembering the woman I'm supposed to be madly in love with." I reached down and grabbed the bottle of whiskey. "I'm so confused, because it feels right to be with her, physically, yet my mind is blank. It's just too much. I drink to chase away dreams of Alec calling my name, but I can never get to him. I drink to numb the pain I feel when I see Sam's lonely, sad expressions. She tries to act like everything is okay, but I know it's not. I can't take it anymore, Tamron."

"Oh my God. Emmett, please. No. You'll devastate her."

"Look, it's what I have to do. I don't expect you or anyone else to understand, but I need to do it for me . . . and for her. It'll be better this way, and maybe, if I ever remember her, and she's still interested, then—maybe we can get back together. I'm gonna tell her tonight while she's here with everyone. I think it may be easier having all of your support. Then I'll see if John can drive me back to the apartment."

"Oh fucking hell." She threw her hands up. "This is going to be a clusterfuck of epic proportions, Emmett," Tamron said as she walked out the back door.

CHAPTER 44

Shattered

Sam

I noticed Tamron walk back outside a few minutes after Emmett went in, probably for more whiskey. Her expression was grim, and she avoided my eyes. That wasn't like her at all, and it left an uneasy feeling in the pit of my stomach.

I suddenly felt like I wanted to run far away. I couldn't shake it and began to feel overwhelming grief. When Emmett walked back outside, he wasn't carrying whiskey. He wasn't carrying anything. It was like staring into a great void, looking at him as he walked toward us by the fire.

I caught Tamron watching me as she slipped her phone into her pocket. Emmett slumped down in one of the chairs opposite me. My peripheral vision picked up on Alison checking her phone, and I glanced over as her expression went from wide-eyed to gloomy.

Everyone grew silent as Emmett cleared his throat. I sat up and hugged my knees to my chest, afraid of what he was about to say. Panic started to fill my chest.

"Uh, I need to talk to Sam, but I don't want her to be alone now or when I am done, so I'm going to do it here. It's not as if you won't all know soon enough, and y'all know everything that's going on now anyway."

I kept hearing the word *no . . . no, no, no, no, no,* and I realized it was me, repeating the words like a mantra. I looked around at the pity on all of my friends' faces, but it was Emmett's expression of regret that broke me.

"Sam, I need to leave," he said.

"Okay," I squeaked. "If you're tired we can go home."

"No, it's not that. Please, listen to me. My memories of you aren't coming back, and every night, I dream of Alec. I drink to numb the pain of each of those. I just need some time and space to clear my head. That's all."

I sat there, staring at the fire while he spoke. The flames seemed to be choreographed with the words he was saying . . . mocking me in their flickering dance. It only amplified the pain that I felt.

"I don't think I'll ever be okay if I don't get off the whiskey and face things. But I can't do that while living with you. I feel guilty every time I see your sad face. It tears me up that I am the cause. I wish there was another way, but I just have to go."

When he finished talking, I finally looked away from the fire and saw pain and regret in his eyes.

"I'm so sorry, Sam. Deeply and truly. I hope you'll be okay, and realize that this is for the best. I need a fresh start . . . to figure out this mess."

"A fresh start," I repeated on a choked sob.

It was Alec's words coming back to me all over again, only this time, from my Emmett. I rested my head in my hands.

"Just go," I murmured.

"John, can you drive me so I can get my things from the apartment?"

Emmett looked at me for a long moment, his brow furrowed in sadness, then turned around and walked back into the house. John got up and followed him inside, not even looking in my direction. A few minutes later, I heard two car doors shut and the engine start. Tears streamed down my face as they drove away.

"Sam . . ." Alison began.

"I'm just going inside to lie down. I'm really tired, and want to be alone," I said, holding up my hand in Tamron and Alison's direction.

I stood up, walked into the house, and set my drink on the counter in the kitchen as I passed. Climbing the stairs one step at a time, I repeated Emmett's words over and over in my head. The only room that wasn't occupied was Emmett's old room. Fantastic. My only solace away from everyone, was going to be filled with memories that would once have given me happy smiles, and content thoughts. Now I knew it would only bring me a deep pain that I would feel in my soul.

I went to the bathroom and washed the tears from my face even as new ones continued to flow down my splotchy red cheeks. When I lay down on Emmett's old bed, I hugged his pillow to my chest and lost myself to my sobs.

CHAPTER 45

Empty

Emmett

"Well, that came out of nowhere," John said.

"Yeah well, I've been thinking about it for a few days," I replied.

"You could have given me a heads up, man. You broke Sam's heart back there, and I get you're a mess, but for fuck's sake, Emmett, was that really the right way to do it?"

"I don't think there was a right way to do that, no matter the scenario. At least this way, she's not alone. She's with friends who clearly love her. It was the best solution I could think of," I said.

"If you say so," he answered. "For what it's worth, I think you're making a big mistake. I'm sorry about the whole thing and that you are going through this, and damn man, I'm sorry about Alec too, but you need to cope with that and get back to your life with her ASAP. She's not one to let go. She's one to keep and cherish. One to hold onto and grown old with."

"I know," was all I could say. The rest of the ride back to the apartment was quiet. The only words spoken were John occasionally asking directions.

My rental car was in the parking lot. I grimaced when I saw it. It made me miss my Camaro. I knew I'd have to start looking for a new car soon. The insurance settlement had come in a few days before, but it wouldn't compensate for all the hard work Alec, my dad, and I had done restoring my Camaro.

That damn car had so much sentimental value, and now it was gone, just like they were. I had nothing now. I felt empty as I opened the apartment door with my scratched up key. Clearly, the cut nickel I had on the key ring from Aunt Robin had damaged it. It'd been laser cut with a cross in the center of the nickel, and a ring around the edge from which the chain hung by. Aunt Robin had given Alec and me one after Mom and Dad's funeral service.

"Emmett, are you going to be okay, man?" John asked.

"Yeah, I'll be all right. I'm going to pack up some clothes and a few things. I'll just get a hotel room for now."

"Do you want me to hang here for a while? You don't have to be alone."

"No, it's okay. I think I just really need to be alone for a while."

"Okay . . . I'm going to leave you to it then, and get back to check on Sam. Knowing her like I do, and wish you still did, she probably bolted for the house as soon as you left. She's not one for attention and coddling."

My brow scrunched down at his last words. "Damn it," I swore. I thought I was doing her a favor by telling her among our friends. I didn't want to cause her anymore pain. That was a big part of why I was doing this. "Ok . . . uh, thanks for the ride."

"Anytime, man," he replied. "I'll try to come by next week. I've decided to stay here for a while instead of flying back to Alaska, only to turn around and fly back a few months later for the winter."

He walked over to where I was standing and pulled me into one of those awkward guy hugs. "It's gonna be okay, Emmett. It has to be. Just don't give up."

"Thanks. I hope so. I can't take much more of this hell."

"I know. Listen, call me anytime, okay? I'll see ya around," he said as he walked out the door.

I packed up a few things, fed and watered Gage, then took him for a quick walk. When I came back, I tossed a few dog toys in the middle of the room and made sure to leave out a chew bone so he would have something to do while waiting for Sam to come home.

I loaded my stuff into the rental car and drove to a hotel five minutes away. It was close to campus and, since I didn't know how long I'd be staying, made it easier to get to class.

My phone beeped with a text from Riley.

R: Hey man, are you ok?

Me: Yeah. No. I will be. I don't fucking know, man.

R: You want some company? Quinn and I could come by tomorrow.

Me: Nah, John just asked the same thing. I need to be alone for a while, so I can come to terms with Alec's death. Then maybe I can remember Sam again.

R: Ok, man. Just let us know if you change your mind.

Me: Thanks, Ry

R: Anytime, man.

After I checked in and got settled into my hotel room, I sent a text message to Quinn to see how Sam was. I couldn't stop thinking about her.

Me: How is she?

Q: She cried herself to sleep. In your old room.

Me: Damn. I feel like a jerk.

Q: Look, Emmett, we're worried about you. Are you ok?

Before I could reply my phone beeped again.

Q: Emmett, this is Tamron, I grabbed Quinn's phone. Listen, she'll be ok. Just do what you gotta do and get back with her as soon as you remember again.

Me: I'm trying.

I set my phone down on the bedside table and plugged it in to the charger. Then I threw a couple water bottles into the mini fridge. I unpacked my clothes and put my bathroom stuff away. It wasn't until I sat down and took a long sip of whiskey from the mini bar that I even realized I'd poured it. I decided it wasn't time yet to cut back. I'd just left Sam and felt emptier than I'd imagined I would feel.

I knew Alec would be in my dreams again. He always was. The difference now was, I was alone in my grief. I knew Sam missed and mourned Alec too, but, when I was alone, it felt even harder to bear. So I brought the glass to my mouth again and tossed the contents back, relishing in the burn it left behind in my throat.

Pouring another, I closed my eyes and recalled Sam's expression when I told her I was leaving. I felt torn, relieved that I wouldn't have to see her disappointment every time she looked at me, but there was also the part of me that felt like a complete and utter asshole for leaving her.

I found myself pouring another two fingers of whiskey into my glass and just sat there alone, staring at the amber liquid. I tossed that glass back too, and decided to sleep the day, the night, *and* the whiskey off. Lying down and closing my eyes, I let my mind drift off to oblivion.

But that night, unlike so many nights since my accident, I didn't dream of Alec. Instead, I dreamed of beaches and sunsets with tangled bodies and wide-open black skies with shimmering stars, of laughter and teasing smiles.

I dreamed of Sam.

CHAPTER 46

New Realities

Sam

When I woke up the next morning, I went downstairs to get some coffee and saw John sitting at the kitchen island counter.

"Knew you'd be up for some coffee. I turned the Keurig on already," he said.

I smiled over at him. "Thanks, John. I think I have one of those crying headaches. A cup of coffee and glass of water with some ibuprofen is just what I need," I said as I put my coffee cup under the machine's dispenser.

John reached behind him, pulled the bottle of ibuprofen off the counter and slid it across the island to me. "There ya go, Peachy," he said.

I winced when he called me Peachy. It used to make me feel good, and I would laugh at the antics between John and Emmett. But that morning, it made me feel empty. I didn't want John to feel bad, so I just smiled.

"Thanks, John. So, was he okay . . . when y'all went back to the apartment?"

"Not really. He seemed very torn about the whole thing. He wasn't himself. Well, he hasn't really been himself since the accident, but you know what I mean."

"Yeah, I know," I murmured, taking a sip of my coffee. I grabbed my glass of water, and took the ibuprofen, praying to the crying headache gods to let it pass quickly.

Tamron walked into the kitchen with Alison closely behind her.

"You okay, hun?" Alison asked.

"No. I'm not. But I have to be. We were finally in a good place. Just started living together, and moving ahead with our future. Then this damn accident stole him from me. I'll never forget what I felt when I realized he'd forgotten that Alec had died, that look on his face when Ms. Kisner told him. It was like experiencing Alec's death all over again. It hurt my heart to see it. I thought maybe Emmett had recognized Dr. Shaw, because later, when we were home and talking things over, he said there was something very déjà vu about him. But he didn't, and he should have. He was Alec's on-call neurologist at the hospital the night he died."

I set my cup down and swallowed back the ibuprofen with a drink of ice water.

"Then I noticed him drinking that damn whiskey in the evenings, and I found out he'd been dreaming about Alec, that he was alive, but out of reach. There were little things he'd do too, and I'd think he was remembering, but he wasn't. I didn't know what to do. I thought coming here would help. I guess I was wrong."

I could feel the tears filling my eyes. I wiped them away.

"I have to go. I need to get home for Gage. When I woke up last night, I saw a text from Emmett saying he took care of him and had him set up for the night. But he'll need to go for a walk, be fed and given fresh water," I said as I rinsed my coffee cup and poured out the rest of my water.

"Sam, wait," Tamron said.

"Tell me on my way to my car, Tamron. I need to head home while I still feel like I can."

"Okay, Sam. Let's go."

We walked outside and I put my things into my car. "What's up?" I asked her.

"Umm . . . well, I know now isn't really the time to say this, but I know you'll want to know, and I wanted to thank you for your part in talking sense into me the last time y'all were here . . ." she said then halted.

I motioned for her to continue.

"Quinn and I are moving in together. We're going to see how it goes," she said with a smile that reached her eyes.

"That's fantastic!" I squealed. "And you're welcome, even though I didn't really do anything."

"You and Alison talked sense into me, and that was exactly what I needed," she said, hugging me.

"Will you tell Riley and Quinn goodbye for me?" I asked.

Alison came running outside just then, calling, "Wait! Give me a hug, you brat, and remember we're here for you . . . always."

I hugged Alison and Tamron goodbye and left. When I got home, I saw Emmett's rental car in his parking spot and my heart leapt. I hurriedly parked my car and went inside. Emmett was just removing Gage's leash.

"Umm . . . hi, Sam," he said awkwardly while patting Gage's head.

"Hey," I replied.

"I just was stopping by to check on Gage. I didn't know what time you'd be back. I sent you a text to let you know."

"Oh, my battery must have died." I held up my phone and walked over to plug it into the charger.

"Thanks. I appreciate it, and I know Gage does, too."

"You're welcome, Sam."

"Look, I know it's not much, but it's something, and I wanted to let you know and ask you about it, too."

I nodded. "Okay."

"I didn't dream of Alec last night. I dreamed of you and beaches." He told me about his dream, like it was something fictitious.

"That sounds like our trips to Panama City Beach and Hawaii."

"We went to those beaches?" He asked with a shocked expression that hurt like a knife to my heart, because they were memories I cherished deeply.

"Yes," I answered. "You took me to Panama City Beach when we were together the first time, before I knew about Alec being your brother. Then we went to Hawaii to say goodbye to Alec and have his memorial service. It was amazing by the way. We both finally found peace there."

"Hmm. I didn't think I would ever go back to Panama City Beach; it's where my family went when Alec and I were kids. I always thought it would be too painful after our parents died. You know about that right?"

"Yeah, Alec told me," I whispered.

"Oh, okay. I'm sorry. I'm still just trying to wrap my head around the fact that Alec and I have both been with you," he said.

I felt sick to my stomach. He now questioned all of these cherished memories—and that we were together at all—because of the relationship I'd had with Alec.

"It's okay." I murmured. "Just take your time. I don't think we should push your memory anymore. It's clearly stressing you out, and you were right. It was upsetting me. Do you want to just start today over, maybe go and get some breakfast?"

"I'd love to, but I really think I should go."

"Right, of course. I don't know what I was thinking. I'm sorry. I need to drive over to Atlanta and see Mom and Dad anyway."

"All right then, I guess I'll see you around," he said.

"Okay. See you around. Umm, thanks for stopping by for Gage."

He nodded then left, and I leaned against the wall and slid down to the floor. Gage came over and lay down next to me with his head in my lap.

"I know, buddy, I know," I told him, petting his head. "I miss him, too."

CHAPTER 47

One Day At A Time

Sam

I drove over to my mom and dad's house and parked my car in my old spot on the side of the driveway. I felt depressed as I climbed the stairs to the front porch. Opening the screen door and walking through the foyer, I heard my parents talking.

"No, Vance, I don't think we should tell her. It'll just make her feel worse, and he may remember at some point and wouldn't want her to have found out that way." Mom's voice broke.

I wasn't sure what that was about but I knew, if it had to do with Emmett, I didn't want to hear anything about it anyway. Whatever it was didn't matter anymore, because he was lost to me. I needed some happy time with my parents, and that was exactly what I was going to get. This was an *Emmett Free Zone*.

I walked into the kitchen and saw Mom and Dad sitting at the breakfast table, drinking coffee with their newspapers up in front of their faces.

"Hey Mom and Dad," I said.

"Oh hi sweetheart," Mom blurted as she stirred the cup in front of her.

Dad smiled. "Hey, princess."

"Would you like some coffee?" Mom asked.

"Always."

"Maggie, dear, would you mind making me a refill?" Dad asked.

"I'll get it, Mom, while I make my own."

"Thanks, princess," Dad said, handing me his cup.

I made our coffees and sat down at the table with them. Sitting in my old seat felt oddly comforting. I tried not to think of Emmett in his hotel room, alone with a bottle of whiskey. I wished his Aunt Robin would get back from Europe, but she and Kent had extended their trip again. I reminded myself that this was an *Emmett Free Zone,* and I needed to rein in my traitorous thoughts.

"We have a surprise for you, sweetheart," Mom said, smiling.

I glanced toward Dad and saw his excited expression. That's when I heard a car door shut outside. I didn't know who else was coming, so I just sat there and waited.

"Who is it?"

Then the screen door opened, and I heard Tricia call from the front hall.

"Where's my awesome sister?"

I jumped up and ran to her. Tricia wrapped her arms around me and hugged me tight.

"Hey . . . hey, easy, Sam. I missed you, too, but you don't have to cry over me coming down," she teased.

She took the tenseness right out of the room, and I was able to compose myself again.

"So . . . what are we doing today?" Tricia asked.

"I don't know. Anything. Everything!" I squealed.

"Good answer. I already called before I left my dorm, and made appointments for a full spa day," she said.

"Do you have time for coffee before you go?" Dad asked.

Tricia laughed. "Of course, Dad. What kind of daughter do you think I am?"

We sat and laughed at the bantering that always ensued

between our parents. When it was time to leave they walked us outside.

"So, what happened with Emmett?" she asked nervously, as she pulled onto the interstate.

"Not much to tell, really. He had that car accident and forgot me. *Only* me . . . he remembers everyone else. Just not me. Oh, and he forgot Alec died," I whispered at the end.

"Oh my God," she said. "I am so sorry, Sam."

"Yeah, he came home from the hospital, back to normal, everyday life, but apparently, that didn't help as the doctors expected. So now, he's left me and is staying in a hotel near campus."

"Wow. That's a lot to deal with. I'm guessing he didn't take Alec's death well."

"No, he threw up when the hospital's grief counselor told him, so upset, the nurse had to sedate him."

"Well, let's put all that aside for now, spend today relaxing and not thinking about sad things. You need a day of happy, little sis, and I'm going to make sure you have one," she said.

We got to the spa and signed in. They took us back to the massage room right away and started our hot stone massage, leaving us on the table for our facial massages. I could feel the stress and tension of the last month seeping from my body as the masseuse worked her magic.

The relaxing music and aromatherapy candles were so soothing, that I fell asleep. The next thing I knew, Tricia was gently waking me up for our time in the sauna. We sat on the benches, and I leaned my head back against the wall. Wrapped in towels, Tricia and I let the heat engulf us. We didn't even talk, just sat back and closed our eyes.

We ended our day with manicures and pedicures. As we drove back to our parents' house, Tricia shared some words of wisdom.

"Sam, don't give up on Emmett. I think he's just overwhelmed. Remember when you were dealing with the grief of Alec's death? He's going through that all over again, only this time, he feels alone, because the first time, he had you to share the grief with. This time, he doesn't remember you, so he's lost that added strength. You and I both know he loves you, and I think, with time, he'll remember."

"Okay."

It was all I could say. I didn't want to think too deeply about it. I knew she was right about what Emmett was going through. I just hoped she would be right about him remembering what we had.

CHAPTER 48

In Between

Sam

C lasses were starting again. I was in my sophomore year at Auburn. But what should have been the time of my life, was now marred by the grief of Emmett leaving me. Don't get me wrong. I understood it. I just didn't like it and worried he'd never remember me and that I'd lost him forever.

Like a banshee, I cursed fate daily for all that had happened to us. While I loved Alec, and Emmett, and cherished the time I had been lucky enough to share with them. I cursed fate yet again for making them brothers, and for taking Alec away from us. And I cursed fate for a third time, for Emmett's car accident, for making him forget me, but mostly for making him forget Alec had died. It was cruel that he should go through that loss and grief all over again. That he was doing it alone tore at my heart every minute of the day.

My last class on Monday was English Lit. It saddened me to walk into the room, picturing Alec there waiting for me to arrive. He'd loved English Lit. That class was even more unbearable because I couldn't talk to Emmett about it. If there was anyone else on the planet who would know how hard this was and understand it, it was Emmett. I felt empty without him.

I sat in the back of the class, not wanting to engage with

anyone. There was only one other guy sitting back there with me. He was cute . . . I could appreciate that. But that was as far as it went.

Until he leaned over and cleared his throat. "Hi, my name is Aiden Thompson."

"Hi. I'm, um, Sam Lang," I murmured.

"Well it's nice to meet you *Um Sam Lang,*" he teased.

I chuckled. "Sorry, I only had a half cup of coffee this morning, and I'm just not feeling class today."

"It's okay. I haven't had my orange Tic Tacs yet either," he said with a serious expression that made me break out into laughter. He looked affronted. "What? Don't you eat Tic Tacs? Everyone loves Tic Tacs. It's as American as apple pie."

"Sorry, you just surprised me when you said it. Yes, I love orange Tic Tacs," I said, shaking my head.

The professor walked in and class fell silent. In the middle of the lecture, Aiden passed me a note when the professor wasn't looking. I opened it to see what he wrote.

> Umm Sam Lang,
>
> Would you like to get some coffee after class so you can be just Sam Lang again after your brain wakes up?
>
> Mark an X for YES or an X for YES.
>
> Sorry NO isn't an option.
>
> :-) Aiden

I looked at him and his cute, expectant smile and nodded. What could a cup of coffee hurt? I didn't feel like being alone, and he provided pretty damn good comic relief at a time when I desperately needed it.

When class was over and we had our syllabus, I shoved it

and Aiden's note into my bag. Following him out of the classroom, we headed to the parking lot for our cars. It turned out we were parked in the same lot. When we arrived at Starbucks, I was happy. I could practically taste the Salted Caramel Mocha Latte. I had so many favorites, sometimes it was hard to decide, but the end result was always the same—happy.

Aiden was parked and out of his car before me. He walked over to open my car door and waited for me. What a nice guy.

"Thanks, Aiden," I said as I stepped out of my car.

"You're welcome," he replied.

As we walked inside, I felt his hand at the small of my back. After I ordered my latte, I waited at the other end of the counter for the barista to make it. She shook the salted caramel on top of the whip cream and caramel syrup, making my mouth water.

Aiden cleared his throat next to me. "So, Starbucks was a good call I take it."

"Yeah, I am kind of a caffeine addict."

He laughed. "Don't worry Umm Sam, so am I."

I smacked his shoulder. "Are you ever going to stop teasing me about that?"

"Hmm, that would be a yes and a no. Yes, for as soon as you drink said needed coffee, and no, for when I feel like teasing you in class Wednesday morning," he said with a smirk.

He was fun to be around, and his brand of humor was exactly what the doctor ordered.

"Well, Aiden Thompson, I'm glad we met. It's nice to have someone around who understands my addiction." I giggled.

He smiled, and I could see the hopefulness in his eyes. I knew I'd need to be clear from the start that I wasn't looking for a boyfriend. There was no way that was happening. I was in love with Emmett, and that wasn't going to change. Ever. I figured I could work it into a conversation. I didn't want to lead him on. We sat outside at one of their little tables.

"So, tell me about yourself, Sam."

"Well, now that I'm just Sam, I'd be happy to," I joked.

Continuing in a more serious tone, I said, "There really isn't much to tell. I'm studying to be a psychologist. I've always wanted to help people. I'd also like to be an advocate for people with mental illnesses. I want the world to stop looking down on them and recognize that it's as valid as any other disease out there."

"That's great, Sam," Aiden replied. "You have a good heart."

I smiled, "Thanks, what about you?"

"Oh, me? Well, I don't really know yet. My dad wants me to be a surgeon like him, but it's not my thing. So, I'm going here to spite him, and be closer to my mom. They're divorced. My mom is the most caring person in the world. She's never said a mean thing to anyone."

"Did you grow up around here?" I asked.

"Sort of. I spent most of my childhood floating between Auburn and Maryland. Mom lives here, so I'm staying with her while in school. Dad lives in Maryland, and works at John Hopkins in Baltimore."

"I'm sorry. That sounds stressful, Aiden."

"Eh, it's okay. Anyway, as for what I'm going to school for . . . my MR degree," he finished.

"I thought you said you didn't know what you were going for."

"Well that's true, I did say that, and I don't know, but I may as well work on my MR degree while I'm here. You know, MR, as in mister, as in looking for my Mrs. Right," he chortled.

I shook my head, laughing with him.

"Oh my God, Aiden. You're too much." I laughed again.

"Tell me about you, Sam. I want to know about you as a person." He winked.

"Oh. Well, I'm kind of in a relationship . . . sort of," I answered.

His eyes grew wide as his brow scrunched together in confusion.

"We're just taking a break." I sighed. "Look, it's really a long, sad story, and I don't want to get into it right now."

"It's okay. We don't have to talk about it."

"Thanks. I'm not looking for another relationship now, that's for sure. So if that's what you're after, we may as well stop right here before anyone gets hurt. I'm broken Aiden. My heart's taken, and that'll never change." I dropped my eyes to my lap.

He reached across the table and gently lifted my chin up so my eyes had nowhere else to look but at him. "That's not what I'm after, Sam. I mean, you're absolutely gorgeous, but if you only want to be friends, that's okay with me. Let's just be friends."

I smiled at him. "I'd like that very much."

"Maybe someday, you'll tell me this long, sad story of how you're kind of in a relationship. I have to admit, even taking a relationship break, that's a new one for me."

"Yeah, maybe someday," I said. "Look, Aiden, I'm gonna go. I want to stop by my apartment and check on my dog. I'll see you in class on Wednesday." I got up and slung my backpack over my shoulder.

"Okay, Sam, see you Wednesday."

From that point on, Aiden and I had Starbucks together after class every Monday and Wednesday. He took my mind off Emmett, and that was what I needed, because when I wasn't hanging out with Aiden, I was sad about Emmett leaving me and worried I'd lost him forever.

He was so funny and full of life. It was a relief just being around him. On Tuesdays, I couldn't wait for Wednesday to get a good dose of *Aiden Comic Relief.*

CHAPTER 49
As Days Go By

Sam

A month had passed since Emmett had left, but I was getting by pretty well. I still had my moments when reality would smack me upside the head and say, "He's gone!" I'd inevitably break down in the ladies' room or while sitting in my car at a stoplight. It was never a nice reality to face. But I had to face it . . . repeatedly. Fate was a cruel bitch, and I'd had enough of her games, constantly toying in our lives. I wondered many times if fate was a real, breathing, conniving thing. I mean, it had to be with the level of turmoil it had caused Alec, Emmett, and me.

I thought about Emmett every minute of the day, wondering how he was coping with Alec's death, how he was he able to get by each day dealing with it alone. We'd barely survived and recovered from Alec's death when we were together. I couldn't imagine facing that without Emmett by my side.

I wanted to call him. It was a battle I won every day to *not* call and check up on him. I knew he had to be suffering, but also that I couldn't help him. Otherwise he would have stayed. He wouldn't have walked out of my life and left me alone. All of our friends were great about checking on me. They said Emmett was hanging in there when I'd ask about him. Emmett deserved better than just 'hanging in there' though. He needed his life back. He needed me, and I needed him.

I was meeting Aiden for a study-lunch for an exam we had coming up in English Lit. When I pulled up to the restaurant, I saw his sporty, little car parked in the back. He got out when he saw me. He really was cute, and I tried to think of who I could set him up with, but all of my friends were already in relationships.

"Hey, Sam!"

"Hey, Aiden. Ready for a mad study-lunch combo?"

"Yup. Let's go get a table."

We walked inside the bistro and waited to be seated. The hostess came pretty quickly to lead us to our table. As we turned the corner, I felt Aiden's hand at the small of my back, and tingles spread across my limbs. I was so startled by it, that I tripped, causing Aiden to catch me in his arms.

"Oh! Sam, are you okay?" he asked as he helped set me straight on my feet.

"Yes, I'm fine. Sorry. Trippy feet is all," I murmured, embarrassed.

We sat down across from each other in the booth, and I struggled to look anywhere but directly at him. I needed to regain my composure.

"Alexis will be your waitress this afternoon. Can I get your drink order to start with?" she asked us.

"Yeah, I'll have a Coke," I said.

"An iced tea, please," Aiden replied.

She gave him a flirty smile. "Would you like that sweet or unsweetened, sir?"

"Oh sorry, I'd like that sweet. I need all the sugar I can get," he said, winking at me.

I laughed. I couldn't help it. I loved it. Aiden was constantly making me laugh and have happy, relieving moments. The hostess shook her head with a giggle and walked away.

"So," Aiden said.

I peered over my menu and waited for him to continue.

"There's a frat party on Saturday night. You wanna go? We can flip a coin for designated driver." He smiled.

"Okay. Sounds fun. But why don't we take a cab so we can both have a drink," I suggested.

He winked. "Sounds like a plan, Sam."

The waitress came and took our order. We discussed the English Lit exam study guide while we ate.

"I think we're both about as prepared for this exam as we're gonna get," I said.

"Yeah, it'll be cake."

"What time should we meet Saturday?"

"I'll have a cab pick you up at seven pm."

"Ok, see you Saturday, Aiden," I said, waving goodbye.

"Saturday it is," he said, smiling.

He had to be one of the most carefree people I'd ever met. I just hoped he really realized I meant it when I said we needed to just be friends. The occasional touches here and there had me worried. I drove home and parked. I couldn't tear my gaze away from Emmett's empty parking spot. The lightness I felt at Aiden's humor was instantly gone, and my heavy heart returned.

I walked into my apartment, and Gage met me at the door, wagging his tail.

"You want to go for a walk, buddy?" He started jumping around with excitement when I grabbed his harness and leash. I hooked him up, and put a couple poopie-bags into my jeans pocket. I grabbed my ear buds off the counter on my way out. I fished the wire down the front of my shirt and stuffed one of the buds in my ear, leaving the other one hanging so I could still hear traffic. I turned on my playlist and, with music in my ear, lost myself in my walk with Gage.

We walked down to the dog park where I let him off his leash to run and play. I saw a text come in from Heather.

H: Hey girl, how ya doing?

Me: I'm good. At the dog park with Gage.

H: Cool. You coming to the frat party Sat night?

Me: Yeah. Aiden asked me.

H: Whoa. You're hanging out with that dude a lot. Anything I should know?

Me: No. We're just friends. It's all good. He makes me forget the pain sometimes, and I kinda need that.

H: No judging. You can do what you want to, but . . . if you're so quick to defend your friendship with him, maybe you should look a little deeper at your feelings. There could be something meaningful there.

Me: No. Really, he's just a friend who makes me laugh.

H: Ok. So I'll see you at the party then?

Me: Yup. See you Sat.

Heather was perceptive. But she was wrong this time. I only had room in my heart for Emmett. Well, and Alec, but he had a corner that was all his and always would be. Emmett understood and was okay with that. I sure as hell didn't have room in my heart for another guy. While Aiden was attractive, he wasn't my Emmett. My eyes started to fill with tears as I thought about Emmett again. It was that way most of the time. It was like he'd taken a piece of my soul with him when he left.

I called Gage over and hooked his leash back up then walked us back home. I couldn't shake Emmett from my mind. I hoped, wherever he was, that he was okay. I curled up and watched a movie with a spoonful of mint chocolate chip ice cream. After waking up on the couch, I got up and turned the TV off, went into the bedroom and pulled my PJs on before dropping into bed. With tears in my eyes, I stared at the empty space where Emmett should have been and dozed off.

I'd just finished getting ready for the party when I heard a horn honking out front of my apartment building. I grabbed my compact and lip-gloss and stuffed them in my jeans pockets along with a key to my apartment and my phone.

Locking the door behind me, I turned around to see Aiden, sitting in a cab, waiting for me. I ran over and got in. The driver took off to the address Aiden gave him.

"You look fantastic, Sam," he said.

"Thanks. You, too," I replied.

We arrived at the party, and it was an event to behold. There were cars parked everywhere in the street, and even a couple almost up in the front yard. The music was thumping, and there were people standing inside and outside of the house. It was a complete contrast to the first frat party I'd been to the night I met Emmett. Thoughts of him started to turn my mood somber, so I pushed them right out of my head. Tonight was supposed to be fun, and that was what I was going to do. Have fun.

"You really do look fantastic, Sam," Aiden said, leading me into the house.

"Thanks, Aiden. Um, look, I really want to be sure you understand I meant it when I said we could only be friends."

"Sam, when are you going to open up about what this guy's done to you?" he whispered.

"I'm not. I told you, it's not up for discussion. It's a long, complicated story anyway. Besides, we're at a party. Let's have some fun."

"Yeah. Okay," he murmured.

We made our way through the house to the kitchen where Aiden grabbed us each a beer. They were playing beer pong in the dining room, but we passed through to the back so we could go outside. There were people dancing in the grass and lying on lounge chairs by the pool.

A couple was in a kissing embrace in the pool. The DJ started a new song when the last one finished, and even more people started dancing. Aiden and I danced our hearts out. After consuming a few more beers, we ended up sitting next to each other in lounges by the pool to catch our breath.

"I think I'm ready to go home, Aiden."

"Okay, I'll call a cab to come pick us up."

It was a fun night, but I was exhausted and ready for an eight-hour nap. Good thing it was night and well past my bedtime. I remember thinking that, for once I would just pass-out and not have to cry myself to sleep like every other night. Maybe there was something to Emmett and his turn to whiskey after all. I'd file that away for evaluation on another day.

We took a cab to my apartment building first. When the cab stopped in the no-parking zone, Aiden got out and opened my door for me. I held onto his hand as I climbed out and felt those now familiar tingles spread up my wrist and arm. I think Aiden felt it, too. He startled before giving my hand a light squeeze as I stood to my feet.

We got to my door and stood there a minute while I reached into my jeans pocket, pulling my lip gloss and compact out to get to my key.

"Here it is," I said, giggling as I held my key up in the air.

"Good thing. For a moment there I thought I was gonna have to take you home with me," Aiden taunted.

I glanced up at him. He was staring at me intensely.

No, please don't do this. Don't ruin our friendship.

I broke the moment by turning back toward my front door. The heel of my boot caught on the uneven pavement where the step began and I dropped my stuff and key and stumbled toward the ground. Aiden caught me at the last second before I hit the pavement.

"You know, we really have to work on your walking skills. It's a good thing my arms are always around to save you," he teased.

"Sorry. It's that damn step. I'm going to have to call maintenance and report it. Maybe they can level it out somehow."

As he stood me up straight, my face was an inch from his. My nerves were shot, and I couldn't move. I continued to stare at him as he stared back. Our lips were so close, I could smell the orange Tic Tacs on his breath. He leaned into me, and our lips touched as our breathing sped up. Closing his mouth over mine, his hand wove into the back of my hair, and I reveled in the feel of affection . . . until I began to panic. I pulled away and stepped back. With my hands fidgeting, I hurried to unlock my door then stepped inside.

"I'm . . . I'm sorry, Aiden. That shouldn't have happened," I blurted.

"I'm not sorry," he said as he licked his lips and backed away, still staring at me.

I watched as he turned around and walked over to where the cab was parked, its engine still running. He got in and the car drove away. I backed up slowly, closed and locked the door, leaning back against it as I sank down to the floor. Gage came over and lay down at my side. I closed my eyes and wondered how the hell I was going to save our friendship after that.

CHAPTER 50

Mine

Emmett

It had been over a month since I left Sam. I felt incomplete. But I'd also stopped having dreams of Alec. I only dreamed of Sam. When I woke up, I was no longer gasping for air at Alec being out of reach. Instead, I was reaching across the bed for Sam . . . only to find an empty space.

The morning I realized I wasn't dreaming about her, but rather remembering her, felt like a punch to my gut. Then it all hit me.

Oh God, what had I done? I was in a panic about the time I'd spent away from her.

"Fuck!" I slammed my toothbrush down on the bathroom vanity. "What if she moved on without me? Got tired of hurting and decided to push the pain away with some other guy? What if she no longer loved me?" I rambled aloud to myself.

I hoped I wasn't too late.

I'd seen her in passing one day after class at Auburn on my way to the cafeteria. I decided to wait in that spot and ask if I could see her again. I was afraid to go to the apartment. I didn't know what I would do if she had some other guy there.

I sat on the ground beneath a big weeping willow where I had a view of the walkway. I put my ear buds in and opened the iTunes app on my phone. I was listening to "Run" by Snow

Patrol when I saw her. She was laughing and walking with a guy. *Fuck me.* My worst fear had come true. She'd moved on. Well, fuck that. She was mine, and I wasn't about to let some pansy ass, college pretty boy, asshat take my Peach.

As she walked closer, her beautiful smile widened as she laughed with him. Then she looked up and caught me staring at her. The coffee mug in her hand slipped from her grip, hitting the ground and shattering into pieces on the walkway beneath her. She never even looked down at it.

Her gaze remained locked on me. Good. Her cute little ass was mine, and I'd be damned if anyone else was going to have her, the *too-close-to-her asshat* especially. I tried to convey in my expression, my exclusive ownership of her heart, and as she wasn't able to break her gaze away, I think I succeeded.

I stood up and brushed my jeans off. I didn't have any books with me, just my phone, wallet, and the keys in my pocket. I walked over to her. She stood frozen in place. The asshat was talking to her, but she wasn't answering him. I could tell he was getting frustrated. Good. Fucker was clearly trying to take my Peach.

I stopped in front of her, as said asshat stood and pursed his lips, his eyebrows scrunching together, looking back and forth between Peach and me like he was watching a tennis match. I would have knocked him on his ass if he even said the wrong thing. He didn't know what he was encroaching upon.

"Hey, Peach," I said with a forced smile.

"Emmett," she whispered. It was one word. Just my name, but it held the weight of everything I'd dreamed about her over the past month.

"You . . . you've remembered. Haven't you?" she tentatively asked.

I knew she was afraid of the answer, so I relieved her anxiety immediately.

"I remember everything."

Tears welled in her eyes, so I gestured to the asshat.

"Why don't you take a walk, kid? My *girlfriend* and I have some things to discuss."

He stared at her, his eyes widening with shock when I referred to her as my girlfriend. Good. Fuck him. *Move along asshat.*

"It's okay, Aiden. I'll . . . see you in class on Wednesday," she murmured.

"Okay, Sam," the asshat said as he turned, and strode off in the opposite direction. I didn't care where, as long as it was out of my Peach's life.

I wiped the disgusted look off my face. I knew Sam. She was a loyal friend. I didn't want to upset her by offending the asshat any more than I already had. I had enough to fix as it was.

"Peach, do you have any more classes, or can we go somewhere to talk?"

"No, I'm done for the day. I have a heavier schedule on Tuesdays and Thursdays. Mondays, Wednesdays, and Fridays aren't bad. I'm done before lunch," she rambled like her mind was on autopilot.

"Great. Do you want to go grab lunch somewhere?"

"No. I'd rather we just go home. I need to let Gage out anyway."

"Okay, let's go. Did you drive? I can meet you there."

She stood there, stunned, with her lips slightly parted. Her eyes had yet to stray away from mine. It was like she couldn't believe I was real.

"Yeah, my car's in the parking lot. I'll, uh, see you soon," she replied, walking backward like she was afraid to look away from me.

I wanted to sweep her into my arms and kiss her right then and there, but I refrained. There would be time for that later. There would be a lifetime of that. I knew this because, when I told her I remembered everything, I meant it. I remembered how truly and deeply we loved each other. I remembered the engagement ring I'd had made for her, too.

When I pulled in behind her at our apartment building, I parked in my old spot. I opened her car door after she pulled in and shifted her car into park.

"Hey Peach."

She smiled up at me as she stepped out. "Hi."

We walked into the apartment, and she set her bag of books and purse down. I dropped my keys on the counter in the same spot I'd tossed them countless times before. She looked from my keys on the counter, to me and back at my keys again, with a small smile on her face.

"You do remember," she breathed.

"Yes, Peach," I said, walking slowly toward her. "I do."

I knew I was probably looking at her like I wanted to devour her, because that's exactly what I wanted to do. My body hungered for hers. At that moment, I didn't want to talk. I wanted to touch, kiss, and feel. I wanted to make love to her.

I pulled her to me and tilted her mouth up to mine, taking possession and sending her all of the passion I felt and held inside me all this time without even knowing it. She wrapped her arms around me and ran her fingers up and down my back. I swooped her up into my arms and kissed her heatedly as I carried her to our bedroom. When I placed her on our bed, I knelt down above her and ran my fingers through her hair.

"I love you, Peach," I whispered.

"I love you too, Emmett," she said, taking my mouth with hers again.

We lost ourselves to our passion as it overtook us. She consumed every part of me, until I wasn't sure where I stopped and she began.

CHAPTER 51
A Bright New Day

Emmett

I woke up and stretched my arm out to the side and felt Sam there, with me, sleeping. I smiled so big, that it almost hurt my cheeks. Finally, we were together again, and I had my memory back. I thought about Alec. I thought about what I had gone through while my memory was gone. At least I had peace about it again. I would always miss him, but I could make it through my days without all the anger I'd felt, and without hitting the whiskey at night to get some semblance of sleep.

I rolled over to my side and watched Sam sleeping. God, I'd missed this without even realizing what it was, but now I knew. This was the emptiness I felt each morning. I felt like I'd come home. I had to make sure she knew what she meant to me. I would spend forever making her happy, so she could forget what we'd been through. In that happiness, I knew I would find happiness too, and hopefully could forget the feelings of pain and loss. I wished peace for both of us.

I ran my fingers through her hair and gently down the side of her face. Her eyes began to flutter awake, and she turned her head toward me. Her lips turned up into a beautiful smile.

"Hi."

"Hi Peach," I replied. "Did you sleep well?"

She stretched her arms up. "Yeah, I slept better than I have in a long time."

"Me, too." I leaned over and kissed her forehead. "Let's get some coffee, my little caffeine junkie."

She smiled and nodded. "Sounds good."

She sat up and the covers fell from her chest. I thought briefly about pulling her back down and postponing the coffee, but decided there would be time for that later. I wanted to get my things from the hotel and move back home where I belonged. Plus, Gage was now sitting at the foot of the bed, whimpering to go outside.

I nodded toward the dog. "I'll take him out while you get the coffee going."

"Deal," she replied.

I put Gage's harness on. She'd bought a new red one, and I could see why; it was a good color on him. Hooking his leash to the harness, I slipped on my shoes and unlocked the front door. We walked outside, and Gage did his business. I decided to take him for a short walk around the apartment complex. When we returned and walked through the front door, I saw her texting on her phone. She set her phone down on the counter and looked up at me. I cocked an eyebrow in question.

"The girls. I couldn't wait to tell them you remembered and came home. They're going to tell the guys." She smiled.

"Cool."

She walked over and hugged me hard. "I just needed to feel you again, to know you're real and actually here, and not some cruel figment of my imagination. It feels good having you home again."

"Yeah, it feels good to me, too. I love you, Peach. I just can't say it enough. I'm so sorry for what I put you through."

"Don't say that, Emmett. You didn't put me through anything. We were both victims of a cruel twist of fate that took your memory from you. I was constantly thinking about you mourning Alec alone, and it made me sick to my stomach. I was so worried about you."

"Oh God, that was hard. But when I left you, I stopped dreaming of Alec, and started dreaming of you. The moment I remembered you was one of the best and worst of my life. I was afraid I was too late, afraid that you'd moved on. Then, when I was waiting for you at school yesterday, I saw you with that . . . guy. I felt my worst fears had come true," I told her.

"Oh, Aiden? No need to worry. He's just a friend. I told him right away I wasn't interested in anything more. He's actually pretty cool. I think you'd like him. He's very funny."

I breathed a sigh of relief. "That's good to hear. No way I could handle someone trying to steal you away from me. Especially right now."

She walked over to the Keurig and made herself a cup of coffee. Her smile as she tasted her first sip was beautiful. Content. Happy. It made me feel good.

"Hey Peach, I have an errand to run, and I want to pick up my stuff from the hotel. Do you want to meet back here after class this afternoon? I only have one class this morning," I said.

"Yeah. Sounds good."

I dressed in a pair of jeans I'd left behind. It was a good thing I only took one suitcase of clothes when I left, or I'd be wearing the same clothes as yesterday. Pulling a t-shirt over my head, I walked into the bathroom and brushed my teeth. I ran a comb through my hair, Sam liked it messy, and that was fine by me; less time in the bathroom.

I walked out of our bedroom and saw her flipping through the newspaper ads. She looked up at me and gave me a small wave. Something was off about it though.

"What's wrong?" I asked.

"I'm just worried. I mean, the last time you went to run errands, you ended up in the hospital and had forgotten me completely. What if something else happens? I can't go through that again." She ended on a sob.

"Nothing will happen, Peach. And if, for some crazy reason, it did, we'd overcome it. We always do. Please don't worry."

"That's easier said than done, Emmett."

I sighed. "I know, but it's not like I can stay here forever. I still have to live life."

She stood up and wrapped her arms around my waist, hugging me to her. "Well, I can think of things we can do to pass the time while you stay here forever." Her eyes sparkled with mischief.

I leaned my head down and captured her lips with mine. Smacking her on her cute little behind, I stepped back toward the front door. "I gotta go. I'll be back soon."

"I love you. Be safe," she called.

"I will. Love you, too, Peach."

I got in my rental and drove to the hotel. As I packed up my things, I threw the empty and half-full whiskey bottles in the trash. I couldn't imagine what the housekeepers must think of me always throwing away empty whiskey bottles. Whatever . . . that was done.

After I loaded up the car with my things, I went to the front desk to check out. Getting in my car, I fought the urge to drive back to the apartment. She was probably in the shower and I'd just make her late for class. I headed to the jeweler instead, to pick up the engagement ring I ordered what felt like a lifetime ago.

I wasn't sure when I was going to ask her, but I just wanted it with me, so it was ready when the time was right. I didn't want that time to come and not be prepared for it.

I smiled knowing she was going to be my wife. She was going to be my forever.

CHAPTER 52

Once Something Is Said, It Can't Be Unsaid

Sam

E mmett had been home for a couple months. Everything was great and back to normal. We argued, we loved, we both spent time trying to forget the hell fate, and our choices had put us through. One day while he was gone, I actually went to the library and researched fate. It basically came down to whether one believed in it or not. I had a hard time not believing in something that had so cruelly toyed with our lives. I still cursed fate for all it had put us through.

I'd been feeling sick for a few days and meant to get more rest, but every night we got caught up in a movie or each other. I took vitamins and drank a lot of water, determined to shake whatever it was.

I locked up the apartment and drove to school. After I parked, I pulled my phone out to call my sister.

"Hey, Tricia, it's me. I just wanted to see if you're coming home next week for Dad's birthday. I miss you. Call me back. Love you. Bye."

My phone chirped a minute later as I was getting my backpack out of the backseat. I leaned against my car and saw it was from Tricia.

T: Yeah, I'll be there. I'm heading into class right now, so I can't talk. Miss you, too.

Me: OXOX

Good, I thought. I'd call and let Mom know. So far, it would be Mom and Dad, Tricia, Emmett, and me. I loved family gatherings.

As I walked toward the buildings, I saw Aiden sitting in his car. I waved, but he just sat there, his hands rubbing the back of his neck. Usually he got out and met me at the walkway. I wondered if something was wrong, so I walked over and tapped on the driver's window. He looked up, and his mouth, at first in a hard line, turned up into a smile when he saw me. He got out and slung his backpack over his shoulder.

"Hey, Sam. What's up?" he asked.

"Not much. I was wondering the same about you. Everything okay? You looked upset."

"Nah, I'm okay. Just tired. I didn't sleep well last night," he evaded.

I knew that wasn't all of it. There was something he wasn't telling me. I hoped he would confide in me. I was worried for my usually carefree friend. He'd been there for me, and would have listened had I chosen to tell him what was going on with Emmett. It wasn't his fault I couldn't bring myself to talk about it.

"Let's go, or we'll be late," he urged.

I looked at my watch and back up at him, nodding as we took off running for class. We reached the door just as our professor was walking over to lock it. He didn't permit interruptions during instructional time. Giving us a disapproving glance, he stepped back and let us pass. We walked to the back of the classroom and took our seats.

I caught Aiden staring down at his blank notebook a couple times, so I passed him a note when the professor's back was turned.

*After our last class, Starbucks,
and you're coming clean about
what's bothering you.
No, there isn't a No option.*

He looked over at me and smiled with a nod.

Our professor droned on about the chapter we were studying. And with as sick as I felt, I was grateful when he said class time was over for the day. As he stood to leave, I reached out and squeezed his hand.

"I'll always be here for you."

His eyes widened briefly before his cheeks relaxed into a soft smile. "I know Sam. Thanks."

The rest of my day seemed to crawl at a snail's pace, but I somehow made it to the end of my last class. I met Aiden at the walkway, and we strolled back to our cars together before he followed me over to Starbucks. We placed our order, his treat, and sat down with our lattes and scones. I looked up and saw him staring at me.

"Okay, lay it on me. Whatever is bothering you, don't think, just spill the beans. You shouldn't keep it to yourself. You'll feel better when you get it off your chest," I told him with a stern voice.

He looked at me, the corners of his mouth tipped slightly down, his eyes focused on his coffee cup. His physical reaction alarmed me. I twisted my bracelet in my lap as I waited for him to open up to me. My normally funny, upbeat friend had something eating away at him. If someone had hurt him, I was going to give him or her a piece of my mind, for sure.

"Okay. You really want to know?"

"Yes, of course I do. What kind of friend would I be if I didn't?"

"I'm in love with a girl," he murmured.

I smiled as profound relief swept over me. "That's fantastic!" I squealed.

His pained expression remained.

"What's wrong?"

"She's in love with someone else." He slumped back in his chair.

"Oh. Damn, I'm sorry, Aiden," I said. "Do you know that for sure?"

He looked down at his scone and latte and nodded. "Yeah. It's painfully clear."

"Oh God, Aiden. I don't know what to say except how sorry I am. She doesn't know what she's missing. You're a great catch. But, if she's in love with someone else, then you need to try and move on. You deserve happiness."

"Don't you think I've tried?" he hissed.

"Well, I don't know, Aiden. Who is she? Do I know her?"

"Yeah," he said. "You know her." He looked up to the sky and sighed before turning his gaze back on me.

"Well, who then?"

"You, Sam. I'm in love with you," he whispered.

My mouth fell open and my heart sank. I didn't know what to say. He'd stunned me silent. A part of me feared this would happen, but I'd needed his positive friendship and laughter in my life. He couldn't be in love with me. I'd told him since day one that we could only be friends. I was in love with Emmett. Looking at him sitting there, his leg bouncing, and his eyes downcast, my stomach knotted up for what this would mean for our friendship. I wasn't sure we could recover from this revelation.

"Look, Sam, I tried not to, but I love everything about you. You're the highlight of my day. I don't even give a shit about the rest of the week, just the days I get to see you. English Lit and our coffee dates are my favorite parts of the week. I think about you all the time, and even as much as I hate Emmett being back in your life, I'm happy for you, because I can see how happy you are now that he's returned."

"I don't know what to say," I whispered.

"There's nothing to say. It is what it is, and I'll have to get over it. But I need some time. I don't think I can keep spending time with you out of class. It's gonna suck as it is when I see you there. I know I'll still crave those times, but knowing I can never have you outweighs that more and more every day." He stood up and leaned over, giving me a lingering kiss on my forehead. "It's not your fault, Sam, so don't beat yourself up over this. You were clear from the beginning that your heart was taken. I guess we just can't help who we fall in love with."

He turned and walked out. My eyes filled with tears. I picked up our plates and cups and threw them in the trash. Walking out to my car, I kept picturing his face and hearing his last words to me.

CHAPTER 53

I Didn't Expect That

Emmett

S am had been acting funny for the last few days. I knew she hadn't been feeling well for a couple weeks. She was usually happy when she came back from her English Lit class, which I suspected had to do with the asshat. I know she liked him only as a friend, but I couldn't shake the feeling that he was after more than her friendship. I decided to get to the bottom of the change in her mood. She came out of the bedroom dressed in shorts and a tank top, with her hair wrapped up in a towel. I handed her a cup of hot chai tea.

"Hey, Peach," I said. "How're you feeling this morning?"

"I'm okay. Just didn't sleep well last night, I guess. I don't feel rested enough."

"So, did something happen at school to upset you? Usually you come home happy on English Lit days. You're home earlier than you used to be, too. Did you stop having coffee with Aiden after class?"

"Umm, yeah. We aren't really hanging out anymore," she answered.

The relieved feeling I should've had wasn't there. Instead, I was sad at her sullen expression. Clearly, his friendship meant more to her than I'd realized.

"I'm sorry, Peach. I know you really liked him." I walked over to where she was standing, and pulled her into my arms.

"It's okay. He just has a lot going on right now and needs to focus," she replied.

"All right," I said. "Well, how about we eat an early dinner and call your mom in case she needs anything for your dad's birthday dinner tomorrow?"

"Good idea," She'd just walked over to the sink to rinse her cup out when she yelped and grabbed her belly. I ran over and pulled her to me. Looking her over quickly and not seeing any blood, I breathed a sigh of relief.

"Are you okay?"

"No, I'm having really bad cramps. It hurts."

I picked her up in my arms and carried her over to the couch. Setting her down, I touched her forehead, but she didn't feel hot. She continued to moan and hold her midsection. I didn't know what to do.

"What do you need? Is there anything I can get you?"

"I have to go to the bathroom. I'll be right back," she said as she got up, still holding her stomach and disappeared behind the bathroom door.

I pulled my iPhone out and Googled urgent care clinics to see where the closest one was. I found one off of Opelika Rd.

When I went in the bathroom to check on her, she was rinsing her shorts out in the bathtub, and the water was running red. I figured it was her period and she would be all right.

"I'm fine, Emmett. My period finally started. I've been pretty stressed lately and sometimes that makes it late. But it came on so suddenly." She shook her head.

"Okay. Well, let me know if you need anything," I told her.

Walking out, I went into the kitchen and grabbed the heating pad and a couple ibuprofen. I filled a cup with ice water and walked over just as she sat down on the couch again.

I handed her the ibuprofen and water and set the heating pad on the couch beside her then plugged it in. I sat down and pulled her feet into my lap. Rubbing them, I looked over at her as she gingerly placed the heating pad on her abdomen.

"So since we're staying in, is there anything you want to get caught up on TV or a movie you want to watch?" I asked.

"Yeah, I'm a few episodes behind on *The Vampire Diaries* if you don't mind watching it," she answered.

"It's okay. I'll admit, I'm kinda wondering what's gonna happen with Damon and Elena," I said with a smirk. I knew she liked Damon's bad-boy character.

She smiled as I turned the TV on and selected the DVR. I chose the first of three recordings and settled in for the show. We were watching a scene where the witch, Bonnie, was trying to cast a spell, when Sam shrieked, dropped her water, and doubled over in pain.

"Cramps getting worse?" I asked her.

"Yeah, it was a bad one," she clenched her fists. "I need to go to the bathroom again."

I helped her up and to the bathroom. While she was in there, I waited by the door in case she needed anything. I heard the toilet flush and the water in the sink run. She opened the door looking really pale.

"I think I need to see a doctor, Emmett," she said. "There was a lot of blood that time, even more than the first. That's not normal for me. I think something's wrong."

"Okay, there's an urgent care clinic over off Opelika Rd. We can go there or to the ER if you think that would be better. Are you ready now or do you need a few minutes?"

"Let's just go to the ER. The clinic would probably send me there anyway. I'm gonna wash off and change my clothes. I need to throw these into the washing machine before we leave or they'll be ruined." She winced in pain.

"You take your shower and I'll get the wash going. Don't worry about it."

She went into the bedroom, and I grabbed her clothes and headed for the laundry closet. As I started the washing machine, I worried about her. I'd never really paid much attention to a girl's cramps before Sam, so I didn't know what was normal and what wasn't.

I took Gage outside for a quick walk then hurried back inside. As I was undoing his harness, Sam came out of the bedroom with her wet hair swept up in a ponytail and wearing a pair of Falcons pajama pants and a black sweatshirt.

"Ok, let's go," she said.

I drove her to the emergency room, and when we arrived, she looked relieved. Hopefully, they'd be able to give her something for the pain. I'd never had to worry about her medically. She was very healthy. Her only real vice was having a drink socially. I parked the car and helped her inside. I signed her in at the front desk and took the clipboard over and handed it to Sam.

"Here ya go, Peach. We need to fill this form out and give her your driver's license and health insurance card. Do you want me to fill it out for you?"

"No, I can do it," she said as she dug out her wallet.

I startled when she screamed with pain. The nurse at the desk ran over behind me to check on her.

"Hey, hey, easy. Come here, Peach. Lean onto me."

I rubbed my hand up and down her back as she shivered in my arms.

"We'll call her back soon. There's only one other patient ahead of you," the nurse said.

"Okay, thanks, ma'am," I replied.

"I'm sure you'll be fine, don't worry. It's good we're here though; you're looking really pale. How are you feeling now?"

"The pain comes and goes." She let out a deep breath. "But it's not really any worse than it was when we were at home."

They called the family with the sick little boy back, and we continued to wait our turn to be seen.

"When they call you back, do you want me to come with you or wait for you here? Whichever you want is okay with me."

"I'd like you to come back with me if you don't mind."

She leaned her head on my shoulder, still holding her stomach. I ran my hand up and down her back, trying to comfort her as best I could. I hated the feeling of not being able to make her better.

A nurse opened the door and looked around the room until her gaze settled on us.

"Samone Lang, you can come back now."

I helped her stand, and we slowly walked over to the nurse and followed her to a room.

"Come on in. I'm just going to take your vitals and ask you a few questions," she said, to which Sam nodded. "What brings you in today?"

"I've been having really bad cramps and bleeding, but it's a lot more blood than normal," Sam replied.

"Do you have any other symptoms?" the nurse asked.

"Well, I haven't been feeling well for a few weeks now, and I've been tired a lot lately," she replied.

"Are you on any medications?" the nurse asked as she took Sam's blood pressure.

"No, just vitamins. I did take some ibuprofen for the cramps about two hours ago," Sam answered.

"I'll let the doctor know you're ready. He'll be in as soon as he can."

Sam lay back on the hospital bed and closed her eyes. I stood by the head of the bed and ran my fingers through her hair. When the doctor finally came in, Sam had fallen asleep.

"The doctor is here, Peach," I whispered, gently waking her up.

"Hello, I'm Dr. Roberts. How are you feeling, Ms. Lang?" he asked.

"Not very good," she replied.

"I see that your blood pressure is a little high, which could just be the pain. I'd like to run a few tests, draw some blood," he said then turned and walked out the door.

A phlebotomist came in and took a few vials of blood from her arm. She sat there like a champ through the whole thing. I could tell she was still in pain by the grimaces on her face.

We'd been waiting for a while before I excused myself to use the restroom. When I returned, Sam was asleep, still moaning in pain. I was just about to lose my patience when the doctor finally came back in, his face serious, a sign that didn't bode well for Sam and shot my nerves to new heights. I tapped her shoulder and gently woke her up.

"Ms. Lang, we've got your blood tests back. Maybe you'd like your friend to wait outside while we discuss your results?" he suggested.

Sam's eyes shot to mine. "No. I want Emmett to stay," she replied, her voice shaky.

The doctor looked pointedly at me then and said, "Let me get the nurse back in here."

I looked at Sam as he called for the nurse. She returned and closed the door as Dr. Roberts rolled his stool over and looked at Sam. We peered back at him expectantly.

"You have elevated levels of HCG in your blood. It's the hormone produced during pregnancy. The cramping and heavy bleeding mean that you've likely had an early miscarriage. I'll order an ultrasound to confirm it. Then we'll need to do a D&C to remove the tissue," he explained. "I'm so very sorry, Ms. Lang,"

I felt flushed. Shocked. Numb. I looked at Sam as she murmured her thanks to the doctor. She turned and looked up at me, her eyes flooded with tears. I slipped her hand in mine, and rubbed my thumb over her fingers. Neither of us knew what to say, so we just sat there and stared at each other.

Sure, we were young and still had college ahead of us, and the timing was awful considering we weren't married, or hell, even engaged, but we'd created a life, and it had been snuffed out before it ever had a chance in the world. My throat felt tight as tears welled from the corners of my eyes, but they were nothing compared to the ones that streaked down Sam's splotchy red cheeks.

I was overcome with anger, frustration and helplessness as her eyes told me she was thinking the same thing as I was. Fate had fucked us again.

CHAPTER 54

Healing Doesn't Happen Overnight

Sam

old. I was so cold. I snuggled under my covers as I laid in bed for the third day in a row. I wished I hadn't stopped taking the birth control pills when Emmett left me. We could have avoided this hell. I knew we weren't ready to have a baby. But it was a life we lost just the same.

It was half me, and half Emmett. It was our love. And now it was gone. Taken from us. Before we even knew about it. We didn't even have a chance to love it.

I went into a panic every time I had to go to the bathroom and saw the blood evidence left behind in the toilet, as my body slowly began to heal. It was fate's cruel reminder. I was numb.

I closed my eyes and fell back asleep.

CHAPTER 55

Helpless

Emmett

It was Sam's third day in bed. She'd gone straight under the covers when we got home from the emergency room on Saturday and only gotten up to use the bathroom since. She'd barely eaten the sandwich and salad I brought her on Sunday. She got up when I did on Monday, and I'd hoped it was to start the day, but she just used the bathroom and went right back to sleep.

The doctor had said she might need to rest for a few days. He also said she may experience some depression. Even though it was an early miscarriage, she still had the pregnancy hormones, and would likely be emotional for a while. I was ready and could handle it. I would be her rock to lean on. But I was still angry, *and* depressed, and I didn't have the excuse of those hormones in my body, so I could only imagine what my Peach was going through.

I would have used her phone to text Aiden to get her English Lit assignments, but given they apparently weren't talking anymore, I decided to leave well enough alone. She could get the assignments when she returned to class . . . hopefully soon.

I walked into the bedroom and saw her lying awake in our bed.

"Hey, Peach," I said. "I'm going to take Gage to the dog

park. Do you want to come?"

She looked at me. I could see she was torn, but ultimately her sadness won out. She shook her head and rolled over.

"Okay, I'll be back soon. If you need anything, call me and I'll come right back."

She lifted her hand in a thumbs-up and dropped it back to her side.

With a sigh, I retrieved Gage's harness and leash and got him hooked up. "Let's go buddy," I said, opening the front door.

On our way to the dog park, I saw a blue 1969 Chevy Malibu with a For Sale sign in the window. I snapped a picture with my iPhone so I could call later. I also took a picture of the car to show Sam when she was up to looking at it. If it was as good on the inside, and under the hood, as it looked on the outside, I'd try to make a deal with the owner.

I let Gage off the leash to run and play at the dog park. As I sat there on the bench, I turned Gage's water bottle over and over in my hands. My mind kept wandering to the baby and what could have been. I'd hoped to ask her to marry me soon, but now I wasn't sure if that was a good idea. I thought it might upset her, for us to be happy after experiencing another loss.

I decided to call John. I needed to vent and he was the best choice to talk me back to normalcy.

I scrolled through my contacts and pressed his name, bringing the phone to my ear, I sighed heavily.

"Hey, Emmett." John answered.

"Hey, man," I said.

"Wow, dude, you sound bad. Something happen?"

"Yeah," I said. It was hard to say the words out loud. I wasn't sure I even could.

"Well, what's up? Peachy okay?"

"No . . . yeah, she's okay. Or she will be."

"Oh shit. What's going on, Emmett?"

I sat there in silence. I couldn't find my voice.

"Is it that bad?" he whispered.

"Yeah. It's pretty bad, John. Peach had a miscarriage."

"Fucking hell. I'm sorry, man."

"She started having massive cramps and was bleeding like crazy. We didn't even know she was pregnant until they told her she'd had a miscarriage. She's depressed and hasn't gotten out of bed in three days. I don't know how to help her. I'm at the dog park with Gage. Thought I'd call you."

"Emmett, man, I don't know what to say except I'm here for you guys. Do you need anything?"

"I don't know. Let's talk about something else for a while. I need a distraction."

"Okay. Well, I'm just getting some work done out back for Riley and Quinn. They busted the picnic table, so I thought I'd fix it while they were at work. The girls are coming over for dinner. They'll probably ambush Quinn about the rental houses Tamron wants to check out. I swear, if the living together part doesn't work out for those two, I don't know who the hell else would tolerate the shit they give each other. It's only a matter of time though until Quinn gives in. So . . . you want me to drive over?" he asked.

"Nah, it's okay, man. Stay there and have fun. I just needed to vent, you know, say it out loud."

"I really don't mind. If you change your mind, send a text or call, and I'll be over as soon as I can."

"Okay. Thanks for listening, John," I said then ended the call.

It was getting dark out, so I whistled and called Gage over to me. I thought about Sam back at the apartment and was angry I'd left her there alone the whole afternoon. Gage and I sprinted home. I was so worried about my Peach and was breathing hard when we stopped at the apartment door and I dug out my keys. It was silent inside as I unlocked the door and walked in.

I ran to our bedroom to check on Sam. She wasn't lying in bed. My heart dropped as I heard the water running in the bathroom. She walked out and stopped short when she saw me standing in the doorway.

"Hi," she whispered, looking down at her feet.

"Hi," I said back, hoping this was a step forward.

She walked back to the bed and crawled under the covers. When she turned to her side, I knew the conversation was over before it even began, but I had to try.

"Peach, can we talk?"

"I don't really feel like talking right now, Emmett."

"Well, I think we need to."

She rolled over and looked at me with devastation in her eyes. "I just can't right now."

I walked over and kicked my shoes off. Lying down on the bed, I pulled her into my arms. She laid her head on my chest and lost herself to her sobs. I tried to be strong for her and not to break down, but my heart was broken about ten ways in one, and I didn't catch my tear before it dripped on her arm. The second she felt it, she erupted into shaking cries.

"Why Emmett, why?"

I held her tighter to me and rubbed her back. "I don't know, Peach. But it's gonna be okay. *We're* gonna be okay. Because that's what we do; we make it through these tough times, and we always come out stronger."

She sniffled and squeezed my hand.

"I promise, Peach, someday, we *will* have a family, and we'll love each other forever."

CHAPTER 56
One Day At A Time

Sam

I woke up with Emmett's arms wrapped around me. He was still asleep. After three full days, I was finally ready to get out of bed. I tip-toed through the apartment and turned on the Keurig. Then I grabbed Gage's leash and took him outside. We walked around the apartment complex a few times. It was nice to breathe in the fresh air. When we returned home, I was kicking off my shoes as Emmett walked out of the bedroom. He looked at me with surprise, relief, and hope in his eyes.

"Do you want some coffee or tea?" he asked.

"Coffee would be great."

"So what do you want to do today?" he asked.

"I don't know. I haven't really thought about it. It's Tuesday. Maybe I'll go catch my afternoon classes. Get back into the swing of things."

"All right. I have a class at one. It'll be good to get things back on track. Are you feeling okay? Physically, I mean?"

"Yeah, I'm fine."

The tense set of his shoulders relaxed. I loved him so much. I was sorry I'd caused him pain while we were both hurting and in shock.

"Peach, I think we should probably talk about it," he said tentatively.

"No . . . Emmett. No. I'm not ready. Just let me get through the damn day," I hissed.

He looked like I'd slapped him. I felt horrible the second the words left my mouth.

"You're not the only one who suffered a loss, Sam. I know it was really early in your pregnancy, but it was my baby, too," he yelled back.

I started to cry. Backing up against the wall behind me, I covered my face with my hands. I was being selfish. He needed to talk about it, but I just couldn't. He ran over and pulled me into his arms.

"I'm sorry, Peach. I didn't mean to yell."

"I'm sorry, too. Can you just give me a little time before we talk about it?"

"Okay. I love you."

"I love you, too. Never doubt that, Emmett, please. No matter what I'm am doing or how I am acting, please don't ever doubt how much I love you." I reached my head up and kissed his cheek.

Emmett helped me up off the floor and I took a shower. I let the hot water beat down on my back as if it were washing all the pain of the last few days away. I was glad it was Tuesday and not an English Lit day.

I showered, dressed, then grabbed my car keys, purse, and backpack and headed for the door.

"I'll see you this afternoon," I called out as I walked out.

The roads were pretty clear of traffic and I made it to campus in record time. As I walked to class, I felt my phone vibrate in my pocket. It was a text message from Emmett. I sighed, hesitant to open it. I didn't want to start crying again. I swiped it open regardless.

E: Hope your class goes well, I love you.

Me: Thanks. Yours too. Love you.

He really was amazing. I was lucky to have him in my life. I knew I didn't deserve him. I just hoped I could get back to normal, and stop causing him pain. I knew he needed to talk about the baby. I only wished I felt up to it.

I got to class and listened to the professor. I couldn't focus and ended up doodling in my notebook. I had missed all of my other classes for the day. At least I made the effort to get back to normal. I rewarded myself with a latte from Starbucks.

As I walked up to the apartment door, I saw Emmett and Gage turn the corner.

"Hey, Peach."

"Hi babe. How are my boys?"

"We're good. Just finished up a walk."

He smiled and held the door for me as I walked in. There was a beautiful, large floral arrangement sitting on the counter. I looked back at him as he shut the apartment door.

"Where did these come from?" I asked. "They're beautiful,"

"I picked them up for you," he said. "I thought you'd like them."

"I love them. Thank you, Emmett." I reached up and kissed him. "What sounds good for dinner, chicken cordon bleu or a veggie stir fry?"

"Stir fry," he said with a nod.

"Okay, I can start that right before we want to eat. It cooks quick." I walked around and got us both a glass of sweet tea.

We stood there on opposite sides of the counter, looking at our glasses of tea then up at each other and back again. The silence was deafening—and awkward.

"Emmett, we can talk about it if you want to," I said.

His eyes snapped up to mine. But he just looked at me. He smiled softly and cleared his throat.

"Well . . . I mean, only if you're ready," he said, and I nodded for him to continue. "Hell, Peach, I don't even know what I want to say. I mean, I know we're young and in college still, but . . ." He paused.

"But that was our baby, a product of our love," I finished for him.

"A life our love created," he added.

"I know," I said, looking down at my hands.

He walked around the counter, took me in his arms, and held me tightly to his chest.

"I love you so much, Peach," he whispered into my hair.

"I love you, too, Emmett."

"Are you okay?"

"I will be. *We* will be. We can always remember it. I'm not sure if I wish we knew whether it was a boy or girl, or if I'm relieved that we don't know. Part of me wants to know so we could name it, because I hate thinking of it as *it*. I *want* to remember, but not as an *it,* as a *who*," I said.

"We could name it Dakota Bailey. Those are both names that could be used for a boy or a girl," he said.

"I love it. It even feels right. Dakota Bailey Walker," I said, looking at him with a small smile.

"Dakota Bailey Walker," he repeated.

I reached up and kissed him deeply. I poured all of my emotion into that kiss so he could feel even a fraction of the depth of my love for him. He was an amazing man, and I planned on making him know just how much he meant to me and how wonderful he was. We had a name. It helped start the healing process. Remembering Dakota started to be a healthy thing for us.

"Emmett, I don't want to tell anyone else about this."

He looked down at me and grimaced.

"What? Who did you tell?"

"I told John. When I went to the dog park with Gage. I'm sorry, Peach, I just needed to talk to someone and . . ." He paused.

"I wasn't talking," I admitted.

"Yeah. Basically." He looked down at his hands. "But John won't say anything to anyone. Not even the girls, or Riley and Quinn. I know he won't say a word."

"I know. I trust John completely. He's a vault. It's okay, babe."

CHAPTER 57

Lost In A Good Way

Emmett

A few months later, we were planning a party at Riley's. It felt weird not to say Riley and Quinn's since they'd been there together for so long. But eventually, all things change, and Quinn and Tamron had moved into their rental house together.

Sam was excited, as always, to see the girls and had made them both door wreathes for the holidays. She was one of the most creative people I knew. She made one for us, too. I have to admit, it was cool, and I was excited to spend the holiday season with her.

I heard the lock turn at the front door and knew she was home from class. It was officially winter break, and not soon enough. We'd both crammed for exams, and our brains needed some down time. When she walked through the door, all I wanted to do was get lost in her.

"Hey, babe." She set her bag and purse down and dropped her keys and phone on the table by the door. "How was your day?"

I smiled at her. "It was good, Peach. How about you? Class good?"

"Eh, it was okay. Aiden is at least talking to me again."

"That's good. You guys get coffee?"

"No. But it's a step in the right direction, so I'm happy," she said.

"You know you really gotta cut the guy a little slack. I know, first hand, just how easy it is to fall in love with you."

She blushed ten shades of red, and I probably had that smirk on my face she loves so much.

"Emmett, don't say things like that. You act like I'm an angel or something. I'm more like the harbinger of mischance."

I walked over and wrapped my arms around her. She melted into me. I tilted her head up and kissed her passionately as I ran my fingers through her hair and backed her up against the kitchen wall.

"I love you, Peach."

"I love you, too," she replied, her voice husky with need.

She reached her hand down and twined her fingers with mine. Stepping around me, she pulled me along as she walked backwards, her eyes locked onto mine. I followed her into our bedroom, and as she let our hands drop to our sides, she leaned into me, looking down and resting her forehead against my chest.

"I want you," she whispered.

"I'm yours."

I shivered as she skimmed her nails down my back. She was igniting me, and she knew it. My little vixen. I reached down and slowly unbuttoned the shirt that now stood in the way of what I wanted. As I finished the last button, I swept the shirt off of her shoulders and took her in.

I kissed her softly, nipping her lip with my teeth, tasting strawberry and wax in the lip-gloss she wore. Deep in need, she wrestled to unbutton my jeans. I pushed her back onto the bed, where she lay staring up at me. Her expression was heavy with passion, and I wanted her . . . I needed her.

I nestled my head in the hollow of her neck, groaning as the soft scent of her vanilla perfume registered in my brain. I breathed it in deeply and trailed kisses along the soft curve of her ear, relishing in the way she sighed, and turned her head to the side for more.

Looking back at me, she held my gaze with her passionate, brown eyes wide. I smoothed her hair back and ran my fingers down the side of her face and neck, settling on her shoulder. I slid the strap of her lacy, blue bra over her shoulder. She bit her bottom lip and slipped her arms out. My breath caught as I popped the button of her jeans open and lowered the zipper, watching her while I pulled them off and kicked them to the floor.

I braced my weight with my arms on either side of her while she pulled the hem of my shirt up and over my head, lifting each hand in turn before tossing it aside. My back arched as she ran her fingertips down its length, resting at the waist of my unbuttoned jeans.

I kissed her again, drawing back to see the love in her eyes. She smiled coyly as she pulled me back to her, embracing me in a kiss that had both of us breathing in fast, shallow breaths.

As I reached down and pushed my jeans off, I hovered above her and took what she offered. Her soft body pressed against mine. I began, slow and teasing. I knew how it drove her crazy, so I gave her what she wanted, what her eyes told me she needed, and taking what she gave me in return. I got lost in her.

CHAPTER 58

Good Tidings

Emmett

G age woke me up with a lick to my hand. I stretched my arms above my head and sat up before kicking my legs over the side of the bed and patting his head.

"Mornin,' Gage," I said. "Well, come on then. Let's go outside."

He padded behind me, nudging me on. I laughed as I grabbed his harness and leash then tip-toed to the front door so I wouldn't wake Sam up.

While I was waiting for Gage to do his business, I scrolled through the pictures on my phone. I came across the one I snapped of my new car and texted it to John. Well, it was new to me anyway. I'd bought that blue '69 Chevy Malibu I'd seen on the way to the dog park. I was so happy to be rid of the rental. Fortunately, they'd cut me a good deal.

I came across a picture of Sam and me from our last night in Hawaii. An older couple was nice enough to take the snapshot for us. Sam had demanded I text it to her immediately. I had laughed at her impatience, earning me a swift smack on my ass. I chuckled at the good memory.

Gage came running back over to me.

"You all done there, buddy?" I asked with a pat to his head.

"Well, let's get back inside."

It was pretty brisk out for Alabama. We had another cold front come in. I filled Gage's food and water bowls, then went back into our bedroom and crawled under the covers with Sam. I rolled over to my side and watched her sleeping peacefully. I lightly ran my fingers through her hair as her eyes fluttered open and locked onto mine.

"Good morning," she whispered.

"Morning Peach," I said. "Did you sleep well?"

She stretched out. "Mmm hmm. I slept really well. What time is it?"

"A little after nine," I answered.

Her eyes opened wide, and she jumped out of bed. "We gotta get ready if we're going to make it to Riley's in time." She ran around, grabbing clothes from drawers. "I'm going to jump in the shower. Can you take Gage out?" she called on her way to the bathroom.

"Yeah, I already took him out. I'll put some bagels in the toaster and make us some coffee."

When I heard the water turn off in Sam's shower, I set our bagels and coffee out on the breakfast bar. I sat and sipped my coffee as I waited for her to join me.

We arrived at Riley's a few hours later. As Sam and I pulled into the driveway, we saw Tamron and Quinn getting out of Quinn's truck.

"Hey, guys!" Sam yelled.

"Sam! Emmett!" Tamron called back.

Quinn waved as he guided Tamron into the house. When we got inside, we saw John, Riley, and Alison sitting in the living room. Alison jumped up and ran over to Sam and Tamron, and the girls took off for the kitchen. I dropped down onto the couch next to John and nodded my hello to Riley, while Quinn got comfortable in the recliner.

"Damn, man, I really miss my chair," Quinn sighed.

We broke out in laughter as Riley shook his head.

"You could have taken it with you, man," Riley said.

"Yeah . . . no. You know Tamron hates this chair. It doesn't go with anything else in the house," Quinn huffed.

"Just lay it down, Quinn," John said.

Quinn looked at John, "Lay what down?"

Riley and I both looked at John, too, waiting for his explanation.

"The fucking law, man. Lay it down. You like the chair . . . take it home. It's your chair. Let her get used to it," John said with a smirk.

Riley swung his head back around to look at John. "Did you forget who Tamron is?"

"Yeah, man, 'pick your battles' my dad always used to say. Sadly, my comfortable, broken-in chair isn't one of them. A happy wife equals a happy life, as the old adage goes. We may not be married, but well, y'all know my Tamron. We may as well be," Quinn finished.

"I'm gonna grab a beer," I said laughing.

"Yeah me too," John said.

We walked down the hall toward the kitchen. "Hey, man, can we talk out back?"

"Sure," I replied then walked into the kitchen and stole a quick kiss from Sam. "Hey, girls. Just grabbing a couple beers and going out back."

"Okay, love you," Sam said as her eyes lit up with a smile.

"Love you, too," I said, kissing her on the forehead as I passed her again on my way out to the back doors.

John followed me out, and we ended up sitting up on the brick wall again.

"So, what's up, man?" I asked.

"Well, I just wanted to see how you and Peachy are doing, you know, since the miscarriage," he said quietly.

"Oh. Yeah. We're doing okay. It's hard still, but we finally talked about it and named the baby Dakota Bailey Walker so we could grieve and remember. Every time we discussed what happened, the only way we had to describe the baby was as *it,* which upset us both. Since we didn't know if the baby was a boy or girl, we couldn't say him or her, so naming the baby helped," I answered.

"Dakota Bailey. That's nice, man. Real nice."

"Look, John, Sam still doesn't want anyone else to know. She knows I told you, but she trusts you won't say anything to anyone else, not even the girls. She just doesn't want to deal with everyone saying how sorry they are, constantly bringing it back up. Neither of us can take that," I added.

"Gotcha. I get it. That would make it harder to move forward," he said. "So, are you really okay, man?"

"Yeah. She makes me okay. Everything we've faced has made us stronger. Her love makes every day a new slate for me."

"That's good to hear, man, good to hear. Well, you know I'm always here for both of you, anytime."

"Thanks, John."

When I walked into the house, I sensed someone behind me. I turned around and saw Sam staring at me.

"So . . . what were you and John talking about?" she asked leaning against the counter.

"Oh, he just wanted to see how we were doing. You know, privately," I whispered.

Her shoulders slumped as she exhaled a labored breath and she looked down at the floor.

I pulled her in and wrapped my arms around her. "It's okay." I kissed the top of her head. "He was just worried and didn't want to upset you by asking directly."

"I know. I'm okay. Did you . . . did you tell him we named the baby?" Her voice hitched.

"Yes. He loved the name and thought it was a good idea."

A small smile perked her lips up as she looked up into my eyes. "It kinda feels good to share it, but I still don't want anyone besides him to know."

"I know. It's okay. It's just John. No one else will know, unless you decide you want to tell them," I said, kissing her softly.

"Okay," she whispered.

I reached into the refrigerator and pulled out the bowl with the veggie skewers.

"I'll grab the seasonings and follow you out," Sam said.

When we went back outside, everyone was sitting around the fire, except for Quinn, who was flipping the steaks on the grill. I walked over and laid the veggies out on the grill while he held the lid open. Sam gave him the seasonings and went over to sit by the fire. When we had everything on the grill, Quinn and I joined them all by the fire.

"Do we have marshmallows?" Alison asked.

"Uh no. I don't think so," Riley said.

Alison looked at him and shook her head. "Well, then I guess you better drive to the store then," she said as she took his beer from him.

"Hey woman!" he yelled.

"Oh relax, Riley, you haven't even popped the top off yet. Now please, Riley, go to the store and get me some marshmallows," she said in a sing-song voice.

"Damn. All right, fine," he said.

Alison clapped her hands and kissed him on the cheek. "Thanks, baby."

Riley shook his head, stood up and put his phone in his pocket. "Anyone want to go for a ride?"

"Yeah, man, I'll go with ya," John said. "I want to pick up some more beer. May as well make use of your sober ass while I can."

As Riley and John left for the store, we all settled back around the fire. The girls talked while Quinn and I sat and watched the fire. Every once in a while, Sam would peek up at me and smile. She was happy. She was content. Life was getting better every day. Even with all that we'd been through, I couldn't help but hope for good things in our future. No matter the risk to our hearts.

CHAPTER 59

The Next Step

Emmett

I t was time. I'd made my decision while sitting around that fire at Riley's place the other night. The time had finally come for me to ask Sam to be my wife. I was so happy, I could hardly stand it. I walked over to my dresser and pulled the drawer open. Moving aside a stack of white t-shirts, I found the blue velvet box I was looking for.

I glanced around to be sure I was still alone before peeking at the ring. It really was beautiful, and I knew she'd love it. It had a princess cut diamond in the center, flanked by two smaller princess cut diamonds on each side of it, all set in a platinum band that I had the jeweler inscribe with an infinity symbol and three tiny stars on either side of it.

I closed the box and put it back behind my stack of shirts, closing the drawer just as Sam walked into our bedroom with Gage on her heels. I walked up to her and pulled her into me.

"Hey, babe," she said, smiling up at me.

"Hi there, my sweet Peach," I teased as I kissed her forehead.

"What are you doing in here still?" she asked. "You aren't going to have time for breakfast before class."

"I'll just grab a coffee to go and one of those breakfast bars,"

I replied. "I have a couple errands to run later, so I'll be home a little later than normal."

"Ok, maybe I'll meet up with Tamron and Alison for coffee then," she said.

"Yeah, that's a good idea. Then tonight, we're going out to dinner," I told her.

"Oh, that sounds great." She reached up and wrapped her arms around me.

"Keep this up and neither of us will go anywhere," I teased.

She smirked at me and turned on her toes, walking out of the bedroom. I went into the bathroom and ran a comb through my hair, then met her in the kitchen. As she handed me my coffee and a breakfast bar, I kissed her again heatedly, then patted Gage on the head.

"I'll see you tonight. Love you," I called as I walked out the front door.

"Ok. Love you, too."

CHAPTER 60
The Stars In The Sky

Sam

The girls and I met for coffee at Starbucks. I nearly laughed the whole time as Tamron kept harassing Alison about moving in with Riley now that she had the apartment to herself. Anyone who knew her could see she wasn't even close to ready for that step.

As I got in my car to leave, I saw a single yellow rose laying on my passenger seat. I opened the attached note. It read:

Peach,
I love you.
Emmett

I smiled, holding the note close and smelling the beautiful yellow rose. Tamron, riding shotgun in Alison's car, rolled her window down to see what was holding me up.

I held up my new treasures. "Emmett left me a surprise in my car."

"Aw, you know, Sam, he really is the sweetest."

"Yeah." I smiled. "He is. I'll see y'all later." I waved as they drove off.

I went to the Farmer's Market on the way home to pick up some things for dinner. Walking out with my purchases into the bright Alabama sunlight, I sighed as I took in the striking clear blue sky. I walked over to my car and stopped short when I saw balloons and flowers filling the backseat.

I smiled as I opened the door and spied a big heart-shaped box of chocolates. Good thing I wasn't in the market long or they would have melted. I opened the note attached to the chocolates.

Peach,
Happy 'I love you' Day.
Emmett

He was unreal. I felt spoiled and loved, and with a grin plastered to my face, I took a deep breath in and relished the flowers' sweet aroma. On the seat next to them sat a plush teddy bear.

When I returned home, I saw Emmett's car in his spot and smiled. He must have finished up his errands early to beat me home. I was happy we wouldn't have to wait long to eat dinner. I carried the chocolates and rose up to the door, figuring we could come out and bring everything else in together.

I couldn't believe my eyes when I walked inside our apartment. The lights were off and the curtains were drawn. Everything was covered in strands of tiny, white lights, all strung from the ceiling and curtains. With the apartment so dark, and the lights everywhere, it felt like we were in the middle of the universe with countless stars surrounding us.

Emmett was standing in the middle of the living room. I set my stuff down on the table by the door and walked over to join him, looking around in awe of what he had done.

"Hi Peach," he whispered.

"Hi." I stood on my tiptoes and kissed him lightly on the mouth. "Today's been filled with amazing surprises. What's this all about, babe?"

"You." He smiled down at me. "I love you so much."

"I love you, too," I breathed.

I gasped as he dropped to one knee in front of me. My hands flew to my mouth when I realized what he was doing.

"I love you more than the number of stars in the sky, Peach. I always have and I always will. You're it for me. My soul mate . . . my one true love. I've never been more complete than when I'm with you. Sam, would you do me the honor of being my wife?"

I couldn't believe my ears. My heart started racing, and happy tears filled my eyes. There was only one answer that felt natural and real.

"Yes, yes, I will marry you, Emmett." I answered as he slipped the diamond ring onto my finger, holding my hand in his. I dropped to my knees in front of him, his thumb rubbed back and forth over the top of my hand.

He leaned forward and rested his forehead against mine. "Thank you," he whispered. "Thank you for loving me, for letting me love you. For never giving up on us."

"I love you so much, Emmett, I need you like I need my next breath, and will love you from this life into the next."

He pulled me close and glided his lips over mine. I straddled his lap, wrapped in his tender embrace as his fingers ran through my hair, holding my head in place for our heady kiss. As our tongues wove together, his minty breath left a cool trail across my lips.

Our love had survived Fate's cruel torment, and I couldn't wait to see what our future held.

Acknowledgements

To my critique partners Tricia Zoeller, Alison Gaskin Bailey, Lisa Regan Prodrutti, and Dana Mason, your help and feedback was invaluable. When I look back on the versions that you read, I kind of want to cringe.

Thank you to my beta readers, John Holmes, Tamron Davis, Michelle Pace, Kim Anderson Bias and Laura Wilson.

Thank you to AL Jackson, you've supported and encouraged me from the beginning.

Kindle Buddies group, thank you for your support and encouragement.

Nellie Tice Bailey Zeis and Cindy Darnell-Fagan, thank you, so very much for listening to me read those dreadful early drafts over the phone.

Nancy S. Thompson, my amazing editor, and cheerleader. There is no amount of thanks enough, to show you how grateful I am.

Robin Harper, of Wicked by Design—Fabulous cover design, thank you.

Tami Norman, of Integrity Formatting—Amazing formatting, thank you.

Heather Davenport, of Book Plug Promotions- Fantastic organization of my promotional events.

Brandy Ezelle—Thank you for the Auburn area kayaking information.

Thank you to the Admissions Office at Auburn University— for taking time to answer my questions regarding the admissions process.

To my family, Mike Darnell, Austin Darnell, Nellie Tice Bailey Zeis, Penny Bailey Adamo, Tom Adamo, Kara Adamo,

Love's Secret Torment

Erica Adamo, Cindy Darnell-Fagan, Dick Zeis, Paul Zeis, Ron Bendixon and Charity Drumm Hale—Thank you for your endless support and excitement of the pursuit of my dream.

To my dear, sweet neighbor, Kim Marie Rodriguez, thank you so much for your support, encouragement and excitement. You may not have known it, but it meant a lot to me.

About the Author

Stacy L. Darnell

Stacy is a New Adult/Contemporary Romance author. Her debut novel, "Love's Secret Torment" releases March 17th, 2015. Her second novel, "Sweet Conundrum" due out later that year.

Stacy lives with her husband Mike, son Austin, and chocolate lab Gage, just outside of Atlanta, Georgia. She loves the seasonal weather changes, taking walks with Gage, and spending time with her family and friends.

While happily addicted to Starbucks, writing is her passion, and sharing her stories with the world is a dream come true.

"Love's Secret Torment" on Goodreads:

https://www.goodreads.com/book/show/22887142-love-s-secret-torment

"Sweet Conundrum" on Goodreads:

https://www.goodreads.com/book/show/23520343-sweet-conundrum

love's Secret *torment*

Follow Stacy on social media:

Facebook:
http://www.facebook.com/StacyLDarnellAuthor

Twitter:
@StacyLDarnell

Instagram:
@StacyLDarnell

Blog:
http://StacyLDarnellAuthor.blogspot.com

www.ingramcontent.com/pod-product-compliance
Lightning Source LLC
Chambersburg PA
CBHW021644260626
47154CB00017BA/2196